BITS OF OTHER PEOPLE

Tolu Fapohunda

ISBN: 978-1-969978-10-4

The moral right of the author has been asserted.

Published in Nigeria in 2019 by Eleventh House Publishing Limited, 41, Abuja road, Ire-Akari Estate, Ibadan, Oyo State.

+234(0)8064941239, +234(0)7081923520

info@eleventhhousepublishing.com www.eleventhhousepublishing.com

A catalogue record for this book is available from the National Library of Nigeria.

Edited by Tobi Idowu Cover illustration by Ezeh Kingsley

Layout and design by Bola Branding Agency

For my dad,

I'm yet to meet a better man.

The whites, are my favorite of all your lies and the secrets that you
keep are the darkest I've come by.

— Ahmad Maaroof Mahmood

CHAPTER ONE

The desperate honk across the street finally made me aware that I had been lost in thought again. I glanced at the unfinished portrait and wondered if I would make good on delivery. In that instant, I began to wrap the paintbrush in a wet napkin, done for now until I returned later. My preoccupation with thoughts of her had made me next to useless for some days now. When I heard the honk, which resembled the cry of a strangled dog, again, I contemplated telling Kabiru to go back home so I could just continue the painting. A part of me mocked: You cannot get enough of her. You have to see her now.

I agreed.

At the third time of asking, I shouted, "I dey come, abeg!"

Ten minutes later, I was ready. The car that awaited me was a battered Volkswagen Golf that looked roughly the same age as I was. Slumbering behind the wheel was Kabiru. We grew up in close proximity in the neighborhood. He was streetwise and possessed vast knowledge of the city, so I paid him to drive me around, mostly to the market, church, and art exhibitions.

I tapped him now and went to the other side. I shut the door a few times before I was satisfied it would not drop off on the road. Soon, we were on our way, and I found myself relishing thoughts of her.

"Which kain head I get, eh?" Kabiru lamented, breaking my thoughts with the same line of conversation I had become accustomed to. "Yesterday I played two sure. 4 and 34. I bet my yesterday's money."

I encouraged him to go on with a repeated soft nod.

"Na 3 and 44 comot!"

Close enough, I thought, and let out sympathetic noises.

"You see my life?"

I looked at him. I didn't really think Kabiru believed he could win the sum he often mouthed, but I understood that he at least had hope. Hope is what drives us on.

"Try again."

He produced a piece of paper.

"See this game. Perm'tation."

I accepted and examined it. It showed five random numbers. I nodded my head.

"Maybe you will be lucky today."

"Tomorrow," he corrected.

I gave him back the piece of paper and produced one of my own. It was a sketch of her I kept in my wallet. I looked at it now.

"Fine, sisi," he peered over, the stale stench of cannabis permeating from him. "What time for the afternoon?"

He was asking about my lunch with her.

"One thirty."

"One thirty," he repeated. "One. Thirty. I go play dat today, 1 and 30."

"Fine."

"How did you meet fine sisi, sef?" he grinned. He was missing a few teeth. I had recounted to him a couple of times how I met her, but Kabiru was prone to selective amnesia. Maami felt a head injury from a fight at the bar down the street was to blame, but I was inclined to think igbo was more responsible.

"I have told you the story before," I said and wound the window all the way down to let in more air.

"You no tell me."

I ignored him. He then asked to meet her after our lunch.

I considered.

"Okay. You will meet her after lunch. I will introduce you to her."

He smiled, then declared, "Don't say I'm the driver when you introduce us!"

"I won't call you a driver."

We were almost at the church.

***

I first clapped my eyes on Sade at Freedom Park. It was one of those days when I sought new ideas about what to paint. The ideas, when they came, were as slow as a snail's funeral. Feeling blue as the sky that late morning, I longed for reprieve.

Enter Sade.

As she walked in gracefully, she must have noticed my unflinching gaze on her. With a polite smile, she strode past, taking in the environment with a puzzled expression. Our eyes locked a few times. How can a woman be so beautiful? I wondered. I continued to watch her move from one sculpture to another in dazed fascination.

"It's your first time here?" I decided to shoot my shot by walking up to her. She was standing by the fish pond, not far away from the slave prison.

"Yes." There was a hint of mirth in her eyes that suggested to me that she had anticipated this eventuality.

She asked, almost in tune, "Are you my guide?"

"Not really," I smiled. "But I've been coming here for so long, I can call myself one."

"So you are not a guide."

"I am not a guide, but I can be one for you."

She looked at me and smiled.

"All right. Be my guide. I know you want to."

"You can tell?"

"I saw you looking at me, even though you tried not to show it."

We laughed.

I looked at her more closely now. She had a kind of understated beauty, perhaps because she was so charmingly aware of her attractiveness. Her skin was fair and flawless. Hair, black and long. Teeth, white and even. She was dressed in a simple floral blouse and a dark, knee-length skirt. She was perfect.

"What is this place? I know it's about old slaves... years of slavery, but..."

"It's an old British colonial prison yard," I began. "A former place of pain and sorrow transformed into a heritage space for pleasure and creative expression. It was remodeled from its bad past into a cultural hub. As you can see, there's a lot of green space and lovely art."

She looked around.

"It's really lovely. I like the artworks."

"It wasn't like this some centuries ago. That used to be a place where slaves were dumped after they were killed," I said while pointing to the well by the pond.

She gasped.

"That's horrible."

"It is, and we are still owed a moral debt. Let me show you around."

The park was fairly busy with tourists. We toured the galleries, museum, amphitheater, and food courts.

"I am amazed." We walked past Brooklyn Bistro. There was dull jazz music coming from around it. "You would never know this place used to be a prison yard for slaves!"

"Those massive walls are hiding it."

"Yes! To think I normally pass here without giving it a thought."

"A lot of people say that. I am glad you like it."

She had taken many pictures with her cellphone, and when we got to the sculpture Bembe Drum, she took many more. It was when we sat at the fountain that we finally introduced ourselves.

She was Sade Dairo, a nurse. She was in the area for a retreat that became boring, so she decided to visit the park to cheer herself up during a break.

"Deji Depiver," she said with a hint of surprise. "Isn't that a colonial name, Depiver?"

"I think so, yes."

"Is that why you visit here often?"

I paused.

"I have never made that connection until now that you mention it. I just love the peace and quiet. It helps me think."

"I like the peace and quiet too."

"You can even watch stage plays here on some days. There is a live band too, on Friday nights, but those days are busy and loud."

"I will still like it. I want to come here every day!"

I laughed. We talked some more. The more we talked, the more enchanted I was.

"Do you sing?"

Her eyes bulged.

"So you sing, eh?"

It was an easy guess. Her voice was silky and tuneful.

"Yes! I sing in a choir. I am the choir lead!"

"Choirgirl. Is it a big choir?"

"Yes! One of the biggest in Lagos—Mount Sinai. Have you heard of it?"

I shook my head.

"We are popular in Lagos! I can't believe you never heard of us."

"Where is it?"

"Not far from here."

"On the island?"

"No. But a few minutes once you pass the bridge."

She tried further to explain the exact location, but I wasn't clear on it.

"I will come," I said. "Because of you, I will come!"

***

We arrived at Mount Sinai at about half past nine, later than anticipated. The car broke down. For thirty or so minutes, Kabiru tried every trick to get the car working, and I had almost given up and decided to take the bus when it suddenly stuttered to life. He then pushed the Golf as hard as he could to make up for lost time. I thanked him and promised to pay him later.

The building before me was impressive. Norman arches and stained glass. A concrete monstrosity from the outside, it had the venerable appearance of a cathedral. Inside, it was modern but austere.

Service was midway, but I found a seat in the front pew despite the usher's attempt to sit me at the back. As I'd done a few times since I first came here, a couple of which were unknown to her, I wanted the best possible view of Sade. I saw her where I knew she would be. She sat in one of the front pews of the choir on the podium. She saw me and smiled. I smiled back, resisting the urge to wave.

I wondered if she knew how obsessed I was with her. I didn't think she did or comprehended it. Like the rest of them, she had her robe on, which tended to exude a kind of intellectual beauty.

Reverend Benson Brown was yelling vociferously into the microphone.

"...and giving cheerfully in your days of need is tantamount to receiving multiple folds in your days of abundance! It is the covenant of reciprocity from God, and givers never lack. That is the covenant! God loves a cheerful—"

"Giver!" the church acquiesced.

My attention fled from him faster than a thief at the sight of police, returning quickly to Sade. Soon, I was transported in my head to a lunch date only a few hours away.

***

My second rendezvous with Sade was a more relaxed affair. We met at Bar Beach. She was having a picnic with a group of friends. I was at Freedom Park, and she thought it would be a good idea if I came by. It was a humid Saturday afternoon.

"Ah, finally," she yelped as the scrawny-looking jockey helped her down from the horse. "I kept praying not to fall off. I was bouncing on it like a jumping jack."

"It's a strong horse," I admired the black beast, and it seemed to agree with a nicker.

"Mekina won't fall you down," the boy protested. "Mekina never lets anybody down!"

"Na-so!" replied Sade with a tired laugh. "That was what they told my friend, Bimbo, last year. She is still on crutches till today."

After the boy led the horse away, I handed her a coconut drink and looked at her. Something radiated from within her that rendered her irresistible. A haunting beauty.

"Thank you." She took a sip. "It's nice, yeah?"

"I like it."

"It's just not cold enough."

"I was going to say that."

The weather was hot. She fanned herself with her hand.

"Let's go to that shade over there." I pointed to a thatched structure. "The beach is only perfect in the morning or evening."

"Is it empty?"

"Yes. I saw some people leaving the place."

I led her to the shade. After we played with a few marine crabs and threw a few pebbles into the ocean, she asked as we watched people fool around, "So tell me about your painting, Deji. You didn't tell me much about it on the phone. And before you start, I used to paint too when I was a child, so no do shakara for me."

"You used to paint? Why did you stop? Painting is beautiful."

"I know," she fluttered her eyes. "Maybe I didn't have too much interest in it like that. I think I just prefer singing."

"Singing is a big talent too."

"Not like painting. I remember I used to think painters were weird people. Lonely and weird people."

"Painters are not weird people," I said in mild shock, "but I agree that it is a lonely profession. Sort of."

She gave an elegant laugh.

"I'm saying I used to think that when I was small. Now I don't think so anymore."

"I know what you mean."

"Painters are creative people. There's a painting in our resident doctor's office that I really like. It's a group of market women selling fish and vegetables. I really like it. It made me remember storybooks I read when I was small."

"African mothers. I do that sometimes."

"That's the type of painting you do?"

"Sometimes. But I prefer to do abstract impressionism."

"What's that?"

"It's a kind of painting," I replied, looking at a couple taking photographs, "where I express myself through the use of colors without having any clear objective in mind. Just splash and see how it goes. Anywhere belle face—that's what my friend Somto calls it."

Her eyes met mine.

"Oh…" She appeared delicately confused.

My God! Those eyes, I thought. Wide-set and enchanting.

"You are confused, abi?"

She nodded, deliberately demure.

"Don't worry. When you come to my studio, I will show you. It's a nice art, but people don't really appreciate it in this part of the world."

"Oyinbo people kind of painting," she remarked, toying with a hermit crab.

I did not always agree with this, but nodded my head.

"I understand it now," she said. "I told you I used to paint when I was small. Crayon and watercolor painting. I know you will say it's not painting, but—"

"It is," I cut in. "Every painting is a painting. I paint mystical stuff too. Paintings that are less ordinary and more extraordinary."

Her eyes twinkled.

"And it's not like abstract…"

"Abstract impressionism, no." I chuckled. "It's different. Like this painting I did of a monarch sitting on a throne, surrounded by maidens with pots of fire on their heads."

She grimaced at the thought of it.

"You don't like it? It's beautiful."

"I'm sure it's beautiful, sha," she said in a voice that betrayed her emotion.

"There's another one of a woman I did some time ago, a woman breastfeeding a toddler with blisters all over his body. One of her breasts was larger than the other."

Sade cringed.

"That's…sad."

"I don't think it's sad."

"It's sad," she insisted. "And beautiful. It's…sadly beautiful!"

I responded with a laugh.

"I like how you said that. Sadly beautiful. I think my next painting will be something along that line…sad beauty. You know, Sade, I have never heard anybody tell me that kind of work is beautiful except my good friend Somto. And you have not even seen them with your eyes!"

"Everything is beautiful," she said, tossing the crab away. "When I hear you speak, all I hear is beautiful euphony."

She smiled, raised her eyebrows, and extended a manicured hand.

"So when are you going to paint me?"

"I already did."

"You are lying!"

"I'm not lying."

"When?" she yelped, excitedly at the sudden realization that I meant what I had said. "Where is it?"

"It's at home in my studio."

"How—?"

"I won't tell you how I did it," I said.

She pouted.

"But—"

I pulled out a pencil and a piece of paper from a satchel I carried.

"I will draw you now and go home and paint it on the canvas. This one will be for you."

"Really?" She jumped and pulled me up, delighted. "Let's do it now. I like this! Yay! I feel like a queen!"

"You are a queen. Stand here," I said after I'd managed to tame her wild excitement, "so that the beach will show behind you."

I looked at the sun setting.

"It's a beautiful time. Perfect."

She tried a few positions before I was satisfied. She was a natural, smiling and steady.

"You sing like an angel too."

"You have not heard me sing before." She was conscious not to ruin her pose.

"Are you sure about that?"

Her eyes bulged.

"Did you…? You came!"

"How else did you think I painted you?"

"Why didn't you tell me?"

"I wanted it to be a surprise."

"Surprise? But you didn't tell me." I shrugged.

"You see that I'm right now?" she snickered. "Painters are weird people!"

"It's not like that now, come on," I protested. "I just… I wanted to observe you without… without—you have a fantastic choir, you know."

"Don't change the topic!"

I grinned.

"Your choir is amazing."

"We are," she agreed. "We hear that a lot. I'm the best of them, sha. Without me, they won't be that good." She paused. "Don't you think so?"

I nodded.

"You are an angel. Your voice is… damn!"

"You are a tease!"

"Don't open your mouth too much. You will ruin the sketch."

"But I have to smile."

"Yes, but not much."

One of the picnickers came to her.

"Sade, we'll be going soon."

"Where are they rushing to, eh?" asked Sade stiffly.

"You, wait for me, jare. This gentleman is drawing a sketch of me. He will paint it. It won't take too long, will it?"

I shook my head.

The lady became slightly agitated, but Sade insisted she wait for her. The interloper glanced at me for a few seconds, then walked away.

"Who is she?" I asked without taking my eyes off the sketch.

"That's my friend, Lara. She's in the choir too. Didn't you see her when you came to spy on me?"

I shrugged.

"You look alike."

"That's what people say. I am prettier than her, sha."

She smiled, then asked, "So what will you call this painting when you finish it?"

"*Sade Nightingale on the Beach.*"

***

The choir rendered beautiful numbers. Their voices were almost like angels', notes soaring over the clouds, graceful notes echoing among the masonry, dancing on the staves. At the heart of it was Sade. She was magnificent. After they had returned to the stand in the wake of raucous adulation, I found myself wondering how a woman could be both beautiful and talented. It boggled the mind.

I watched her now, smiling at something I could only imagine another member had said or done to her. Such a demure smile, I thought. Reverend Benson barked something into the microphone that made me react with a jolt. The woman next to me raised a questioning brow, and I responded that all was well with a reassuring smile. For a few minutes, the clergy had my attention before losing it again.

My eyes strayed back to Sade, and what I saw now drew a puzzled frown on my face. She looked frightened, horrified, as though she had seen a ghost. It was a startling transition from just a few minutes ago. She appeared stiff, looking back into the church, very afraid.

What is going on with her? I wondered.

Still confused, I followed the path of what I thought was her gaze, which was somewhere back at the congregation on my right. I didn't see anything out of the ordinary, just a sea of heads.

Then I saw her gaze shift to the man next to her, the choirmaster, who in turn appeared to be looking in the direction of where I sat. On second thought, he appeared to be looking at the drummer who was just near my position on an elevated platform. The drummer appeared impassive, I think, as his face was not in full view.

Strange, I thought. Very strange.

I would later recognize the significance of these exchanges. By the time I looked back at Sade, she appeared at ease again. Almost as if nothing had happened.

Had I imagined it? I wondered.

A stern-looking usher exhorted a slumbering man in front of me. By the time I looked again in the direction of the choir, Sade was no longer there. Disappeared. I saw a few movements in and around that area. There were a few empty seats around where she had sat that were previously occupied. I thought it was strange, but I didn't really dwell on it.

The remainder of the service rolled on without any event.

I was just set for the exit after Reverend Brown announced the end of service when I heard the scream. It tore through me like a shard of glass. It came from the direction of the choir stand. It was a woman's.

Then it came again. Desperate. Terrified.

A wild panic ensued. I saw now that the source appeared to be somewhere backstage. Instinctively, I pressed forward. A woman flew out and fell into the grasp of another.

"It's Sister Sade!" she cried madly. "It's Sister Sade o!"

My stomach flipped.

"What happened to her?" asked the other woman.

"Her head! Somebody smashed her head!"

There was a horrified gasp from the audience. A great cry broke from a woman next to me.

"How can this happen?" an elderly, bespectacled man howled. "In the church?!"

"Who would do something like that?" a frail young lady asked.

The woman wailed on, "I don't know o!" She flung her arms widely and staggered. "Blood! Blood! Blood everywhere!"

"Is she alive?" asked the other woman.

"Yes! But she is not moving! She is not moving o!"

There was a period of chaos and uncertainty that seemed to last forever. I stood there almost transfixed.

Was it the Sade I know? Or was there another Sister Sade? I wondered.

Finally, a group of men carried her out like undertakers.

"She's still breathing!" one of them yelled.

"Hold her still!"

"Hospital! Straight to the hospital!"

"Get out of the way!"

"*Comot*!"

As they carried her past, I saw her. Her face, so beautiful in life, was frozen. Eyes open, grotesquely. Mouth slack, blood dripping.

For a moment, her eyes held mine, and in those fractions of a second she was there, and then…

CHAPTER TWO

Sade died that afternoon. I knew because it rained, the first of the year. As it fell in crazy, hypnotic drops, I stared, lost in space, at *Sade Nightingale on the Beach* and wondered if it had all been just a dream. A twisted, diabolical joke. A harsh, delirious nightmare.

As I stared at the smile on her face, the bloodied image of her face suddenly juxtaposed into view, evoking a profound, atavistic sense of loss. A strange, indescribable sensation poured over me. I shivered. Waves and waves of nausea washed through me.

Why, oh why, death, did you take her away?

I leaned against the easel as the events of the day rewound in my mind. I wondered if I could have done anything to save her. Could I have warned her of danger? Helped her?

My deep thoughts were interrupted by the door flying open.

"Na here you dey!" Somto exclaimed, waving a few wet bills at me. "I don finally collect back my money from that merchant. Stupid man. You should have seen the way he was arguing with me. Arrogant display of ignorance!"

He chuckled, pocketing the cash.

"Thomas Punk shirt is not the same as Thomas Pink!" A tiny hiss escaped his mouth before he added quietly, "If I wan' buy Thomas Punk, I know where to go. Nonsense!"

Somto was my friend for many years. He was funny, irreverent, and ate like a thief. He glanced at his watch now.

"Anyway, that's not why I'm here. Where is Kabiru? I've been looking everywhere for him."

Without disconnecting my gaze from her, I shook my head.

"You neva see am?"

He paced about, knocking a few items onto the floor.

"Chai! That guy should work with the power company as something, anything! They are a match made in heaven. Unreliable! He promised to take my niece to the airport this evening, and her flight leaves in two hours!"

He threw his hands up in frustration and pulled open the drawer where I kept a box of crackers. After a few more seconds of agitation, he grabbed a pack.

"He's been acting funny too," he continued, chewing noisily. "When I called him the driver in front of my niece, he got angry. I mean, I don't understand. Is he a pilot?"

I sat on the old recliner chair and sighed.

Somto pushed the drawer closed.

"You should go to the store and buy more crackers, biko. It's almost finished here, and I don't think there will be any left to pinch tomorrow. You want me to starve?"

I sighed again and buried my head in my hands, wishing somehow she would communicate with me. Tell me it's not true. I tried to conjure my last memory of her, not the bloodied, garish one, but the alluring smile that permeated to me shortly after I arrived at the service.

How was I to know that was the last time we would regard each other?

"Why do you look like a man with the biggest problem in the world, eh?" Somto asked, annoyed at my uncharacteristic sullenness. "Did someone die?"

The aptness of his question caught me off guard.

I got up and circled around the easel.

My friend froze for a moment.

"What's wrong?"

"Someone died."

"You are just making that up, silly!" He laughed. "I know it's not your mama because I still saw her on the street before this rain started. Who died? Rocky? No, not possible. I heard it bark when I entered, so who died?"

Slowly, I pointed to the painting.

"Sade? Mbanu!" he dismissed with a wave of his hand, then stuttered. "You funny. Wait… is she…? I heard some people talking about a girl attacked in… my God! Is she the one?"

Somto covered his mouth, distressed.

I nodded.

"How did it happen?"

"Didn't know today would be the last time I would see her again."

"You told me you would be having lunch with her today. Chineke!" he cried, pulling a stool and sitting down. "How did it happen?"

I told him what I knew, what the woman said, and how the men carried her away.

"In the church!" he cried again. "I mean, it's not like it's a club or a hostel or something where bad things like that can happen. I have never heard of something like this before."

"It's strange."

"So nobody saw anything?"

"I don't think so." I shook my head. "I—"

"Wait, wait, wait, first." He interrupted me with a dubious finger. "She was carried away still alive, and I think I overheard something like that too. How did you know she's dead? She could still be ali—"

"She is gone," I cut in. "I saw it. I saw it in her eyes that she was going to go. This rain confirmed it."

"Rain?"

My friend looked perplexed.

"What has the rain got to do with death?"

Almost as soon as he made that statement, he jerked as a loud crack of thunder exploded. Outside, Rocky let out an eerie howl.

Somto blinked at the ceiling, dismayed. The rain intensified.

He stayed silent for a while.

"Maybe you are right."

I picked up an HB pencil and snapped it in half.

"I was too stunned to react. I wanted to follow them. The people who carried her away."

"What would you have done if you followed them?"

"I don't know." I snapped the broken pencil into smaller pieces. "But I just feel I could have been there for her, you know. I could have done something."

"Like what? I think you are hurting. But how can a girl be attacked like that? Any reason?"

I was silent and listened to the drumming of the rain on the roof.

"I barely knew her. I just know she's a nurse and a nice girl. Someone I want to spend some time with. I told you how we met, abi? I don't know much about her life. That is what is most painful. I was just getting to know her."

"Eyah," Somto said, looking at her painting. "Even from the painting, I know that she's a nice person. Very innocent-looking. I wish I had met her too. But, eh, how is it possible?"

"It's a mystery."

For the next few minutes, Somto and I remained in puzzled silence, punctuated occasionally by his snorts of shock and disbelief.

The rain receded. Outside, the gate opened, and Rocky yelped.

"What did she do?" I whispered almost to myself. "Who did she offend? I want to know! Her face was very bloodied… I barely recognized it."

A premonitory chill traced its icy way down my spine as I remembered the frightened look on her face some moments before the attack.

Could it be…?

The door creaked open.

"Thank God for the rain!" Maami exclaimed, coming inside. Rocky darted in after her, shaking its body vigorously. "You are here. And you too, Somto. I was just entering Mrs. Ajayi's house when it started."

"I saw you, ma," Somto said and greeted her.

"How is your mother?"

"She is better."

"Thank God."

Still ecstatic about the rain, she continued, "My vegetables will grow better now. Green and big. I won't have to ask you to water them for me. I will plant some okra this time. And waterleaf, too. I will ask Kabiru to do that one for me. Do you think I should plant some ewedu too? They didn't grow well last year, if you remember."

I shrugged.

"You still have not finished Iyabo's painting, eh?" she pointed to Mrs. Banjo's unfinished oil on canvas and continued with a scowl.

"How long will it take you to finish it, eh? It's how many weeks now? Five?"

"About that, Maami."

"Ah, oga o. Finish it quickly, tori'olorun. I don't want her to eat me alive."

I nodded.

"This one is very fine," she remarked, pointing to *Sade Nightingale on the Beach*. "Very beautiful. I have not seen it before. You just painted it?"

"Yes."

The corners of her mouth curved downward in a scoff. She held out a contemptuous hand.

"You can paint fine sisi very quickly because she's young and beautiful. But you are taking your time to paint Iyabo because she's old an' fat. Old like your mother, abi?"

"It's not that, Maami."

"Then how is it o'jare?" she asked with a wry smile. "You men will be men!"

A sound escaped Somto's mouth. Maami eyed him jocularly.

"She will eat me alive if I tell her he has not finished it!"

"I will finish it soon."

"How many portraits have you done for her?"

"Three, four. I can't remember." I can't think!

"This one took too long," she observed again and turned to leave, then stopped short at the door.

"Eh-ehn!" she exclaimed in sudden recollection of something. "She called me this afternoon and told me a girl was killed in her church, the one you have been going to lately."

"We were just talking about it before you came," Somto said after a moment's hesitation from me.

"Everyone is talking about it," said Maami, full of pity. "I heard it on the radio in Mrs. Ajayi's house. This world is getting more and more wicked that a girl is not even safe in the church. And she is the only one of her parents! How sad."

"Did she say she died?" I asked.

"That's what she told me," replied Maami with a puzzled frown. "She died at the hospital she was taken to."

I shrank in my chair. There was a loud ringing inside my head. A part of me had wanted to be wrong, wanted her to be alive even though I knew she was gone.

My head whirled. It felt like I was spun around repeatedly. I placed a hand over my eyes.

"Kilode? Did you know her?"

I told her. I told her the sisi in the painting was the girl murdered. Maami sank into a chair and whimpered.

Tears welled in my eyes.

By the time they both left, I was so physically and mentally exhausted that I went to the recliner chair and slept in it.

That evening, I had a dream. In it, we had the lunch date, and everything was smooth until she started to cry. She cried until I woke up from it, sweating profusely and feeling horribly ill.

I couldn't get back to sleep, try as I might, for the rest of the night. The dream kept coming to my mind's eye the minute I closed them.

The next day, still filled with memories of her ghostly face, I succumbed to an impulsive desire to stroll. I needed to clear my head. The weather was gloomy and underpowered, hungover from yesterday's rain.

Ahead, the street stretched long and tarred, fairly busy. I wandered on foot, taking in the different activities: schoolchildren returning, mai ruwa pushing carts, a few indolent youths arguing about football.

I walked past Rendezvous, the only bar on the street. It was a small spot that came alive when the sun went down. Now, there were a few patrons having a drink or two, a subdued ambience about it. One of the customers was Kabiru, and he was in the company of a friend, and they were serenading a voluptuous woman who had just entered the bar.

He did not see me, and I did not bring his attention to my presence. I just walked on.

I continued walking and reached the intersection, and crossed to the other side. Here, the road was unpaved and full of trenches and mud-filled potholes. I wore only flat flip-flops, and soon my feet were enveloped in a purée of mud. It didn't deter me. I marched on and only stopped at the foot of a high-tension tower.

A small crowd had gathered around it. They were urging a man atop it to come down. He refused until his demands were met. He wanted His Excellency, the President of the Federal Republic of Nigeria, to fly a chopper and unload a huge sum of money on him. He wanted a rain of money. A huge chunk of it, too, must be sent to his father-in-law in Benin. He also wanted his wife and three children back.

Lastly, he wanted an American visa. Some evil forces were after him, and America was going to be his safe haven.

The crowd grew agitated. A couple of teenage boys hurled rocks at him. The man began to cry.

I left the place when a policeman showed up.

I got to another road. It lay before me like a tarmac ribbon. A white line ran down the middle as far as the eye could see. Old houses and stalls lined the sides, and cars zipped past in either direction.

I walked, now in labored steps, with my head full of thoughts.

It began to drizzle, and I contemplated going back. When the intensity moved up a notch, I turned back. Almost instinctively, I looked across the road and saw her.

She was dressed in a loose blouse and a flannel skirt. Her dark hair gleamed as she crossed the road in quick, lithe steps.

It was like a vision.

It came so quickly, like a flash.

"Sade…"

I held out a hand to her shoulder and instantly recognized my mistake. The slap came quickly, an explosion of stars.

"Leave me alone!" the startled lady cried. "Madman."

I thought I had seen her.

I stood still for a moment and watched the lady run wildly away from me. She slipped near a rubbish bin and cursed.

I'm sorry. I didn't mean to.

"Bro, you dey okay?" asked a lad smoking a cigarette in a kiosk. He had witnessed what had happened and was now looking at my muddied feet.

I nodded and turned back in the direction of home.

CHAPTER THREE

"Did you sleep well?" Maami asked as I sauntered into the sitting room. She was seated on her favorite chair with a view of the garden. Somto sat on the rug, his legs crossed.

They were both reading *The Guardian*. For Maami, it was a ritual she picked up shortly after Father disappeared when I was only a boy. *The Guardian* was his favorite newspaper, and Maami continued to subscribe in his memory. For Somto, it was a habit he picked up the week after he lost his job.

I shrugged, went to the fridge, and poured myself a glass of cold water.

"I had another dream."

There was a slight look of worry on her face that quickly disappeared when I said, "It's not bad this time."

"What did you dream about?" Somto's voice was anything but concerned. With his gaze still fixed on the paper, he added flippantly, "The kain dream I want to be dreaming is Baba Ijebu jackpot for tomorrow's game. That is the only dream worth dreaming, I tell you."

"How often do you say that?" I asked, sitting on the sofa near him. "That you wish a powerful being would give you the winning numbers just like that. I've lost count."

"It will happen," Somto said. "You man of little faith, it will happen. You will see."

"The dream, or you winning the lottery?"

There was a confused look on his face.

"Both."

"I don't know," I said, shaking my head, "who is crazier. You or Kabiru."

"It is Kabiru," Maami said with a quiet laugh. "Did I tell you what his wife said to me last week?"

"No."

"Ah-ah," she clucked. "She told me he was going up and down the street begging that madman at the junction—what is his name again o—?"

"Lugbogi."

"Ehn-o! Lugbogi—begging him to give him numbers!" Maami screeched with laughter. "Is that not madness?"

"Does he have special powers?" I asked, a little amused. I've heard of people begging for winning numbers from people suffering psychiatric problems, and they supposedly, sometimes, get winning numbers from them, but not one this close to home.

"How will I know?"

"So it is possible they can see things?"

Maami shrugged her shoulders and tapped her thigh with the back of her hand.

"Risi told me some people have been asking Lugbogi for numbers and they have been winning o—yes, that is what she said."

Somto closed the newspaper, his eyes gleaming like those of a wild beast.

"What?" I asked. "You want to go and beg Lugbogi for numbers too?"

"Beg?" he replied, mildly incredulous. "Mbanu! I want to go to the junction and beat him up. Then I will ask for the numbers."

Maami let out a wild laugh.

"Be careful when you attack a madman," I warned. "He can hurl feces at you just to defend himself."

"Don't mind your friend Somto," Maami said. "It is what you think of yourself that will happen to you."

"You hear that? At least I'm playing the game. To win a lottery, you have to buy a ticket, Oga. You, my friend, cannot win a lottery because you won't buy a ticket. Not possible."

"I don't want to win the lottery. I just want to be happy with the little I do. Money doesn't have such a big effect on me."

Even though my gaze was on Somto, who had just returned to the paper, I could feel Maami's lingering look on me. I didn't meet her gaze.

"You sound just like your father, Deji," she said wistfully. A bit sad even.

I said to Somto, "So what about your interview? The one with the oil company. How did it go?"

He dropped the paper on his lap and cried, "Worst day of my life!"

His outburst surprised Maami, who asked, "Kilo shele, my dear?"

"They embarrassed me, ma. Chai! Nothing Musa no go see for gate for dis Lagos."

"What happened?"

"I can't say it. I am too ashamed."

"Don't be ashamed of yourself, my dear," Maami said to him. "The worst they can do is say you are not qualified."

"If only that's what they said, ma, I will be happy."

"What did they say?"

He cleared his throat.

"I got there early enough. Seven o'clock. Powerfully dressed. You know me now. I thought they were interviewing me for a position like financial analyst or auditor—dat kain ting—but guess what? I should have known."

He cried with renewed bitterness.

"I should have suspected it from the time I got there and left quickly before they poured shame on me. Every applicant in the waiting room was dressed like a primary school teacher. Some even wore monkey jackets—can you imagine? I was surprised, but I thought maybe we were there for different interviews. Chai! I was wrong.

"When the lady came out to call us in, and she saw my dressing, and I saw the look in her eyes, Deji, I saw the look in her eyes, she wanted to laugh! I asked her what I was being interviewed for, and she said, 'Doorman.' Doorman! I wanted the earth to open up and swallow me. I wanted to die."

"And you went powerfully dressed?" I mocked him. "How did you get the invitation?"

"I must have applied years ago for a position, but they forgot about it and spooled randomly when they needed applications for doormen, clerks, and co."

"You must feel terrible."

"Don't worry, my dear," Maami soothed. "Things like this don't last for long. Just be patient."

"Worst day of my life," he repeated, picking up the paper.

"What did you dream about, Ayodeji?" Maami asked abruptly. Her eyes watched me.

"It's not bad like the first few ones."

"You think too much about her," she said after a while. "It will only stop when you get it out of your mind. Maybe you should go out more often."

I nodded and pulled at my ear.

"Eh-ehn!" she exclaimed suddenly. "I wanted to tell you something, but I always forget. My friend Iyabo told me that somebody sent a painting of the girl to her parents yesterday. Se'wo ni?"

I heard the sheaf of newspapers collapse. Somto stared wide-eyed at me. I rubbed my cheek. Maami, with a dramatic sigh, rested her head in her palm and fixed her gaze on me.

"I sent it yesterday morning."

"Ah-ah, shuo!" ejaculated my friend. "Why now? Why do you do something like that? Don't you know they may think you are a person of interest?"

"Who?"

"The police."

"I'm not a fool," I countered. "I sent it anonymously. I just wanted to do something for her family. I wanted to make them feel not alone. Something alive to remember their daughter by. It's not a crime."

"Well, they are looking for the person who sent it!" Maami thundered. "Sho'tan!"

"You see your life?"

"Did you tell Mrs. Banjo you think it was me?" I asked her.

"Haba! Why will I do that? I am your mother. You know Iyabo will tell anyone that cares to listen exactly what you have cooked that burned the house!"

She was right. Mrs. Banjo had a reputation as the town parrot.

"I didn't even tell her you and the girl knew each other."

"Which one did you send to them?" asked Somto. "*Sade Nightingale on the Beach*?"

"No. I sent the first one. *Singing Angel*."

"Ah," muttered my friend, relieved. "I thought you sent *Sade Nightingale on the Beach*. I would have asked to check your temperature. That's your best work. A masterpiece."

"I kept it for myself."

"How did you send it, by the way?"

"I went to their street and paid a small boy to deliver it."

"And in your eyes, that is anonymous?" he asked. "Someone saw your face."

"It's only a small boy."

"Is he a blind boy? He saw your face! I hope this thing will not come back to bite you for yansh o."

"You are overreacting. My intentions were good."

"The police don't see your intentions, Deji. They see your actions and, from your actions, connect things that probably aren't there. Your action connects you to the victim. You don't want that. Police wahala is a serious wahala!"

"You did a good thing," Maami said after a spell of rumination. "It should make you feel better about yourself."

She pushed herself to her feet and disappeared into the kitchen.

I picked up the newspaper that Maami had just dropped and glanced at the headlines. The economic situation was dire, as always, and another bomb had just gone off somewhere in the northeast. This had been the recurring narrative for a few years now, and I didn't think it would make any difference if you picked an older issue to read. You'd still be abreast of things.

I lost interest after turning a few sheets. My mind returned to the scene at the church and fixated on that look of fear I saw on her face.

"A fine girl like that will have enemies," Maami said, returning with a tray laden with amaranthus. She must have read my mind.

"She was a nice girl, Maami. She couldn't hurt a mosquito."

"Everyone has enemies, Ayodeji." She picked up a shoot and plucked its leaves. "Even the corn that grows in the fields has enemies. This vegetable has enemies. If you look at it very well… eh-ehn, look! Do you see this insect? Enemies!"

"But they don't get killed just like that, ma," said Somto reasonably. "Especially in a place as open as the church."

"People don't just kill for no reason," said Maami with a robust shrug. "There must be a reason, ke. The reason this insect kills this vegetable is to make a living. We know people kill for money. People kill for revenge! There must be a reason."

"Why was she killed?" I said, almost to myself.

"Why was she killed?" she echoed. "You can have enemies in the church too. There's no place you can't have them. Enemies in the church, enemies in the choir, envy and jealousy everywhere…"

"What if," speculated Somto, "someone died on her watch, and an aggrieved family took revenge? Or maybe she switched babies? Or sold a baby? Terrible things like that we hear nurses do."

All three of us went at each other on the possible reasons for her murder without a unanimous verdict that satisfied.

Maami suddenly stopped picking the vegetables. She pulled out her cellphone from inside the arm of the chair and began punching.

"Let me ask my friend, Iyabo. She will know something."

Maami placed a call to her friend and put it on speaker.

"Rolake! Thank God you called." Mrs. Banjo's raspy voice popped on. "Oremi, where are you?"

"How are you? I am at home. Listen, Iyabo, I want to ask you something—"

"Always at home! You must be smelling of your house by now. What are you doing sitting at home?"

A pause.

"I am just home. I want to cook vegetable sou—"

"What is the use of the soup if you don't know what's going on around town, eh? You don't know what is happening, Rolake! Ha! We have been friends for how long now, and you still don't look like me, eh?"

Maami laughed.

"What is going on in town, Oremi?"

"Now you are talking! See, party kan wa…a coronation party for Oba Akin…Akin…I have forgotten his name o'jare! Anyway, there is a party, and we are going together!"

"Today?" Maami couldn't resist. "What time?"

"The time is this afternoon. I heard my neighbor talking about it."

"Which of your neighbors?"

"The one I told you has three grown children from three different fathers. Don't let me wear something better than you!"

"Owambe!" cried Maami in delight.

Mrs. Banjo reciprocated with a screeching laughter that sounded like something from a witches' coven. She stopped laughing abruptly.

"Why am I hearing myself laughing, Rolake?"

"I put you on speaker, Oremi."

"Why? Is your ear hurting?"

"I want my son to listen to what I—"

"Deji? So you are there!"

"Yes, ma," I called. "Good morn—"

"I will pay the police to lock you up for six months, and there is nothing your Maami will do about it. Where is my portrait?"

"I'm almost done with it. It will be ready soon."

"I want it ready yesterday. You hear?"

"It will be ready yesterday."

"Good. Eh-ehn, Rolake, what did you want to ask me about?"

"It's about that girl that died in your—"

"Sade! Hmm. Everybody is still in shock. You know, I told you somebody sent her parents a painting of their daughter?"

"Yes."

"Did I tell you the police are looking for that person?"

Maami gasped.

"I hope they don't find him—"

"Why? Ki lo kan e? How is it your business?"

"What else are you hearing about it, Oremi?"

"You won't believe what I have heard."

"What did you hear?"

"I hear they suspect the four people who were with her that day she died. They think one of them did it!"

"Four ke?" asked Maami, surprised. "Kilode?!"

"Are you asking me? That's what I heard."

"Who are they?"

"They are people in the choir. Just like her."

Maami flashed me a knowing glance.

"Is that so?" she cajoled. "I was just saying that to my son, too. Do you know them?"

There was a clunking sound in the background, like a dish opening, followed by a cry.

"Ehn?!"

"I'm asking if you know the—"

"Toiba! Toiba!!" Mrs. Banjo yelled in the background. "I asked for fish. Fish, not meat. Useless girl. Toiba! I will kill you today. You will go back to your wretched village, people. Today!"

"Iyabo—"

"Toiba!"

The line went dead.

"One day she will kill that girl," Maami shook her head and examined the bowl of plucked vegetables. Satisfied with the quantity, she began gathering them on a platter before letting out a hiss.

"Knife!"

"Let me get it for you, ma." Somto rose swiftly.

"Thank you, my dear. It is by the cooker."

"You heard what she said," Somto returned with the knife. "They are looking for you."

"It's not a crime to send a painting."

Maami made a sound that seemed to agree with me and began chopping the vegetables.

I immediately seized on a thought that had been teasing my mind for a while.

"Somto, don't you have an uncle who is a divisional police officer?"

He frowned.

"If you mean DPO, yes. But I haven't spoken to him in years. Stingy man like that. One of those yeye uncles everyone has. And hates."

I said carefully, "Do you think you can get something from him? Something about the four people?"

"Did you hear what I just said?"

Irritated, Somto dropped the paper he held and picked up the one I had dropped earlier.

"But he's your uncle."

"What am I even going to say to him to get that kind of information?"

"Just get through to him first. You never know."

"Okay, I get you now. I will go to his office and say, 'Uncle, how far? How body? Abeg dat girl wey die for inside church—Sade, yes, abeg give me the name of dem suspects I wan consult oracle to find out which one is responsible.' Yeah—"

His sarcasm cut through me.

"That will really work."

Maami gave a quiet chuckle that quickly compounded into a cough.

I became numb for a while.

"Tell him you know the girl," she said, gathering the chopped vegetables into another bowl. "He will feel some pity. Does he have a daughter?"

Somto nodded.

"Eh-ehn! Tell him you know her, and he will tell you what you want. Men are not that difficult."

"He is your uncle," I said again.

Somto considered.

"I will try. But what do you want them for?"

"I will tell you when your uncle tells you what I want," I said.

Maami's questioning gaze lingered.

Somto returned to flipping through the papers again.

"Slavery! Modern-day slavery! I would rather sit at home and play Baba Ijebu!" he boomed. "Listen to this…Hesperidium Consult is looking for a financial analyst with a strong auditing background and at least five years of experience, but the job description includes, and I quote…"

Somto returned two days later. Maami was on the veranda, knitting a sweater, and within earshot.

"Okay, so this is what I found out from my uncle, and you owe me big time," he began. "Sade was bludgeoned. Someone hit her hard in the head with something. It must have happened when the service was about to finish, in a room at the back of the pulpit. I think they sometimes use it, but I'm not very clear on what they do there."

Maami was making a few mournful noises in the background.

Bludgeoned, yes. That explained the garish look on her face as they carried her away.

"A room they sometimes use?" I was confused. "What does that mean?"

"Like a changing room or something. I don't know! My uncle was vague about it, but I'm thinking it's for a quick change. Something like that. Na dat kain church me I for like to dey go sef." Somto licked his lips. "Guys and girls changing in the same room?"

Maami groaned.

"I don't think it will be that fun, but go on."

"Okay, there were five of them in the room. Sade was there too, but all four of them told the police they returned to the service and that she was alive when they left her there."

"They all said this?" I asked, perturbed. "They all left at once?"

"That's what he told me."

A flurry of muddled thoughts.

"What was she doing there alone?"

"I don't know." Somto seemed to have lost interest in the matter after he had given the information I needed.

"Waiting for the killer?" I prodded.

"I think," he conceded, "from what my uncle said, the five of them are like a clique."

"A clique?"

"Yes. Accomplished singers. The church's best—blah blah blah, something like that."

"Who are they?"

"I was just getting there. Why your blood dey hot?" Somto meant, Why was I so much in a hurry? He drew out a piece of paper from his wallet and read, "Sade, that's the victim; Lara, her best friend; Nike; Modele; Jimi, the choirmaster."

"All of them are women," Maami observed, "except for that man Jimi, abi what did you call him?"

"One of them killed Sade," I concluded aloud.

"Yeah. That's what the police think. Naturally, the suspicion is on the guy." Somto folded the piece of paper and put it in his mouth.

"Women kill too," Maami's voice carried through.

"She was bludgeoned," said Somto. "Someone struck her in the head. Wham!"

"I thought women killed by pouring acids or using poisons," I said. "I remember stories of gammelin-20. Things like that."

"Or juju," added Somto. "Voodoo. That's my personal favorite. Why kill by physical means when you can just say the words?"

Maami poured scorn on my assertion with a derisory laugh.

"Omode o'moogun ounpe l'efo. You see that stick in the kitchen?" she asked. "The one I use to knead amala…? A woman can kill with that. She can even kill with her stiletto too."

Somto mumbled something unintelligible.

"She just has to do it right. Or don't women shoot?" argued Maami. "What a man can do, a woman can also do."

"I thought they did it better," Somto whispered to me. "Isn't that the saying?"

"They don't do it better." Maami clearly heard what he had said. "Women who say that don't believe it themselves."

I sat back and thought for a while, my thoughts punctuated by Rocky's incessant barking.

"Now that you have the names," said my friend, returning from the fridge with a piece of cake, which Maami protested but ultimately fell on deaf ears, "what are you going to do with them?"

I picked up a currant from the plate, squashed it with my fingers, and tasted it.

"I am going to find them one by one and interview them until I know which one of them killed Sade."

For a moment, we didn't speak. An ominous silence appeared to have wedged us before Somto broke it with an unexpected screech.

"Can you do something for me?"

"What?"

"I want you to find the nearest river to this place—"

I sensed where this was going, but still raised a quizzical brow.

"—and wash your head thoroughly at the riverbank, with black soap, to appease the gods! Because something, my friend, is pushing you to play with fire!"

"You are dramatic."

"You want to meddle with murder? If katakata bursts, I will not go to my uncle for your sake."

"I need to do this."

"You don't understand. It's like doing the police's job for the police."

"Relax. I have a plan."

"Let him ask around, Somto, my dear, if it is troubling him so much," I heard Maami say as I approached the door. "He liked that girl so much. Maybe it will even stop those dreams you are having?"

I nodded and whistled for Rocky.

CHAPTER FOUR

If you looked down from the highway with keen, telescopic eyes, you'd probably still miss the little settlement of Lafenwa. A rustic place of scenic beauty located just on the outskirts of the city. It was from here that I began my investigation into the murder of Sade with a visit to Nike, the first suspect.

The VW Golf groaned and ground to a halt in front of a nondescript bungalow at exactly 3 p.m. The houses were unnumbered, but it was easy to find this particular one. It was the only house with a green rafter roof, just as she had described to me.

Kabiru pulled from his dirty buba a neatly wrapped stick of igbo. He struck a match and lit it. As he did so, I got out of the car and looked around the agricultural setting, almost envying the peace and tranquility the dwellers here enjoyed. After noticing how sparse and far apart the homes were, I approached the gateless property with the pomp of a tax collector. It was new and freshly painted.

I knocked, and the door opened.

"Are you the man coming to see my wife?" The tone was more accusatory than welcoming.

"She agreed to see me, yes." I was looking down, with a degree of perplexity, at the man before me.

"Good afternoon." He regarded me with mirth.

"Afternoon, Mr. Reporter. Nike is in the bathroom. Come in."
The voice, like the face, was boyish.

I entered the cozy apartment, trying to hide my amusement. The man, you see, was a proportionate dwarf. He was about the size of an obese seven-year-old. He bounced ahead like a big pool ball.

"You are a reporter, eh?" he asked, looking back at me. His grin was cutesy and warm.

"Yes."

I looked around. The living room was reasonably big, made modern by the oversized television and state-of-the-art home theater. But what caught my eye were the color schemes. The walls were painted in a garish neon carrot-and-magenta palette in an attempt, albeit one that failed, to be aesthetic. It made the shade of pink of the L-shaped couch even more ghastly. With a few discothèque lights, I said to myself, you'd have the rudiments of a clubhouse.

"I'm a comedian," he announced with the ebullience of a child handed a toy.

"Oh, that's…" very fitting, I wanted to say, but said instead, "a rewarding job nowadays."

"Yes-o. Comedians make good money now. Unlike before. Sit down. Nike, hurry up!"

"You don't have to rush her, please," I said. "I can wait."

"My wife can bathe for an hour!" he whispered, almost conspiratorially.

"Women take their time. Unlike us men."

"What are we washing to take that long?" He spread his hands, bemused.

"I don't spend more than one minute in the bathroom. Time na money."

"Where do you get your jokes from?"

"Anything." He shrugged, throwing his arms in the air. "Everything. Like this, your beard, uncle."

I rubbed it instinctively. "What about it?"

His expression was suddenly deadpan. "They make me remember Olente, my father's goat in the village. Stubborn animal like that."

"Did he enjoy the meat last Christmas?"

"Who eats goat for Christmas?"

We laughed. The dwarf, I soon realized, was a seasoned talker. He prattled about his childhood, bullies, and discovery as a comedian. I listened attentively. It occurred to me that he was one to relish the company of a good listener.

"Comedy is big business now," he added lavishly. "I even want to set up a school."

"A school of comedy?"

"Yes."

"You will be the principal?"

"No. Secretary!"

We laughed again. His careless joke about my beard had caused me to become conscious of its imperfection. There was a wayward strand I had been meaning to pluck out for some time now. I did so presently while looking around.

"Where is Nike now?" he wondered, echoing my very thoughts. Almost as soon as he'd said that, Nike walked in, preceded by a soft waft of fragrance. Her demeanor was very respectable, somewhat mournful. She greeted me with all the politeness you'd expect from a well-mannered lady and sat next to her husband, who, unsurprisingly, looked like her son.

"Good afternoon, Nike," I responded. "I called you earlier on the phone."

She nodded.

"What took you so long, my darling? I hàve been telling this man jokes he's not paying for."

"Do you want anything?" She sounded tired.

"No. I'm fine. Thank you."

"You must take something," the dwarf insisted. "Otherwise, you have not visited us." The couple spelled out an assortment of refreshments: wines, juices, apples, bananas, and biscuits.

"An apple will be fine," I said finally. "Thank you."

"Let me get it." The dwarf bounced to his feet and rolled off. Nike smiled, amused by something.

I studied the woman before me. Nike was not the sort of woman guys at the bar talked about. She was of good height, but that was as good as it got. She had very dark, oily skin with a large, broad nose. There was a mark the shape of a kola nut on her chin, and her teeth protruded. In spite of these, she retained an air of savoir-faire.

"Interesting choice of colors."

"I hate it," she replied frankly. "I think my husband is trying to tell our friends a joke with it."

"You don't like them?"

"How can I? I will have it changed soon."

"What do you hate, my darling?" asked her husband. He had just returned with a bowl of apples and was already eating one.

"I was just telling Mr. Depiver… Deji Depiver, abi?"

"Yes."

"Okay. I was telling him that I don't like the colors you painted the house."

"You said you liked it before."

"That was then. Now I hate it."

"Just last week o," he reminded her.

"I don't like it anymore," she said with firm honesty.

"It's not that bad," I said, "but you can try this combination I saw at a friend's house if you must change it. See, you can paint this part of the house mauve"—I pointed to the television area—"that's a lighter shade of purple, but not as light as lilac." She stared at me with sudden interest. "Then you can paint the other part peach or taupe, depending on how bright or soft you want the house to be."

"I like it!" she shouted. "I like it already. Let's do exactly what he said." She wrapped her hands around her husband, who nibbled on.

"No wahala," he said, chewing noisily. "I just hope the week after, you will not hate it again."

"I won't!" To me, she said, "It's a good idea you gave us. Eat some apples."

I nodded, picked an apple from the bowl, and examined it.

"So what newspaper did you say you work for again?" she asked.

"The Guardian."

Her husband stopped nibbling. "Do people still read newspapers in this age of the internet?"

"My mother does," I said with a smile and sank my teeth into the apple, attesting to its deliciousness with a repeated nod of my head like an agama lizard. Nike grinned.

"Who is that urinating in front of my house?" asked the dwarf abruptly. He stood on the couch and peered.

I turned my head and looked through the window. Kabiru was urinating, facing the house in the most peculiar manner. His trousers were down to his ankles. As he urinated, he held his penis, which from my vantage looked like that of a horse, firmly with one hand and, with the other, tapped repeatedly on his forehead.

"Who is that?" Nike asked.

"The company driver," I stuttered.

"Is he okay? Why is he slapping his head?"

"I don't know myself," I said, cursing Kabiru.

For some reason, the dwarf found it hilarious. He tossed his half-eaten apple in the bowl and excused himself. I reckoned he'd recognized another source of a joke. A few seconds later, I could see him talking animatedly with Kabiru.

I smiled at Nike, whose gaze still lingered. Her buck teeth were now even more pronounced in her state of bemusement. I cleared my throat.

She shifted in her seat, suddenly aware of my gaze. "I hope he is okay."

"He is fine."

She nodded. "So what did you say you were investigating for The Guardian, Mr. Deji?"

"Domestic violence against women. There's an uptick here in the West."

"Domestic violence?" she stuttered. She picked up the remote control from the center table and muted the television. "Sade did not die from a domestic kind of violence."

"But she died violently, didn't she?"

She blinked wildly, then nodded. "Yes."

"Then we are saying the same thing," I reassured her with a smile. "What can you tell me about Sade?" I pulled out a pad and a pen. Nike drew in a deep breath and let out a sigh. She paused as though pondering how to begin.

"It's sad what happened to her," she began somberly. "I can't understand any of it or why it happened. Till today, it's still like I'm dreaming. Sade was a nice person. Everyone liked her. She was like an angel."

"That was the impression I got, too."

"Ask anybody. They will tell you she was nice…and for her to die like that…" A tear rolled down her face. She wiped it off with a finger. "God will judge. Only God will judge."

"You were very close to her?"

She hesitated. "We are like sisters, all of us. We are a family. That is why this is so painful."

I scribbled something in the pad and tried my best to look the part. "Tell me about the choir."

She looked up and blinked uncertainly. "We sing for the church."

"Yes, I know," I said with a discomfited smile. "What I mean is your relationship with the others, especially the clique."

"The clique?"

"Yes, the five of you."

"Oh!" she exclaimed in instant recognition. "You mean Big Five."

"Is that what you call it?"

"Yes, that is what we call ourselves. I don't even know who gave us that name." She placed a finger on her temple and dredged up her memory. "Now that I think of it, I think it was Sade. I remember I wanted us to be called Fabulous Five, but then the others preferred Sade's name, so…" She shrugged her shoulders.

"I like Fabulous Five better," I said. "It has a nice ring to it."

"That is what I thought too." Her face lit up momentarily. "But Sade normally won things like that." There was a bitter smile on her face that was soon replaced by a forlorn look. "It started when we wanted to record a few songs. We asked ourselves what we would be called, but we didn't go ahead with the plan."

"Why not?"

"Nothing o. Just that we felt it was not right. Since then, people call us the Big Five."

"So it's not like you are different from the rest of the choir?"

She shook her head. "We are just…well, you can say the best sha, but I don't like to use that word. It's not good for the rest of us."

I nodded. There was a noise coming from within the house that suggested to me there was a third party.

"I think the five of you sit in the front row of the choir?"

"Yes. We sit permanently in the front of the choir."

I scribbled some more. "Did she quarrel with anybody? Did she have enemies?"

"Enemies," she murmured. "I don't know who would make enemies with her. She was a person who made friends with everybody. Very sociable."

"Did she party?"

Nike shook her head, somewhat without conviction. "Erm…she was very quiet. I didn't think she partied like that. Or maybe you should ask Lara. Are you not supposed to be recording this?"

"I don't need to."

"Because the inspector who interviewed me last week recorded everything."

"I prefer to write. I like it that way."

Nike nodded but didn't look convinced. "Can you think of anyone who may have wanted to harm her? Anyone at all?" I tried again.

"I have thought about this too." She wrinkled her face, eyebrows drawn together. "And I'm still thinking about it. I really don't know. It's very strange. But I told the inspector that I saw a man enter the changing room just as the service was about to end."

I stiffened. "A man?"

"Yes."

"What did he look like?"

"That's the problem," she replied with a sigh. "I can't even remember."

"Do you think this man was responsible?"

"That's what I think."

A door opened, and a young girl emerged. She strode cheerfully across the room and was almost out the door when Nike barked with venom, "Come back here!"

The girl backpedaled.

"Can't you see we have a visitor? Can't you greet? Where are your manners?"

The girl greeted me, but Nike wasn't finished. "Where do you think you are going dressed like a prostitute on Allen Avenue, eh?"

"Tutorial," the girl sulked.

Nike laughed. "So how will you dress if you are going to a party, eh? My friend, go back inside and dress properly. And remove that makeup on your face."

The girl grumbled and went back whence she came.

"My sister," Nike explained, looking embarrassed. "She's staying with us until she finishes her exams. UTME."

"I hope she passes well."

She rolled her eyes. "If she study hard and stops trying to be the center of attraction."

"Nike," I said, trying to reconnect to our conversation, "do you know Sade outside of the church?"

"Not really." Her response was swift. "I know she was a nurse and, erm, I haven't been to her place before…abi? I think I have. Once, yes. Her birthday! It was just after she joined the choir. That was, erm, a few years ago."

"Can you be exact?"

"Three years, I think."

"You had been in the choir before her?"

She nodded. "Since I was fourteen."

"Oh," I said, surprised. "That long?"

"Yes!"

"Has it always been that big?"

"No. It was a small church when I joined with my parents back then in 1995." She gazed around her living room. "About the size of this room. There were only a few members then. We grew in size over the years, as all churches do."

"I have never been in a church that long."

Nike smiled and shrugged her shoulders. "Maybe you have not found the right one for you."

"I guess you could say that." I pretended to jot some things down. "About the changing room," I said after I'd stopped writing, "where she was killed…"

"Yes?" she coughed.

"I'm confused. What is a changing room?"

Nike forced a thin smile. "People have been asking me about that. Even the inspector wanted to know. It's nothing really. Just a backstage area where we keep our robes and stuff."

"Were all five of you returning your robes that day or something? Help me understand."

"No," she spoke slightly above her breath now. "Sometimes we go in there to, erm, escape."

"Escape? From what?"

"Erm, well, it's not escape like that. Like if you have an urgent call or something, it's easy for you to enter the room to receive it. Other times, we just go in there after singing and, erm, congratulate ourselves."

"For a job well done."

"Yes!" she said eagerly. "You get it."

"All of the choir?"

"No, usually us and a few others. They gossip there too, you know."

"So on this day, were you in there congratulating yourselves?" I remembered the rendition was splendid.

"No." She paused, then continued, "I don't even know why I went in there. I just did. The A.C. is very cool too. We all like it in there."

"And this was just before the service ended?"

"Yes."

"How long were you in the changing room?"

Nike considered. "Maybe two minutes."

"Two minutes was the time you spent in there?"

Another cough escaped her mouth. "Yes. Two minutes, I think. This one is not good either," said Nike to her sister, who had just come in a second time. "Go back and change."

"What is wrong with this one?" the girl protested.

"The jeans are too tight. You want boys all over you, abi?"

"I always dress like this at home!"

"This is my home, and you can't dress like that. Go back and change."

The girl stormed off.

"What were we saying?" she asked, returning to me and clearing her throat.

"You were telling me how long you spent in the changing room."

"I said two minutes."

"Okay. What did you do during that period you were there?"

Nike paused. "I was just talking to Modele. Have you met her?"

"No, but I will see her next."

"Her house is not very far from here."

"What did you talk about?"

"Her shoes. She was wearing a fine shoe that I hadn't seen on her before."

"Women love their shoes."

She stifled a smile, conscious of her teeth.

"What were the others doing?"

"They were talking too. Among themselves."

"With the choirmaster?"

"Yes."

"What were they talking about?"

"I don't know. I didn't listen." Her eyes wandered to the window. "I was trying on Modele's shoes. They were really fine."

"What happened next?"

"I left them there."

"You didn't all leave at once, leaving Sade there?"

"No. I was the first person to leave. I left them there and went back to the service. Don't you want more?" She pointed to the bowl.

"No, I'm fine."

She picked an apple, bit into it, decided the taste fell short of her expectations, and dropped it back.

My gaze drifted to the couch. I tried again to remember what shade of pink it was. For a desperate fraction of a second, it came to my mind like a flash but disappeared quickly, as though taunting me.

"Is anything wrong?"

"I'm trying to remember what shade of pink this couch is," I said. "A small exercise for my head."

"Is it not just pink?"

"It is pink, but to people like us, it's not just pink."

"Ah!" exclaimed Nike with a scowl, as if to say, the things that bother you anyway.

"I'm sure before I leave here, I will remember it."

Nike gazed at the wall clock and nodded.

"So," I said, shifting my weight, "did Sade show any emotion that would suggest to you that she was afraid of something?"

Nike frowned, then shook her head. "I didn't observe her that much that day. I had a headache, but I thought she looked happy when she led the choir. I don't think I remember her being afraid of anything." She shook her head again. "I don't remember anything like that."

At that moment, her husband walked in with a big grin. "Dis your brother is funny."

"His brother?" asked Nike, surprised. "I thought you said he's the driver."

"With that kind of a car?" asked the dwarf, snatching another apple. "Your company must be selling tomatoes and peppers." He grabbed the remote control, unmuted the television, and flipped through the channels.

Nike got up and went to the window. I saw her jaw drop. She hissed. "Oga o. One would think The Guardian would be able to afford a better car."

"We sometimes like to conduct investigations undercover." I tried not to betray any emotion. "We don't always like to arouse suspicion." There was a glint of secret amusement in her eyes that suggested to me she didn't buy my story. Damn, Kabiru.

"Is he your brother or the company driver?"

"He is the company driver," I said. "He tells people we are brothers so as not to arouse any suspicion." I wasn't sure if I was making any sense, but that's what I said anyway.

"Suspicion of what?"

"The case," I replied as confidently as I could muster.

"Okay." Nike seemed confused. She shrugged her shoulders and left the window. "The television is too loud," she complained, sitting back down. "Turn it off, jare."

"They will soon start showing Laugh Mata."

"He is still asking me questions."

Her husband protested, but Nike fired back. "No! You cannot watch television now."

He dumped the remote, bade me goodbye, and left the room. Nike retrieved it and muted the television. She stared at me with weary eyes. "When are we going to finish? Because I want to go to the market."

"Soon."

"Okay."

"The man you saw," I scribbled, "the one you saw entering the changing room—"

"I don't think I even saw him enter the room. I think I saw him around the room. Wait, I can't even remember if it was before or after Sade died." She let out a tired hiss.

"Who do you think it was?"

"I don't know. It happened very quickly."

"Do you think you've seen him before?"

She shook her head.

"So you did not get a good look at him?"

"I didn't." She covered her face with her palm, breathing heavily. "I wish I had seen his face. I keep telling myself, maybe he is the man who did that to Sade."

"But did you see what he was wearing?"

Nike stopped agitating and appeared thoughtful. "I don't know…something dark…black…or gray. Something like that."

"Think!" I looked straight into her eyes. "Close your eyes, take a deep breath, and think." She obeyed. I could see her eyeballs move under the lids. "Cast your mind back."

Silence, except for the humming of the refrigerator.

"What do you see?"

"I think it was dark. Dark blue or black." She opened her eyes. "I'm sure now."

"You are sure?"

A rapid nod.

"Was it a big man? Or a small man?"

She considered. "I think he's a bit tall. Just like you. He was wearing a suit."

"A suit?"

"Yes. Or maybe a monkey jacket like the one my husband likes to wear. Something like that."

I leaned forward. "Do you think it was a man you've seen before? Maybe around Sade? Was he familiar?"

She closed her eyes again and breathed slowly. Then she began to shake her head. "I can't see anything." She opened them. "I can't see anything. I can't see his face!"

I let out a sigh.

She continued. "I remember thinking it was not normal that someone who was not wearing a choir robe would be around the room. That's all. My mind wasn't there at all. There was too much on my mind that day."

"Personal things?"

She hesitated. "I wasn't happy at all that day." I waited for her to elaborate, but she merely toyed with her fingers.

"So…" My voice trailed off. Her sister emerged with a stony expression. She wore a long skirt and a long-sleeved turtleneck shirt that met with Nike's approval. "Eh-ehn! This is better. You look decent now, like a well-trained girl. But are you not already late for—"

The girl slammed the door.

Nike shook her head and stood up. "I want to go to the market now."

"Just a few more questions," I said quickly.

She glanced at the clock.

"Who found the body?"

"Lara," she supplied. "It was her scream I heard."

I also remembered the blood-curdling scream.

"Her best friend."

Nike nodded.

"And did she see anything?"

She shook her head. "Nobody saw anything. I told you."

"Okay. One final question," I said with a pause.

"What is it?"

"There is no other way I can ask this but, er—"

"Did I kill Sade?" She took the words right out of my mouth. "God forbid!" She ran her fingers over her head in a circle, culminating in a dramatic snap. "The inspector asked the same question, and I will tell you what I told him. I did not. What would I gain by her death?"

"Thank you, Nike," I said and got up, "for your time."

"I have a question for you, too," she said, staring into my eyes. "You are not a journalist, are you?" There was a cool iciness about her now. "Am I right?"

It took me a few seconds to reply.

"Yes, you are right."

"Okay." Her tone and demeanor were blank. "Who is she to you?"

"A friend. Sorry, I lied to you."

A vague nod. "It's okay. I understand."

"Thank you. By the way, it's cerise."

"What?"

"The shade of pink. I told you I would remember before I leave."

"Which one is cerise?" she asked with a taut smile. "To me, it's just pink. Anyway, goodbye."

"My regards to your husband," I said as the door closed behind me.

CHAPTER FIVE

Finding Modele's house was harder than anticipated. Nike's casual remark that it was not far away from her own house was misleading. Actually, we ran in circles.

The neighborhood, when we found it, was typical of suburban Lagos: dense population, malodorous drains, and erratic numbering. Twice we called on the wrong house, but the third time we were lucky. Her home was a small one with surprisingly neat surroundings.

I knocked on the metal door and waited for a response. When I didn't get any, I knocked again. Finally, it opened. The woman behind it peered out with a myopic stare. One could tell from her appearance that she had just returned from somewhere and had barely settled.

"Can I help you?"

"Good afternoon. I'm Deji Depiver. I want to—"

"Wait, wa-wa-wait," she cut me short. "Are you the man Nike is telling me about? Investigative something something?"

"I just left her place not long ago."

"She was saying things I didn't understand," she said, holding on to the door. "I was on the bus, and the conductor was shouting and shouting. I couldn't hear her properly on the phone."

"I think she was trying to tell you I would be visiting."

She peered into my eyes. "If this is about what I told the inspector the other day, I'm not changing my story."

"Oh. What story?"

"About the man Nike said she saw," she replied, a little dismayed. "I didn't see anyone."

"Oh…that. I see."

She hollered at someone behind me. A teenage girl walked into the compound and handed her a grocery bag. Modele checked the contents and, satisfied with what she saw, thanked the girl.

My nose caught a whiff of something from the house.

"I am not changing my story," she repeated. "That man wanted to put words in my mouth. He kept saying, 'Are you sure? Are you sure?' like I'm a baby, and I don't know what I'm saying—what?!"

Finally, she saw that I was pointing concernedly behind her. "Something is burning."

With a throaty cry, she spun around and fled into the house. I waited a few seconds and let myself in, waving away a light stream of smoke emanating from the kitchen. There was a frenzied clattering of metal, a hissing of some sort, and a climaxing simmering sound that conveyed to me that everything was finally under control.

I called anyway, "Is everything okay?"

"Everything is fine. I'm coming."

I assessed her home. It consisted of a sophisticated set of graphite-colored couches, a glass center table, a television, a DVD player, and a refrigerator adorned with stickers and magnets. The walls were painted a tiresome butter color, which seemed to be everyone's choice nowadays.

Across the room hung a painting that tickled my fancy. I drew close to it. The piece, although amateurish, showed great imagination. It was an oil on canvas depicting a very dark woman dressed in white. Her regalia, including her gele and beads, was white, giving her a resplendent yet revered look.

What struck me most about the painting was her eyes. They were omnipresent. No matter which angle you looked at it, she was looking right back at you, a difficult technique. Interesting, I thought, and looked for any caption or signature. I found none. Anonymous artist. Hmm.

"I like this," I said to her about the painting when she returned. "Where did you buy it from?"

"I didn't buy it," she murmured. "It's a long story. Someone gave it to me." She paused before adding, "Someone I don't talk to anymore."

"It's brilliant." I continued to fix my gaze on the painting with renewed marvel. "Not the painting in itself, but the substance of it." Modele's blank stare conveyed to me that we were not on the same wavelength. "Never mind."

"I know it's a good painting. People tell me it is."

"Do you like it at all?"

"I like it," she seemed bemused by the question. "If I didn't like it, I would have thrown it away or used it like a tray to dry my egusi in the sun." She was smiling now.

"You can't do that to a painting like this," I said with a smile of my own. "It would be outrageous if you did."

"That's why it's still on the wall."

I agreed. "I hope all of your food did not burn…"

"Soup," she corrected. "I was able to save some. Please sit down."

"Thank you," I said while assessing the woman before me. Modele was what a man like Kabiru would call full. She was dark as granite with pouty, exaggerated lips. Bold and composed, her eyes were lustful, blinking rapidly like a doll's. She was the sort of woman who looked at you as though she'd seen you somewhere before but couldn't quite remember where. Her braids were large and snake-like, with blond highlights.

"You have made me remember someone from the past now," she said, looking over at the wall and running her fingers through her braids.

"Is it a good remembrance?"

"Not really. Bittersweet."

"Hmm."

She glared at me. "He bought it for me in one of those open galleries by the roadside in Ibadan. That was before we fought sha and scattered everything. He told me the painting fits me."

"You used to live in Ibadan?"

She nodded slowly with a rapid blink of the eye. She's trying to be sensual, I thought. Captivating.

"I like the city. I had my university education there."

"University of Ibadan, abi?" she asked with a humorous glint. "I grew up around there. We are not from there, but it's a nice place. I miss it a lot."

"You relocated?" Sometimes I asked the daftest questions.

"Obviously." Her laugh was impulsive. "I had to. I wanted to leave the place. Get away." There was a quality to the way she said it that made me wonder if she was running away from something.

"Bad experience?"

"Bad memories."

"Oh." I immediately regretted my probing. "I'm sorry to hear that."

"You see what you have caused now, eh? You made me remember a period I didn't want to. All because you liked my painting too much. I'm not giving it to you even if you begged me to," she teased, putting it on display now, which made me smile.

"I didn't mean it that way." I let out a cautious laugh. "It will probably look better in your house anyway."

"Okay." She folded her hands neatly on her lap. "So what is this about?"

"Sade," I said. "But let me introduce myself. I am from The Guardian, and I'm investigating domestic violence against women in Lagos and the West in general. See if there is a cultural link to the rise we are noticing."

She nodded mechanically.

"Too bad what happened to her." She was shaking her head now. "We are all shocked."

"She was very popular?"

"Yes. Can I get you anything? A cold drink?"

"No, thank you. I'm fine."

"Okay." She sank further into the couch and looked expectantly at me.

"What can you tell me about her?" I asked. "What was she like?"

"What is there to tell?" Her dark eyes looked at me severely. "She was a pretty girl who destroyed other people's happiness."

I reacted with a jolt. So taken aback was I by her statement that I felt a momentary paralysis, complete with delirious confusion.

"You are surprised, eh?" There was a mocking tone to her voice. "Why are you surprised?"

"I did not expect that. What you said. I did not expect it at all. Yes, I am in shock."

"What did they tell you? I think you have met with everyone. I hear they are calling us suspects."

"I've only met with Nike. I will see Jimi next. Then Lara."

"Ha! Lara," she scowled. "That witch! But Nike, what did she tell you? Sweet things, abi?" She chuckled. "I am not surprised. I am not surprised at all. The choir is full of liars and pretenders. You won't find anyone authentic."

She snatched a fan and fanned herself, even though the ceiling fan was circling.

"I have my own opinion of her too, you know. Sade was a nice person."

Modele raised an eyebrow.

"We met before. Twice."

She eyed me with contempt. "You think I didn't know you are an impostor? Nike said something like that. I was looking at you like, 'Okay, continue with your lies.' It's funny. Anyway, how did you meet Sade?"

I didn't reply immediately, but when I did, I said, "I met her at Freedom Park."

"And?" She leered at me.

"And what?"

She rolled her eyes. "Don't you know what I'm trying to say?"

I shook my head.

"Like nothing happened between you two?"

I was incredulous and, at the same time, hesitant, casting my mind back to that fateful day. It was a coincidence, wasn't it? "Nothing happened."

With disdain in her eyes, she crossed her legs. "I'm listening to what you have to ask."

Not sure how to continue, I tried. "So what were you talking about?" I dropped my pen and pad. "When you said she destroyed other people's happiness?"

"She's a slut," she blurted out. "Sade slept around the church."

"You don't like her very much, abi?"

"We tolerate each other. Hi, hi. How are you? How are you?" She must have seen the dismay on my face because she said, "It's not like we don't see eye to eye or something like that. It's just that we don't have much in common."

I nodded. "Did people know…erm, that she's…well, what you said?"

She frowned. "No. She hid it very well."

"Then how did you know?"

She made a face like she was disappointed in me. "It's not a very big choir, Oga. Words get around. I can count about three men she had affairs with." She recoiled, shaking her head in disgust. I let my gaze drop to her long, fake scarlet fingernails. They quickly reminded me of the prostitutes on Allen Avenue that Nike chided her sister about.

"Can you tell me the names of the men?"

"I can't tell you that," she replied, examining the hem of her skirt. "As you see me so, I don't gossip." She paused for a thoughtful moment. "I didn't actually see them with her or anything like that. I just heard."

"You know it's possible those men could be involved."

She shrugged, indifferent.

"Okay, who told you? Where did you hear it from?"

"I can't tell you either." She fluttered her eyes. "It's something I overheard."

I clasped my fingers. "So you overheard somebody telling another person that Sade had affairs with men of the church?" I thought I sprinkled enough mockery in that question to provoke an instant rebuttal.

"Look," she snapped, "this is what I can tell you, okay? I heard about the other two. They happened, I think, before I came to the church. The third one…" She shrugged. "Maybe it's just a rumor."

I let out a tired yawn. It seemed an inopportune reaction. "Tell me about this rumor."

Modele was now uncomfortable. "You want to know everything. Must you know everything? You will like gossip o. And I don't gossip like that." Something about the way she expressed her reservations conveyed to me a shade of subterfuge.

"Me, I like gossip—"

"When you are not a woman!"

"It's not about that. Anyway, you know you can tell me anything," I soothed. "And it could even be something important."

Silence.

"If you don't hear it from me," Modele shrugged her shoulders after a while, "I know you will hear it from someone else."

I agreed with a nod. "So, who was it? It's someone important, isn't it?"

She picked at her braids.

"Is it a deacon? A patron? The reverend?"

"It's Jimi," she said finally.

"The choirmaster?" I heard a loud whistle in my head.

"That's why I didn't want to tell you."

"It's significant," I said.

"It's a scandal," she muttered.

"Was it common knowledge? The affair."

"No-o. They hid it well. Jimi is married."

I paused, thinking.

"So it's not a rumor."

She shook her head. "I just said that so you won't bother me."

"How many people know about the affair?"

"How am I supposed to know that?"

"So you don't know anyone who knows about it apart from you? Is that what you are saying?"

"Is there anything hidden under the sun? There is nothing hidden under the sun."

For a while, I didn't say anything. I became momentarily lost in thought. "Jimi…"

Modele giggled. "Why did you say his name like that?"

"Like how?"

"I don't know," she shrugged. "Like you are thinking of him."

"I am thinking about him."

"Me too," she let slip.

Slightly alarmed, I asked, "Are you trying to enter my head?"

"He's just every woman's dream," she laughed playfully. "He's tall, handsome, not dark like most girls want, and he can sing! He always reminds me of someone." Her eyes went to the painting.

"Are we still talking about the same man?"

"Yes," Modele said. "He's obsessed with me."

"Now I'm confused."

"I think I'm talking too much." She suddenly got up. "I need some water. Excuse me."

She hurried to the kitchen. I remained thoughtful, chewing at the end of my pen. Could there be, somewhere in here, a fatal love triangle? I wondered. Modele returned with a pleasant smile. "Anyway," she said, "now that Sade is no more, Nike can go back to being the lead again."

"Lead? You mean the choir lead?"

"Yes."

"I didn't know she was the lead before," I said, surprised at the abrupt change of topic.

"She was. Until recently."

"What changed?"

"Jimi just woke up one day and changed her. Just like that."

"Did they fight?"

Modele shook her head.

"Was she bad?"

"Nike?" she laughed. "Nike is the best. Although I know if you ask Lara, I'm sure she will tell you it's her friend Sade, but…" She shook her head. "Nike has a better head voice." She paused before continuing, as though in soft recollection. "Those two were always competing with each other. Nike's upper register is thin, but her voice is always clear like a school bell. Her mid-register is very good, too. She can sing almost any song."

"I've heard Sade sing too," I said. "She sings like an angel."

She agreed with a reluctant nod. "Sade's upper register is good too. She can belt in G5 like she's possessed with mami wata and make you have goose bumps. Do you even know anything about music?"

"No."

"Then you won't understand. Anyway, the congregation liked her a lot when she sang like that, and who can blame them? She has a very good lower range too, but that's my own mata. Falsetto. I'm better than her in that range. I know I am, and nobody can tell me otherwise. Laye!"

There was a soft knock on the door. It was a neighbor who had come to borrow some sugar. They chatted for an inordinate amount of time, and after she closed the door, she said with a hint of regret, "It's lonely here sometimes."

"You live alone?"

"You like asking questions that you know the answers to." She sat, crossing her legs. "Does your girlfriend like it?"

"I'm sorry about that."

"Don't be sorry. It's who you are." Modele giggled. "Are you married? Or you are one of those men who don't wear their rings?"

I smiled. "There's no ring."

She pushed out her bosom provocatively and rolled her eyes around. "Are you sure you don't want anything? I cook very well. It's another thing, apart from my voice, I won't be humble about."

I shook my head. "I'm fine. And it's not nice for you to live alone. This place is big enough for two people. What if you are sick?"

"I used to have a roommate," Modele said with a dismissive wave of her hand.

"What happened to her?"

"We shared this apartment together for some time without any wahala, until she started having accidents."

Out of curiosity, I asked, "What kind of accidents?"

Modele became excited. "That girl is possessed! One time, she fell in the bathroom and broke her leg. There was another time she plugged in the hot plate and got a big shock. Mind you, I had just used the same hot plate only minutes before. Yamayama things like that. One day, she packed up, saying there was a bad spirit in the house. Can you imagine?"

"Where is she now?"

"I don't know. She could be anywhere. She could even be dead."

My gaze drifted to the woman in the painting, and then came a recollection of what Modele had said at the door. "When I came in, you were saying something about a man."

"What man? Oh, yes. I didn't see any man."

"Why did you think I was here because of that?"

She hesitated. "I don't know. I thought that's why you wanted to see me."

I watched her. She appeared calm and controlled. "So you didn't see any man around the changing room?"

"No."

"Let me take your mind back. That day she died," her expansive eyebrow shot up an inch, "there were five of you in the room, am I right?"

"Yes."

"What happened in the room? What did you do?"

Modele looked uncertain. "Nothing, I guess. I remember I removed my robe. It was hot. The A.C. is good."

"The sermon wasn't over?"

"No, it wasn't. We sometimes do that—"

"I heard about it. What happened next?"

She frowned. "I think Nike was feeling my shoes. She was telling me how nice they were, and I was trying to sound as if they weren't that nice. I was surprised because Nike does not know anything about a good shoe. All I see her wear is okrika. Old, used clothes all the time. Horrible shoes my grandma wore back in the day. What does she do with her money, eh? Anyway, I would probably dress like an old lady with a man like that."

"How did she sound to you?"

"Nike?" she drawled. "I don't know. I think she looked somehow. Maybe something was on her mind. I was just happy she didn't ask to borrow my shoes or something. I can't trust her with my shoes, abeg."

"What were the others doing?"

"They were talking." She seemed disgusted by the question. "Chatting. Giggling like fools."

"With the choirmaster?"

"Yes."

"What were they talking about? Did you listen?"

"I wasn't listening to them. Lara and Sade were laughing about something. I didn't know what it was that was funny, but they didn't share it with me. They didn't share anything with me."

I sighed and stayed thoughtful for a minute or two. "Who left the room first?"

"Nike," said Modele with certainty. Then she frowned. "Lara left next, I think. Abi? Yes! She had stopped that annoying laugh. Jimi and Sade were the last in the room because I left them there. They were saying something—whispering—so I wouldn't hear what they were saying."

"How long did you spend there?"

She placed a skeptical finger on her chin. "Maybe three minutes or four. I'm not sure."

"How did Sade look to you?"

"How do you mean?"

"I mean, was she…off? Did she look afraid or anything like that?"

"I don't know. I wasn't looking at her."

"Okay. Who found her?"

"That would be Lara. It was her scream I heard. That girl can scream and wake the dead!" She shook her head in amazement. "If only she could sing just as well."

"Do you think she had enemies? Anyone who might want her dead?"

She shrugged.

For a moment, I thought about nothing; my mind whirling lightly. Circling. Hovering. Homing in on something that appeared vague and without form. The room had suddenly gone humid and stifling.

"I'm getting tired o," Modele announced with a playful smile.

"I won't take any more of your time," I said, immediately rising to my feet.

"You are leaving?" She was surprised.

"Yes. It's getting late. I don't want to take any more of your time. Besides, you said you are tired already."

"I'm tired of talking about Sade. Maybe if you talked about something else, I won't be so tired."

I shook my head and said with an assuring smile, "Another time."

Her nod was rapid, but her disappointment was obvious. "I can't visit your choirmaster today. It's late. I will continue tomorrow."

At the door, I turned and asked, "But I have one last question, if you don't mind."

Her brows shot up again.

"Did you…take her life?"

Her dark face grew darker, and her eyes narrowed to thin, menacing slits. Suddenly, she let out a howl, shook her head, and slammed the door in my face.

CHAPTER SIX

I was getting ready to visit Jimi when Mrs. Banjo announced her presence in the house rather forcefully. Her arrival was timely. I had something pertaining to the murder that I wanted to ask her. Her countenance, however, caused me to be hesitant. I greeted her cautiously.

"What is good about the afternoon, Deji?" she bayed. "What is good about it, eh?"

I stood motionless. With her, you never know what to expect. Something is odd about her appearance, though, I said to myself, immediately resisting an urge to laugh.

"Where is your mother?" she brushed past me. "Rolake! Rolake!!"

"What is it, Iyabo?" Maami came in, half-dressed and alarmed. "What is it?"

Mrs. Banjo's voice broke. "Useless girl! The useless girl you recommended cannot even do a simple makeover. Look at my face, Rolake. Just look at it!"

Maami examined her face. "What is wrong with it? Ah! I see it now. Bawo lo'se se?"

"Look at my eyebrows!" Mrs. Banjo cried. "Do you see what I have become? Do you see? Now I have to pretend to be surprised at everything at Mrs. Ipaye's party."

"About that party, oremi, do you think I should wear—"

"Look at my face!"

Mrs. Banjo ambled around, fuming. "When next I go to that bongafish's salon, I will destroy everything there! She will think a train hit her." Her bleached face grew red.

"You will not do anything like that, oremi."

"You just wait and see." Her many bangles chimed like a tintinnabulum. She half-turned her necklace-adorned head and snapped, "You want to tell me something, Deji, abi why are you looking at me like that?"

I nodded but was unsure whether now was a good time to ask. Modele had alluded to Sade's many affairs, and I wondered if her murder was a direct consequence. I was going to start talking when Maami exclaimed, "That necklace!"

Mrs. Banjo touched her neck and feigned surprise—or was it those nasty eyebrows again?

"Are you just seeing it?" She giggled and turned full circle.

"Gorgeous." Maami went to her. "It must be very expensive!"

"As the eye! Don't ask me how much I bought it! What did you want to say, Deji?"

"It's about the girl who died."

"Ki lo'gbo?" she snapped. "Tell me."

I told her.

"Why do you look so surprised, eh?" she asked with a slight upturn of her nose. When Maami let go of her neck, she dragged herself closer. "She was even having one with that fine yellow choirmaster, too, before she died, but who can blame her? That man is fine."

Maami growled.

I was particularly interested in the lovers before the choirmaster, so I put the question to her.

"I heard about that, too," Mrs. Banjo said. "Deacon Karounwi and that other man who left the church sometime last year." To Maami, she whispered, "The one I told you was caught asking primary school girls to sit on his lap. Wicked, wicked world."

After a slight pause, I asked, "Where is the deacon?"

"He left the country," she replied, then flashed Maami a suspicious look. "You have to find a wife for your son, Rolake, to occupy his mind, because why is he asking me all these questions? He should leave the gossiping to us!"

I fled the house before she remembered to ask about her painting.

***

"Thank you for seeing me," I began.

We sat on the terrace overlooking a small pool. "Your house is nice." I looked around the dainty property. Brick houses were a rarity nowadays. The neighborhood was upper-class, with gardens and alien architecture that suggested old money. Jimi looked proud and smiled broadly. The genial housemaid, who looked too good to be a housemaid, brought us cold water and groundnuts. She knelt in obeisance and, after setting down the treats, departed. I was looking at my host without really appearing to do so, and I thought I caught an affectionate glance from master to maid, but I couldn't be sure.

I drank some water while Jimi dug into the ceramic bowl of groundnuts and chewed leisurely like a ruminating bull. He is a good-looking man, I thought to myself, slightly older than I had imagined. He was light-skinned with slick, curly hair and a well-carved goatee, suggesting an individual who took great pride in his appearance. An aftershave that smelled like peppermint permeated from him. We talked idly about a few unimportant things for a few minutes before we were joined by a mannish, aggressive-looking woman dressed in combat shorts and a loose-fitting camouflage shirt. She was tall, broad-shouldered, with dark skin, prominent cheekbones, and eyes that scarcely missed anything. She sat down and barely regarded me.

"This is my wife, Kofo," he said to me. "Kofo, this is Deji. He is a journalist."

"Good afternoon, Mrs. Smart," I greeted her. "I was just telling your husband you have a nice house, and your compound is neat and beautiful."

She regarded me from head to toe and back. "It's Major Kofoworola Kosile-Smart." Her voice was like rocks rolling down a hill. "People like you call me Major Kofo."

"My wife is an army woman," her husband said with an awkward chuckle, realizing he should have warned me ahead of time. "You know army people now. They don't like people addressing them like civilians."

"I'm very sorry, Major," I apologized.

"You are lucky I'm in a good mood today, else you will be doing frog jumps." To her husband, she snapped, "What is he looking for?"

Jimi fixed me with an earnest look, urging me to state my mission. I shrank in my seat and stared back at him. I was petrified. Major Kofo made me uncomfortable. Something about her demeanor and smart—how apt the name was now—eyes threatened to expose my little charade. So far, I had been in charge of proceedings with the previous interviews, but something whispered to me that things would be a little different today.

"He is investigating domestic violence," Jimi said. "Is that not what you called it?"

"Violence against women," I croaked.

"Okay. They want to know about Sister Sade, the lady who died in our church."

Major Kofo hissed. "How will that solve the problems of Nigeria, eh? I don't like you people from the press. Worst people on earth. You and politicians. All your stories are full of lies! So-so lies! We should go back to a military regime. That is how things will come to order, no nonsense!"

"I think he is honest, Kofo."

"We will say one thing, and they will say another just to sell their papers. Why is he even here? He should be talking to the police for their investigation. Is that not how it is supposed to be?"

"He has talked to them, dear. Abi, have you not spoken to them?"

"They have been helpful," I hurried to say. "They gave me, us, some information. I, er, we only want to know more about the victim. Like what was she like in life?"

"Is this a joke?" Major Kofo showed great disdain. "Go and ask her parents that question. Or did you think she lived here? Bloody civilians!"

"I think he just wants to know things about her in the choir, Kofo. Is that not so?"

I wiped my forehead. "Yes. Things like that."

The bellicose major looked me over again. "Where is your ID card?" Instinctively, I placed my hand over my breast pocket. "Is it not supposed to be around your neck like goats in the market, like you people always carry it?"

I dug my hands into my back pocket, looking for what I knew didn't exist. Then I patted my breast pocket again in utter confusion. "I must have left it in the car." I rose quickly. "Let me go and get it."

"No, no, no, don't worry yourself." Her husband waved me back. "Sit down."

"It will only take a minute. If I can just—"

"Don't worry. Sit down." Jimi was amused. "You like wahala yourself."

It was a gamble that paid off. "Thank you."

Major Kofo's eyes continued to bore through me.

"Drink some water," urged her husband, handing her a glass. When she set the cup down, she said, folding her arms, "We are listening."

The inquiry began.

Jimi's assessment of Sade was remarkably similar to Nike's account. She was a woman of many talents who was selfless and took the church seriously. Everyone loved her. It was a shame to lose someone like her, especially in such a shocking manner. The next questions did not tell me anything I didn't already know until I maneuvered to the tricky part.

"Do you know of anyone who might have wanted to kill her?" A faint sound escaped from his mouth.

"How will he know something like that?" his wife raged. "Is he a magician that he will know something like that? Civilians! Bloody civilians!"

Jimi shook his head. "I don't know anyone who would do that to her. The whole thing shocked us."

"Okay. Modele told me she left the changing room with you and Sade in it. I don't know if that is true."

"Yes, it's true."

"Who left the room first?"

"Did she not tell you? I thought you had spoken to her."

"I have, but I want to be sure what she told me is accurate."

"Sister Nike. Then Sister Lara and Sister Modele. Like that."

"Is that not the girl always trying to be around you, Modele?" Major Kofo now faced her husband.

"She is in my choir, Kofo. She will always be around me."

"All the time? Does she not have anything else she is doing? Are you the only man in the choir? She is around you too much, s'ogbomi. I see it. I'm not blind." Jimi ignored his wife and waved me to continue. I tried to appear embarrassed.

"So you were the last person to see her alive?"

He hesitated, then nodded. "But it should not have been like that. Everything in this life is fate. You see, we almost left the room together. We were almost out the door when she said she forgot something and went back in."

"She forgot something?"

He nodded. "That's what she told me."

"What did she forget there?" Major Kofo interposed, taking the words right out of my mouth.

"I don't know," he shrugged. "I didn't ask."

I took this in with a nod. "And no one else was in there at that time?"

"No."

"What did you talk about?"

Major Kofo shifted in her seat. Her eyes grew bigger.

"Modele said you were talking about something."

He nodded. "She wanted to tell me something important, but I don't think I should be telling it to you. It concerns the church." Major Kofo looked incredulous. I was certain this was news to her. I took another glass of water and averted my gaze in the direction of the calm cerulean pool. I didn't say anything. I didn't scribble. I allowed the talons of silence to claw at his conscience. It worked.

"Okay, I will tell you," he said with a reluctant sigh. "It's about her friend, Sister Lara. Have you met her?"

Major Kofo scoffed before I could open my mouth. "Birds of a feather. What is wrong with her?" There was a pause. I caught a glimpse of irritation in his eyes that I suspected was directed at his wife.

"I have not met her," I said to him. "But I will go to her place when I leave here."

He nodded.

"The Sunday before she died," he began, "Reverend Benson called a meeting with some of us and said someone stole from the tithe basket. One honorable who worshiped with us—I won't mention his name—always paid his tithe in dollars. That's his style, and he has been doing that for years. That day, his tithe was missing. Nobody saw anything, and I didn't think one of my choristers did it. But the day before she died, Sister Sade found some dollars in Sister Lara's purse. She didn't know what to do because they are friends, but she thought it was the missing money. It was a lot of money. She wanted to tell the Reverend about it, but she told me first. That's what happened."

This is interesting, I thought. A new angle.

"Was it in an envelope?"

"The tithe? Yes."

"How did they even know it was missing? What if the man did not place his tithe at all?"

"It was missing jare!" Jimi said. "They found the envelope torn open in the basket."

Major Kofo scoffed. "That girl Lara… always looking about like a market thief."

"We don't know yet if it's true that she stole it, and we may never even know." There was a portentous quality to the way he said it that made me pause to think. I was not convinced.

"So that is all you talked about?"

"That's what she wanted to tell me."

Major Kofo stirred.

Nike said she saw a man around the changing room before her body was found. Did you see him too?

He shook his head. "Did she say who it was?"

"No." I looked straight into his light brown eyes. Like Nike's, when I asked if she had a hand in Sade's death, they told me nothing.

"So she did not see the person?" Major Kofo broke my concentration with vivid curiosity. "I'm talking about the…the face."

"No, she didn't."

A brief spell of silence followed.

"Didn't you say you had talked to the police?" Her tone was accusatory.

"Yes, I spoke with the officer on the case. Very nice, man."

She squeezed her face. "Very local man with body odor. What is nice about him? Or is it not that man with heavy marks on his face? What is his name again? Remind me."

I stammered. "Inspector…Inspector…"

Major Kofo raised her eyebrow so far up it nearly touched her crop-top hair.

"Isiaka," her husband offered. "Inspector Isiaka."

"That's him," I said, relieved. "Inspector Isiaka."

Major Kofo, disappointed her husband bailed me out, asked, "Who did he say did it? Did he say anything like that?"

This was a totally unexpected question. My hands grew cold. "He didn't say." I shook my head. "He only told me everyone in that room was a suspect." I added, "He also told me they cannot rule out someone from outside."

"Someone from outside." Major Kofo seemed to think. "Are you going to write that in your paper?"

"No." I let out a vain chuckle. "We only want to, er, chronicle events that led to her death. Mostly, we will be writing about her life and what people thought of her as a person. Things like that."

"Is she a celebrity that we don't know about?" she wondered. "Because it looks like you are trying to find her killer by yourself and not this chronicle you are talking about."

I stared wide-eyed, unable to respond beyond a shake of the head that lacked conviction.

"If that is what you are doing, it could be dangerous for you. Very dangerous."

Was that a subtle threat or a friendly warning? I wondered. Somto's misgivings about embarking on this personal mission suddenly looked accurate. Am I in danger already?

"When are you going to finish?" Major Kofo asked, and to her husband said, "You remember we are going to Uncle Diekola's place." There was an awkward glance from the wife to the husband, who looked puzzled for a second or two before saying, "Oh, yes. Thank you, dear, for reminding me. What time is it now?"

"Past three," I said, getting ready to leave. "I still have to see Lara, too."

I didn't learn anything new after a few more questions, and I took my leave, thanking them warmly. There was a question I wanted to ask him—about the affair—but I knew that had to wait another time when Major Kofo didn't get in the way. I was about to close the gate behind me when I felt a slight resistance. I let go, and the genial maid who brought us groundnuts stepped out, closing the gate behind her quietly.

"Oga, you don dey go?" A counterfeit smile materialized on her face.

I smiled back, hoping she would not link Kabiru's decrepit car to me. "Yes. I have to go back to the office. There is still much work to do."

"Hope your office is no far from here?"

"No, it's not."

"*Hian*!"

"Hope no problem?"

"No problem o." She folded her arms. "I jus' wan tell you say oga na nice man. Very nice, man. E no get wahala."

"He sounded nice," I agreed. It became clear to me that she had been eavesdropping on our conversation. "You wan' tell me something?"

She looked unsure. I drew closer to her. "But can I ask you one question, please?"

"Ask me anything, oga."

"Were you in church that day?"

"Dat day wey dat aunty die? I dey. I dey church wit madam."

"Did you sit with her?"

She was alarmed. "If I nor sit down with madam, the beating I go chop that day, my mama no go sabi me. I sit down with am like I do, but eh…" she whispered into my ear. "But later, I no see her again."

"She disappeared?"

The maid nodded.

"Where did she go?" I tried to control my excitement.

She shrugged. "She jus' disappear like breeze."

"When was this?"

She pulled back, thinking. "Service remains small to finish."

My heart raced. "You sure?"

"I no dey lie, oga. I never lie for my life."

"Okay. Tell me, wetin your madam wears?"

"Wetin she wear?" She looked puzzled. "She wears a soldier man shirt and, er—"

"I mean that day. That day in church."

"Dat day? Okaaay. She wears an erm, suit. She likes to suit well. She likes am pass man sef."

I froze. "She wore a suit?"

"Yes."

"What color of suit? Do you remember?"

"Wey she wear?"

"Yes."

She paused again to think. "Like blue. Like dis one wey de your bodi so." She pulled at my navy-blue shirt. "Like am."

"Thank you very much."

"Oga na nice man o," she said again. "But madam, wicked. She fit… e fit kill person."

As soon as she said this, I could hear shouting from the compound, like an argument.

"Dem don dey fight again." She began to retreat. "Make I dey go inside. Bye-bye, o."

CHAPTER SEVEN

Lara lived in a slummy neighborhood. As Kabiru descended slowly onto the undulating dirt road, the area conjured up a panorama of despair, despondency, and decay. I watched the residents go about their lives in a dull, lifeless manner. I had never seen so much doldrums. It's like everything here is in slow motion. Everybody is dragging their feet. I would like to do a painting of this place whenever I get the chance. Kabiru must have been looking at me in the mirror because he broke my thoughts.

"Dis place no be like dis o, Deji. No tink am."

"But why is everywhere like a natural disaster?" I asked, recalling what he had told me about the area after we left the Smarts' residence. According to him, it was a place blessed with a profusion of miscreants, thieves, and addicts. Not a place to live or raise a child.

"When night comes, all those thugs and ashewo go come out. E go be like night market."

"But where are they now?"

"Dem dey sleep. Night is for business. You see dat house?" He pointed to a decayed building. "I lived there before. If you wan buy correct gbana, na here you go see am. If you wan fuck gbana girls, na there you go see dem."

"Oh." That was all I could manage. Gbana was crack cocaine.

"Make we park here." Kabiru ground to a halt near a battered shop that sold ogogoro. "Dat hole go swallow my moto." There was a cavernous pothole, discouraging enough that he decided to park and have some cheap liquor.

I observed the area more closely now. It appeared that rain had recently fallen here. The giant crater, filled with mud and detritus, was just ahead. It had, for company, other smaller but equally treacherous potholes, making navigating it on foot ever so daunting. Kabiru's automobile abomination would not stand a chance.

I stood by the car, taking in the bleakness of the street while Kabiru exchanged pleasantries with the woman who owned the shop. They knew each other. After chugging a free shot of ogogoro without batting an eye, he led me into the alleys in search of the house, occasionally stopping to greet old friends and acquaintances.

No. 17 Aboaba Street was a decrepit two-story building that looked like it could collapse any minute. It leaned slightly to the left, and its features were those of ancient architecture, possibly from the 50s. I had an idea it had been built by a discontent blacksmith rather than a proper bricklayer. The peeled, mildewed yellow paint gave it the appearance of a giant leper.

Kabiru went in search of a long-lost friend while I queried a naked boy of about four, where I might find "Aunty Lara." He beamed and pointed up.

"Aunty Lara! Aunty Lara!!"

He grabbed my hand and led me through the dark, smelly passageway and upstairs to a door brown with age. I gave him a hundred-naira note. He ran off shouting for his mother.

I knocked.

"Who is it?" a hesitant voice came from within.

"It's Deji. I called yesterday."

The door cracked slightly open.

"Deji who?"

"Good evening," I said, noticing the sparkling gold necklace around her neck. "I don't think you remember me, but we met before."

"I remember you." She was relaxed now. "At the beach."

"Yes. Are you going out?" She was dressed up.

"Yes. I'm—"

"I won't take much of your time, I assure you."

She eyed me. "Okay. Come in quickly, please, because of mosquitoes!"

I darted in.

Lara lived in a single room, small and cramped. It was a room, like the outside of the house, in need of a little money spent on it. It consisted of a bed, a table laden with creams, lotions, perfumes, and accessories, and two small chairs. Across the room was an obviously new flat-screen television fastened to the wall, and a brand-new fridge just to the left. They looked distinctly out of place, and I wondered idly if this was the stolen tithe put to good use.

I placed myself on the chair next to the table while she sat on the bed, eyes fixed on me. She was a slim, fair woman with a tall mane of hair, a curious expression, and a determined chin.

"What can I offer you?" she asked. "I have Coke in the fridge."

"I'm fine. Thank you." My eyes fell on the picture frame on the table. It was a celluloid still of the two friends giggling at a wedding. To a casual observer, they could be twins. "You two were very close."

She nodded.

"Tell me, how did you meet?"

Lara smiled and recalled. "We met in secondary school. School had just resumed, and there were many new students. I was just coming out of the buttery with my snacks when a girl came to me, calling me Sade, asking me why I took so long. She even took one of my buns. I was confused, thinking maybe it was a prank. Then Sade herself came out with buns, and we just stood there looking at ourselves, the three of us."

"Very confused."

"Yes, confused. The new girl made friends with Sade just the day before. I can never forget that day. So…" she struggled to find the word.

"Unreal."

"Yes! So unreal."

"An innocent case of mistaken identity."

She nodded. "We became friends from there. The other girl left our school, but we kept in touch."

"Nice story." I put back the frame.

"Your place is nice."

"It's not nice. Sade didn't like coming here."

"Why?"

"It's small. And old. Can't you see it? She wanted me to get another place. She even asked me a few days before she died if I had found another place."

"Have you?"

"No."

"I know a friend who is an estate agent. Maybe he can help you. He is cheap, too."

"No. I am not leaving anymore. At least until the end of the year."

I nodded. "When you evaluate your life and make new decisions."

She stared at me.

"What did you say you wanted to see me for?"

Quickly, I told her my mission and why I was there. I watched her expression shift from mild befuddlement to slight admiration, then to quirky unease.

"Are you alright?" I asked.

Lara nodded, patting her chest.

"I think I will take the Coke now," I said. The weather was still hot. She pointed to the fridge. There was a choice of drinks and some cheap wine, but I helped myself to the Coke.

"Will you see her parents?"

I nearly gagged. "Eh?"

"Shebi, it was you who sent them that painting?"

"Oh… yes. It was me."

"I knew it. When they told me about it, my mind went to you."

"How is her family taking it?"

"Not very well. She was their only child."

"Did Sade talk about me?"

A slow nod. "She liked you."

"I see her in my dreams," I confessed. "That's why I need to know what happened to her."

She hesitated, then asked, "How is Jimi?"

"He's fine when I left him."

"Did you see his wife?"

"Major Kofo."

Lara paused, as though weighing what to say.

"He looks rich, by the way, and he is not getting all of that from being a choirmaster. What does he do?"

"His wife is the rich one," Lara said.

Lara snorted. "He married her because of her money. Her father is rich. He is a retired general from Abeokuta. Very popular family."

I thought I had heard that name before, General Kosile. It all made sense now.

"Was Sade having an affair with him?"

"Modele told you that, didn't she? Tell me!" Lara was visibly upset. "That unfortunate girl! She told you, abi?"

I nodded. "So it's true."

"Modele is just bitter because Jimi did not like her. Because he refused to go out with her. Modele wanted Jimi. Everybody in the choir knew it. She was always hopping around him like a badly behaved rabbit, calling him and texting him. So when she found out Jimi liked Sade instead, she began to hate her. Evil, that's what she is."

"Interesting," I said. "Because Modele told me Sade hated her for no reason."

"She lied!" Lara clapped theatrically. "She's the one who hated her. Let me tell you, there was a day after rehearsal that Sade found her handbag torn to pieces with a blade. Modele did it! We just knew it was her. She's evil." She tapped her head. "Psycho!"

"Did you confront her about it?"

"No." Her breathing was laborious now. "But she did it."

I was thoughtful for a minute or two. "When did this happen?"

Lara frowned. "Two or three months before she died."

"So they were having an affair? Jimi and Sade."

Lara nodded without meeting my eyes. "Jimi is not happy in his home. He promised Sade he would leave his wife for her. His marriage was a mistake."

"How long has he been married?"

"Nine years. No child."

"Did she know about the affair? His wife, I mean."

Lara hesitated. "I don't know. But Sade told me one day at the salon that lately she had thought someone was following her. She didn't see who it was, but she felt it. Some weeks before she died, she became so afraid. Whenever she bumped into his wife in the church, she looked at her somehow. Like an evil look."

Almost immediately, I recalled the frightened look on her face the day she died. Did she meet a murderous gesture from Major Kofo? I wondered. I went back to the events that led to her death.

"How did she appear to you that day? Did you have any feeling that something like this could happen?"

"No." Her eyes became misty. "It was like any normal Sunday. Nothing different from other days."

"You found the body."

A pause.

"I will never forget that day. I wish it wasn't me."

"Did you see or notice anything unusual when you found the body?"

"No. I just screamed when I saw her on the floor. I shook her to wake her up, but…" She covered her mouth with her hand.

"She didn't say anything? Maybe mumble a word?"

"No."

I backpedaled. "Modele told me you left the changing room before she did, correct?" I knew I could eke out a good deal from Lara because of her close relationship with Sade, but nothing prepared me for what I was about to hear.

"Yes. I left because Sade gave me a sign to leave."

"A sign?"

She nodded and replied in a clear voice. "She wanted to tell Jimi something. She wanted to tell him she was pregnant for him."

My heart skipped.

"She was pregnant?!" To my ears, my voice came out in a harsh whisper. I don't want to hear this. I don't want to hear this anymore.

"About a month."

Only a little more than an hour ago, Jimi had told me a different story about a missing tithe and hard currency supposedly found in Lara's purse. Had he been lying? I wondered.

Lara had more. "She didn't know what to do about it because of her boyfriend. She was confused."

"Her boyfriend?" I felt a short bout of vertigo.

"Yes." She wiped a tear, smudging her mascara. "Richard. The church drummer."

My stomach tightened in knots. I felt betrayed.

"Are you—"

"Eh?"

"Are you angry about what I just told you? He's actually her fiancé."

"No, no." I touched my forehead. I wanted to vomit.

"But you are hurt? I can see it in your face."

"A little."

"I don't blame you."

"But I really shouldn't be. I mean, I only met her twice."

She nodded. "Sade is like that. Men quickly like her. She can have a choice of men, but I think she wanted Jimi. Richard is good too. He was planning to marry her next year, but she wasn't feeling him like that."

"Did anyone else know about it?"

"She didn't tell anyone. It was a secret."

"You didn't tell her parents?"

"Why tell them?" she cried. "What good will it do? Don't you see? They lost their daughter and grandchild."

"I guess you are right."

"Besides, it's not Richard's. So you see?"

I nodded. My eyes strayed to her tiny, drab kitchen, with a dirty curtain swept behind the door. A rat was in plain sight, gnawing at something. Lara saw it and hurled a shoe, but missed.

"I don't know what to do about these rats," she lamented. "I have tried those gum traps, but these rats are smart."

I allowed myself to smile in spite of how I felt. "I tried them once too. They know how to avoid the gum. The worst part is they tell their friends to avoid it too."

"That's what my neighbor said. I don't know what to do."

"My mother has a special poison to keep them away from her garden. I can get it for you."

"I would like that. Thanks."

"Didn't you say you wanted to go out?"

"It's not so important. I will go another time."

I was having a dead leg and got up to the window. Looking out, I saw scores of rustic roofs and weather-beaten antennas. I let my gaze drop to a tiny path where two shady-looking men were talking. I saw merchandise exchange hands between them. I said, without taking my eyes off them, "Nike told me something interesting when I spoke to her the other day. She said that she saw a strange man around the changing room."

"What did Modele tell you?" Lara didn't seem perturbed.

I looked at her now. She had changed position on the bed, closer to me. "She told you she didn't see any man, abi?"

I nodded.

"Who do you believe?"

"Who do I believe?"

"Yes. Who do you believe?"

"I don't know. Who do you believe?"

"Nike."

"Why?"

"Because I don't believe anything Modele says."

"So you saw a man?"

A vague nod. "I saw someone."

"You saw someone. Was it a man or a woman that you saw?"

"A guy."

I paused. "You saw a guy around the room?"

Lara frowned. "I saw a strange guy talking to Modele that day. I don't know if he was talking to her or if Modele was telling him something."

"Around the changing room?"

"Outside the church," she retorted. "Before service started. He looked like the thugs I see around here, with scars on their faces and red eyes."

I smiled at her description because, to be honest, she could be describing Kabiru. "He wasn't wearing a suit, was he?"

"No." She seemed amused by the question. "I think he was wearing a red pullover shirt. Something like that."

"Red is a vivid color you are not likely to forget. Did he carry a bag or something?" Perhaps the "strange guy" hid the suit in there, because nothing was making sense.

She shook her head. "I don't think so."

I stopped pacing and leaned on the windowsill. "I don't know what to make of this. So much conflict in my head." My eyes strayed to the darkening neighborhood and saw Kabiru meandering through the alleys toward the house.

"What if he's the killer?" asked Lara as I walked back to the chair.

I mechanically toyed with the Coke bottle.

"Let me throw that away."

After handing her the bottle, she eased into the colorless kitchen. My eyes shot to a pair of receipts tucked under a cream jar on the table. I had seen them earlier but resisted the urge to peek, given how almost impossible that would be without alarming her had she been in the room. Quickly, I tore them open. The receipts were for a television and refrigerator from Okwudili and Sons Limited, and matched the ones in the room. The date was only about a week ago. I tucked them back as she stepped into the room.

"I have to mend this," she announced, directing her gaze to the old stiletto. "The heel is broken."

"Damn that rat!" I said, rising to my feet. "I will get you that rat poison."

"You are leaving?" She set the shoe in the rack.

"It's getting dark."

"Okay. I will see you out."

Downstairs, as Kabiru was arriving, I asked, "When is your choir rehearsal?"

"Every Thursday and Saturday, 5 p.m. Why?"

"I want to come around."

She paused. "Okay."

The little boy and his mother, who appeared to have been waiting for me, expressed gratitude for the token. When they left, I said, "I want to ask you one final question."

Lara stopped breathing and braced herself. She half closed her eyes.

"I heard something about a missing tithe. Did you steal it?"

Lara, visibly relieved, exhaled and whispered, "No," like a meowing cat. After a few seconds, she asked, now slightly agitated, "Who is telling you all this? Modele?"

I shook my head and said with an air of mystery, "I can't tell you."

"I didn't steal any money." Her voice quavered, and with her hands raised, she said, "God is my witness."

I nodded. "Good night."

As we drove back home, I replayed the last conversation, specifically the point where I had said, I want to ask you one final question, in my head and analyzed Lara's bodily response to it. Surely she had expected the final question to be did you kill Sade, and was only relieved I asked something of lesser evil.

Well, did she?

CHAPTER EIGHT

I woke up the following morning with a nasty headache. Sade had been in my dreams again. We talked, in fields of green, about nothing. Before going to sleep, and not in every sense of the word, I had stayed up late to finish Mrs. Banjo's painting.

I looked at it now, after swallowing a couple of paracetamols, with utter dissatisfaction. It was a portrait of a smug woman dressed in turquoise sequins, an outlandish gold gele, and an assortment of red beads. My hope, when I finally delivered it to her, was that she would be too carried away with narcissism to notice the overlapping colors and pitiful lack of symmetry around the eyes. I placed the painting gently on the iroko chest and went to the kitchen in search of something to eat. I found nothing. From the window, I glimpsed Somto and Maami in her vegetable garden.

Maami's garden sat on a full plot in the backyard. She grew her own pumpkins, amaranths, celosia, tomatoes, peppers, and garden eggs. It seemed such a waste in a place like Lagos, but Maami liked her vegetables and would not have the land appraised, let alone turn it into a block of flats. The property belonged jointly to her and her husband, so it held sentimental value.

Outside, clouds gathered. Maami was plucking garden eggs, and Somto was helping her pull out weeds. He looked at his watch as I approached and shook his head. "Nine fifteen. What is it they say about the early bird?"

"They get eaten by predators," I replied, and greeted Maami, who gave a vague nod.

"Did you sleep well?"

I shook my head.

"How will you sleep well when you sleep in the garage instead of your bedroom, where you should sleep?"

"I was painting all night."

"Have you finished Iyabo's painting? She might come today, o."

I answered in the affirmative and took an egg from her basket. "It's the reason I stayed up late into the morning." Maami did a little dance. I ate quickly and picked another.

"I want to cook garden egg soup today," she said. "You know Iyabo likes my garden egg soup."

"Everybody likes your garden egg soup," Somto said with a grin that quickly disappeared as Maami let out a frantic cry. He had mistaken some obscure vegetable for weeds, which drew her displeasure and necessitated swift correction and apology from him. Still, she complained for some time about how difficult the plant was to cultivate and only stopped when the first rain began to fall.

"Thank God! My pumpkins need the rain. It has not rained for a week now. Ah, look at that egg!" She was pointing to a fat garden egg partly hidden in vegetation, which truly was a collector's item. I plucked it and handed it to her. "Garden eggs do well with or without the rain, but the pumpkins don't!"

"This rain won't fall," said Somto, gazing at the sky even though a few drops drummed on his head. "It will stop now and only bring heat."

"What does a child know?" Maami eased her way quickly toward the kitchen.

"Want to bet it won't fall?" I teased as he washed his hands, scooping water from the watering can.

"You have been hanging around Kabiru too much! Of course it won't rain."

Somto was wide off the mark. The rain fell so hard that Maami wondered, looking out the window, whether the flood would obliterate her garden. After a late breakfast of yam, fish, and garden egg soup, we sat in the living room with the doors and blinds shut, waiting out the storm. Power was out, and it would have been a surprise had it stayed on, so the room had the ambience of a library. Somto made small talk about happenings in the neighborhood that I was oblivious to and, not getting the responses he craved, soon busied himself with crossword puzzles from an old newspaper. Maami, without the distraction of a television, grabbed a paint bottle and began to paint her toenails. I sat back and let my mind wander a bit before Somto's vocalization of his frustration at the puzzles made me speak out.

"I think any one of them, or even all four of them, could have killed Sade."

It was such an odd statement to make without an accompanying conversation, but it was all I wanted to think or talk about, the murder. Maami stopped painting her toenails, capped the bottle, and heaved forward, just as Somto dropped the papers and glared at me. It seemed to me that they had been waiting for me to say something pertaining to it.

Somto asked, "What have you found?"

"A bucket load. They all have reasons to kill her, even if they try not to show it."

"Including her best friend, Lara?"

"Including her."

"Ha!"

"*Eh-ehn*?!"

Quickly, I told them about the interviews. From the first encounter with Nike to the last, Lara. Maami reacted badly, deeply saddened about the possibility of Sade dying with an unborn child. She cried without actually tearing and cursed.

"So you see," I said to Somto after she stopped swearing, "anyone could have done it."

"What is the motive, though? There has to be one; otherwise, wetin be the point of the crime?"

I gave him a thumbs-up. "You ask a very good question, Somto. What do you think?"

He hesitated. "I think if a woman is killed, it is usually because of love."

"Hmm!" Maami muttered. She appeared in awe of Somto's line of thought.

"So you are looking at the love triangle too. Sade likes Jimi. Modele likes Jimi. Boom! Sade is killed."

"Makes sense."

"Yeah. But it doesn't tell us how, because Modele left both Jimi and Sade in the changing room, so she could not have been physically there to eliminate her competition unless there was another means."

"Like the guy in the red pullover shirt."

"Like the strange guy in the red pullover shirt," I agreed. "But even that is a difficult sell. I mean, how did he gain entry?"

"Yet nobody saw anyone like that."

"Nobody saw anyone like that except Lara, and that was even before service began."

A ponderous silence followed. Nearby, a neighbor's heavy-duty generator roared to life and compounded the drumming on the roof. Maami hissed. "What about Jimi himself?" she asked with exaggerated wonder. "Is he not the last person to see the poor girl alive?"

"Yes. And he's a man too, which puts him at the front of the queue and the last person to see her alive. The needle is pointing in his direction, but if he killed her, what was his motive?"

"Scandal," said Somto.

I nodded. Somto might as well be living in my head. "You know, that's exactly what Modele said, and that's what I'm thinking too. Scandal." But Maami dismissed my thoughts out of hand. A man without a child for so long will not kill his unborn child.

"Well," I said to Somto, "we are back to square one."

"I don't think we moved an inch, to be honest."

"This is just rigmarole."

"But I also think it's okay to analyze the suspects and find a loophole or contradiction. Dat kain ting."

I nodded. "We can all agree that there was no contradiction in how each of them left the changing room. Nike first and Jimi last."

"That's a fact. They all confirmed it."

Maami heaved a troubled sigh, as though something was on her mind.

"Money is another motive if you look at it critically, but it's not really a strong one in this case."

"Are you talking about Lara?"

"Yes, Lara. She stole the tithe. I'm sure of that. But did she stop her friend permanently from telling on her?"

"It seems far-fetched."

"I agree with you. I mean, would you kill me if I was about to go to the police because you stole from a neighbor?"

"Like, how much are we talking about?"

I recalled the brand-new flat-screen television and refrigerator and concluded an estimate. "Maybe a thousand dollars. I mean, the stolen tithe was in dollars."

"Not enough, biko."

"Exactly. But I know people kill for a lot less."

"True. I read somewhere in the papers how an okada man killed his friend because of fifty naira. Ordinary fifty naira!"

"You see? But Lara is poor by all accounts, so I wouldn't put it past her. And that place she lives, she could have access to all kinds of criminal things and ideas."

"Nike nko?" asked Maami after a short period of silence. "What is her own motive?"

"Revenge," I said. "Jimi removed her as choir lead and installed Sade."

"That's lame." Somto was not convinced. "It's like when a football coach removes a captain and puts another one in his place. They don't kill each other because of that. Happens all the time."

"I'm just saying. It's all I could think of."

"Did any one of them weep at all?" asked Maami suddenly. "Jimi won't cry, he's a man, but did the women cry?"

"Lara cried at some point."

"Only her?"

"Yes. Maybe Nike, too."

A thoughtful pause followed. "I am asking because the ones who weep are the ones hiding something." She went on to ask me what I thought of their characters when I interviewed them. "What did your gut tell you?"

"Nike is controlling," I recalled how she ordered her husband and sister around. "She wants to do things her way, and I think she doesn't like people talking back at her."

Maami nodded. "She won't have trouble making friends with my friend, Iyabo. What about Modele?"

"I forgot to mention her husband is a dwarf."

"For real?"

"Very nice guy. Funny too." To Maami, I said, "Modele is unstable."

"How do you mean?" Somto interjected.

"There is a way about her that I cannot explain, but she's manipulative."

"I avoid women like that, tufiakwa!"

"She told me Jimi was obsessed with her, but it's the other way around. According to Lara, she is the one obsessed with him. And I think I prefer to believe Lara."

"The love angle is strong here," Somto reasoned. "Kill Sade and get the man, married or not, who cares?"

"What about Jimi himself?" asked Maami.

"He is cunning. That's what I think of him."

She seemed to agree with my assessment. "Most men are like that. Lara nko?"

I frowned. "Lara is corrupt."

"Didn't you say she was the last person to see her alive?"

"No. Jimi was the last person to see her alive. Lara was the first to see her dead."

"*Oma se o!*" Maami cried.

"You know what I'm thinking," Somto said after a thoughtful pause. "What if Lara was actually the last person to see her alive and then made it look like she only saw her after she had died? You feel me, so? Is it not convenient that on the day her friend spilled the beans was the day she was killed? Maybe even within a few minutes? To think that Lara was first on the scene of her death is too much of a coincidence, biko."

The idea seemed plausible. "But it's all supposition."

Maami frowned. "Lara said Sade only wanted to tell Jimi she was pregnant for him, but Jimi said what Sade told him was that her friend is a thief."

"Which is the truth?" wondered Somto.

I recalled. "Jimi claimed he left her there and that she was alive when he did so. We don't know that for sure."

"Is it possible he killed her then and there when every other person had left?" asked my friend.

"But why would he do that?"

"She was pregnant for him!" Maami dismissed. "Lara said so."

"But how are we sure Sade even told him she was pregnant in there?" I asked. "It doesn't look like a place to be making that kind of confession."

"But what about his wife?" she asked after a while.

"Major Kofo. Her maid told me something very important." Maami shifted her weight and glared at me. "She said she was with her that day in church, but before the service ended, she disappeared!"

Maami gasped. "To where?!"

"I asked her too. She doesn't know. What intrigued me was what she said she was wearing that day."

"Wetin she wear?"

"A navy blue suit."

"Complete with trousers?"

"I should think so."

"Is she a man?"

I ignored him. "Don't forget Nike said she saw someone in a suit around the changing room."

"That's why I asked, na man?"

"You could mistake her for a man," I admitted. "She even cuts her hair short."

"So it's possible that Nike saw Major Kofo?"

"It's possible."

"But," Maami poked an agitated finger, "ma gbagbe pe there is still that strange-looking man Lara said she saw Modele talking to that day."

"I think Lara is lying about that," I said. "But I will ask Modele about it. We'll see if it's true."

"Let's say Major Kofo killed her rival," Somto said. "How did she get past the choir to the backstage and into the changing room?"

"You ask the right questions, my friend! You should be a police officer or detective."

He eyed me. "Is there a back door?"

"In the changing room? I don't think so."

"Abi, she went in through a window, ni?"

"I don't know, Maami. I will have to find out if that's possible."

"Find out, biko. This is exciting."

I looked at him. "Never knew you could say that."

Somto left when the rain stopped and promised to be back in a jiffy. After he had gone, Maami suddenly wore an anxious look.

"What's wrong, Maami?"

"Maybe my eyes are deceiving me. I have been thinking about it since yesterday."

I let my quiet disposition urge her on.

"Iyabo was just leaving, and I saw her off to the junction after Kabiru's father's house," she continued. "It happened so quickly. She was telling me about her rude daughter-in-law, so my attention was on her. You know how she tells good stories. Then I just saw the face in a crowd, and before I could look again, he was not there again."

"Who did you see, Maami?"

"Your father. I think I saw my husband."

I looked at her. Maami is only fifty-seven, fit and healthy, so I imagined any thoughts of dementia were a little premature. "You saw my father, or you saw someone who looked like him?"

"I saw him," she cried.

Maami had always maintained she thought he was alive somewhere, and I recalled I shared that view too as a boy. But as I grew older, it became apparent that such an idea was fanciful, and I quickly accepted he was dead, because what other logical explanation could there be?

"It must have been someone who looked like him."

"Iyabo said the same thing, but I am not mad. I am not seeing things. My son, I am not mad."

I made her a soothing tea of clove basil from the garden and honey after she had exhausted herself trying to make me reason with her, and encouraged her to take a siesta. She agreed and left for her room. I, too, was sipping from a mug when Somto returned.

"Listen," I said after the brief chatter. "Another thing we don't know is what she was killed with. I think it's important."

"You mean the murder weapon. You should start talking more technically, like you mean business."

"Yes, sir."

"Good. According to the report I read, she died from— "

"Wait, you read a report?"

"Totally by accident. I saw it on my uncle's table when I dropped by his office some days back."

"Why did you visit him a second time?"

"Because he promised me some money. I'm out of work, abi you don forget?"

"Did he give you any?"

"He gave me stories."

"Ah."

"What was I saying?"

"The report."

"Yes! She died from a… focal impact upon the head by a… sudden acceleration." He appeared to be saying this off the top of his head, and with some difficulty too. "Deceleration within the cranium… abeg! The koko be say, someone whacked her in the head around the temple."

I recalled that all too well. "It brings into perspective, I think, the motive. Again."

"I don't understand."

"I mean, who kills someone with a—"

"Blunt object. That's what the report said."

"Yes. A blunt object. Don't you think it calls into question the motive?"

"Like how na?"

"I mean, if you are going to kill someone, you will use a gun, right?"

My friend regarded me. "How many people have access to guns, Deji? It's not like the movies."

"I'm just saying! Like Major Kofo. That would be her weapon of choice."

"For sharp-sharp killing, yes. Or a knife."

"Exactly. That shows premeditation. You planned to kill the person in advance. Not always, but most times."

"So you are saying whoever killed Sade did not plan to do so?"

"That's what I think." I took another sip. "She was face-to-face with her attacker. It would be almost impossible to kill with a gun in a church without being heard."

"And a knife…"

"Would have been easier," I keyed into his thoughts, "but she wasn't killed with that either. Which means…" I paused for effect. "It means, Somto, this murder was spontaneous. On a whim."

"It was never planned."

"Exactly. It just happened. What do you think it was? The weapon."

"I don't know. Maybe firewood?"

I looked at him. "Who brings firewood to church, Somto?"

"Okay. A plank?"

"How do you conceal a plank?"

"A short plank. Should fit into a handbag."

I considered. "It doesn't make sense."

"Hammer nko?"

"Be serious!"

"I don't know, please! You are the wannabe detective."

I paused and let my mind wander a bit. A chilly breeze swept into the living room, bringing with it the earthy smell of wet foliage. I set the mug down when a thought suddenly occurred to me. I considered the scenario in my head.

"Deji?"

"Hmm?"

"What are you thinking?"

"Richard."

"Who is Richard?"

"Richard. Sade's fiancé."

"Wetin do am?"

"He is the church drummer."

"So?"

"He sits on a platform. He drums on the platform."

"Wetin you dey talk now?"

"Don't you understand? From where he sits, he should see the changing room. It is in his direct line of sight. I need to talk to him."

"You think he saw something?"

"That's what I need to ask him."

CHAPTER NINE

Modele had been kind enough to give me Richard's number after what was an unexpected call from her. Richard agreed to see me. The call from Modele had baffled me. It seemed odd because she spoke as though we had been friends for years. How was I doing? Had I had breakfast? A new movie was just showing at the cinemas, would I like to see it? I had to cross-check the number to make sure I wasn't mixing her up. I told Somto about the call, and he concluded she was probably lonely. He then asked to follow me to Richard's because he had nothing to do and wanted some excitement too. I agreed, against my better judgment.

We set out a little after one o'clock. Kabiru had bailed on me at the eleventh hour after first agreeing to drive me to the address. He had received a call from a madam to carry some light cargo from the wharf. The woman offered to pay more than I gave him, so naturally, he followed the money. We took the bus and continued the rest of the journey on foot. It was a fine day to do so.

We arrived at the address to find a plain two-story building with a cheeky inscription: Kamson Castle. It was anything but a castle. It looked more like three fat huts piled on top of each other. The mallam who sold at the kiosk at the gate told us Richard lived on the top floor.

We entered the cramped, poorly lit stairwell. As we did so, I almost collided with Lara, who was just climbing down. We both apologized, she more profusely.

"I didn't know you would be here," I said, genuinely surprised.

Lara let out a hollow laugh. Her red-painted lips seemed to stretch across the width of her face. "I didn't know that myself." The dark sunglasses she wore almost fell off her face. "I was just around the area and decided to check up on him. He's not feeling too well. You want to see him too?"

"Yes," I replied. "He didn't sound sick when I called."

"It's just a slight fever."

"I wonder if he will want to see me now."

"It's not serious."

"Okay. Are those little monsters still disturbing you? I haven't spoken to my mother about the poison yet. To be honest, I completely forgot."

"Don't worry yourself. I will have the place fumigated."

"Ah! Better. Let the experts do it."

She hurried down the stairs. "Well, I should be going now. I—I, erm, only came to check on him to see if he's better. Bye-bye." She departed quickly.

"That's Lara," said Somto shrewdly.

I nodded and continued climbing the stairs, wondering about her evident need to justify her presence in Richard's house. When we got to the top floor, I said to Somto, "Don't say anything, my friend. Just let me do the talking, okay?" I expected the trite "no problem," but when I heard "no promises," I immediately regretted bringing him along.

I knocked, and Richard opened the door with such lively promptness he must have been just behind it.

"Deji Depiver?"

Voice deep and buttery, Richard was what you might call ruggedly handsome. Dark, athletic, with hard eyes like a tilapia's. He looked like a good fit for a protagonist in a romantic movie. Sade, I thought to myself, knew how to pick them.

"Yes."

He looked quizzically at Somto. "Who is he?"

I was prepared for this eventuality. Quickly, in rehearsed sentences, I told him that he was a friend who lived in the area and had met him by accident, explaining further that due to the passage of time since we last saw each other, he was difficult to dislodge. He looked relieved and ushered us in, immediately taking a liking to Somto, who assumed a fizzy persona, and soon they were discussing European football matches, which happened to be one of Richard's pastimes. He served him beer from a can, which I declined. His sitting room was about the size of my studio, cramped but adequately furnished. I cleared my throat until I was almost gagging before I was able to steer the conversation to the purpose of my visit.

"Did you see Sade's friend on your way up?"

"Lara," I said. "I almost knocked her over. Your stairwell is dark."

Richard apologized and said, "She came to return some of Sade's stuff." I noticed he didn't meet my eyes as he said that. Somto and I exchanged stolen glances.

"But you were not married. Shouldn't she be returning them to her parents?"

"It's not stuff like that. Personal stuff that belonged to me."

"I see. How is the fever?"

"Fever?" Richard was perplexed.

Lara lied, I thought. "Not you. I'm asking my friend."

Somto, puzzled at first, took the hint. "It's gone. Hallelujah!"

"You should not take beer when you are sick," advised Richard.

"My brother," said Somto in a merry mood, "cold beer like this is exactly what the doctor ordered."

Richard grinned and asked me, "Does her family know?"

"Know what?"

"This thing you are doing."

"Oh, no. I'm doing this just for her."

He nodded and didn't press further. I suspected Lara must have debriefed him beforehand. Soon, he began talking volubly. It was kind of me to be doing this, and only God could possibly repay me. Well, they had met at the hospital where she worked three years ago. He was a patient, and she had cared for him. They had liked each other instantly, he coming from a medical background himself, but having no interest in it whatsoever. He had always wanted to do music. It was what he had always been good at—percussion and drums. That Sade also sang was a bonus. They loved each other and were due to marry next year. What a rude shock it was that she died! And at the hands of another who was still walking free? It was difficult to bear. Richard's eloquence was cut short by Somto, who asked for another beer. I was angry at the interruption, but kept my face blank.

When he returned with the beer, he said to me, "I hear you think someone in the choir did it."

"It's what everyone thinks," I said. "Who told you?"

"Lara."

I nodded. "What did you think when she told you?"

Richard waited a minute before he said, "I don't know what to think. It has to be one of them, abi? There is no other way to explain it."

"I was there that day, Richard. I saw the look in her eyes. Sade was afraid of something. Do you know why she was afraid?" I asked. "Did she tell you anything that might be important?"

Richard squeezed his face like he'd just sucked on a tart orange and shook his head.

I prodded him further. "Do you maybe think she was hiding something from you?"

A pause followed.

"How do you mean?" Richard asked.

"Like a secret life?"

Richard looked baffled.

Somto wiped his mouth, set the can on the stool, and said, "Like an affair, abi? Is that not what you wanted to say, Deji? An affair?"

Richard hesitated, fatally so, and I knew what came out of his mouth next would be false.

"No, Somto," I said between gritted teeth, allowing the tone of my voice to convey that I would appreciate it if he kept his mouth shut. "That is not what I meant at all." It was exactly what I meant, but I didn't need him to say it for me.

Richard looked uncertain. "I told you we were going to get married. Nothing like an affair."

I reflected. Richard knew his fiancée was having an affair. Of that, I was certain. I was also sure he knew it was with the choirmaster, so why claim ignorance?

He said to me, "What do you think really happened back there, eh? Who could have done it?"

"That is a question that has bothered me, Richard."

Somto waded in again. "We know that she didn't kill herself. I mean, how can you hit yourself in the head with a plank or something? It's not possible."

"Did you know Sade, too?" asked Richard, confused.

I said quickly, "Yes, Somto. Did you know her?"

My friend looked like a cornered cat before recovering with a stupid grin. "I didn't know her—mba o—but I read about it in the papers."

"You read a lot of papers, I remember."

Richard frowned. He rose and paced about. "Do you suspect anyone?"

I let my gaze drop idly to the potpourri on the miniature center table. Its smell was strong but indeterminate. I wondered if it contained orange peels or cloves. "I suspect everyone," I replied with an air of mystery, then asked, "From where you play the drums, can you see the changing room?"

His eyes flickered. "Yes. I can see almost everywhere." He sat back. "I saw them entering the room. My eyes were on them. They didn't even spend up to five minutes there. Maybe ten. Lara came out first and went back to her seat. I remember she nearly fell. There were wires and cables on the floor. Then Modele came out next, looking tired. I—"

"Wait, wait, slow down," I spluttered. "Lara came out first?"

"Yes."

"That's not what I heard."

"Yeah," murmured Somto in agreement before realizing his mistake and swiftly correcting himself. "I mean, yeah, sure?"

Richard's face fell. "I don't know anything about that, but I'm telling you what I saw and how I saw it. My eyes were on them."

"This is strange," I said, a throb of anxiety rising in me. "Modele, Lara, and Jimi all agreed that Nike left the room first. Even Nike said it herself."

"Are you calling me a liar?" Richard roared, a flame jumping into his eyes.

"No, not at all," I said with an air of surprise and a shade of apology. "I am just confused. Don't get me wrong."

He shook his head emphatically. "Lara came out first. I'm sure of it. Then Modele. All within a minute. I think Jimi came out next. I'm not sure I saw Nike. Maybe I took my eyes off for a second." His voice drifted, and he began muttering under his breath as though questioning himself.

I let my mind drift a bit. His firm narrative that Lara came out first changed the complexion of the case in my head. Was it consequential? Could he be taken seriously when four other witnesses or suspects stated otherwise? I wondered.

"I'm sure of it," he said again, this time lacking earlier conviction.

I stayed silent for a couple of minutes. Then I made up my mind. "I'm sure there's an explanation for it. Maybe you're right. Ah, that day. I remember it like yesterday. Reverend Brown's sermon was so boring, it was like watching paint dry." Somto let out an unfortunate laugh.

"You were there?"

"Yes, I told you. I was in fact not far from where you sat."

Richard's face lit up. He smiled, then shrugged. "You know, when you are the church drummer, you don't really listen to the sermon. Most of the time, you are looking at everyone and what they wear to church. But that day, I was listening to him. It doesn't happen always, but I was listening to him."

I nodded. "What was he even wearing? Do you remember?"

"Reverend Brown?"

"Yes. I mean the color."

He waited a second or two before replying. "Blue." I nodded in agreement.

"Why do you ask?"

"Nothing. I'm just trying to recall the events of that day. You see, I like colors. They help me think. I'm a painter." Somto eyed me. I knew he wasn't buying my drivel. Richard excused himself and disappeared into a room.

"There is one thing Sade was upset about that morning," he said when he returned. "I just remember it now."

I sat up straight.

"She couldn't find the lucky mic, and she thought someone hid it from her."

"What's a lucky mic?"

"It's the microphone she liked to use. She gave it that name. She doesn't use any other mic except the Lucky Mic."

"What's special about it?"

"It's not special. It is the oldest microphone in the church. The first microphone owned by the church. She just liked to use it."

Somto and I were in a danfo heading back home twenty minutes later. We sat in the two front seats.

"I don't even know why I agreed to let you follow me. Did you charm me?"

We had been arguing since we left Richard's place.

"How am I supposed to just keep quiet when you are talking to him? I'm deaf and dumb?"

"I didn't mean you shouldn't say anything. I meant don't say anything relating to the case. If he were smart, he would put two and two together and walk us out."

"But he didn't."

He slammed his fist like a magistrate's gavel on the dashboard, which drew the ire of the driver.

"Case closed!"

We didn't speak for a while. We reached a logjam at Ojota Bridge.

"Ojota!" cried the conductor.

"Owa!" spat an angry man.

I bought a bottle of water from an elderly woman hawking drinks.

"Why were you asking him about the color the reverend was wearing?" Somto asked. "What is that about?"

"Reverend Brown wasn't wearing blue the day Sade died. He was wearing white."

"So?"

"So if Richard cannot remember the color of a man who preached for over an hour, how are we to believe his testimony that Lara, not Nike, as everyone said, was the first to leave that room?"

"Whoa." His eyes widened. "E mean say…"

"It means," I cut him short, "that Richard is not a credible witness. We really cannot believe his testimony."

We didn't say anything again till we got off the bus. Then he asked what had been boggling my mind the minute I almost collided with Lara.

"So, is Richard having an affair with Lara already?"

CHAPTER TEN

On Wednesdays, I retrieved letters from the mailbox. It had been weeks since I last did so, and usually there were not a lot of them, but today I was surprised to find three. One was addressed to me. It was a reminder from the Lagos State Arts and Culture that this year's exhibition was next Sunday at the National Gallery of Modern Art. I had been preparing for this. The previous edition had been a success, and I was hoping for the same next week. The remaining two letters were addressed to Maami. I shut the gate and ordered Rocky to stop barking. I suspected the fleas he contracted from a neighbor's dog were beginning to bite hard and made a mental note to take him to a veterinary friend of mine later in the day. Inside, Maami and her friend were snacking on fried shrimps. An air of positive camaraderie was palpable.

Mrs. Banjo was telling her friend, "Because that is how I felt, Rolake, osha'amo! The party was not enjoyable, jare. I could not untie and tie my gele in different directions and show them what I am made of. Show them that Iyabo is in town."

"But you said you enjoyed the party when Olori and her people asked about it when we were leaving."

"I lied. What would I have said?" asked Mrs. Banjo, bemused. "That it was a lame party? My tongue is sharp, Rolake, but not that sharp. A party with no live band… is that a party?"

Maami shrugged.

"It's the worst party I have been to so far this year, and you know I have been to many. You will bear me witness. Thank God there are still many more months to go. The food finished too quickly, and the meats were small."

"Olori disappointed me there."

"Olori disappointed herself," corrected her friend.

"Are those letters for me?" Maami noticed my presence and extended a hand.

"Today is today!" cried Mrs. Banjo. Her green veins popped out like a network of estuaries. "I will collect my portrait today!"

"He finished it some days ago, oremi. You said you would come, but we didn't see you."

"I was helping my sister-in-law with her wedding plans."

"Thank God!"

Her friend made a face. "That venue she picked is too small, if you ask me. It wouldn't even accommodate all of my own friends."

"She finally found someone."

Mrs. Banjo shrugged. "Nothing is too late—"

"I am happy for her."

"Although she could do better with the man she picked."

"What is wrong with him?"

"The way I'm looking at him…he's not very rich."

"Beggars can't be choosers, oremi."

"He laughs too much."

"Beggars can't be choosers."

"And then he speaks like he just arrived on the first bus from the village."

"Beggars—"

"*Motigbo*!" cried her friend. "I heard you the first time."

When I gave Mrs. Banjo her painting, she beamed. "I will put this one in our bedroom."

Maami looked up. "Didn't you say you have one there already?"

"Ah, beeni o. If my husband is unhappy about another one, he can move into the guest room."

"When is the wedding?" Maami passed me some shrimp as I sat on a stool. I had been under a lot of stress lately, so I thought I had better lighten up with gossip from Maami and her friend. I enjoyed Mrs. Banjo's presence in the house.

"Three Saturdays from now."

"*Kiakia ni*? So soon?"

Mrs. Banjo nodded. "Before the man changes his mind, abi kiloni mowi?" She cackled at her own joke. From the cavernous bag next to her, she pulled out two gele fabrics.

"I wanted to ask you what was in that bag," said Maami with interest.

"Which one do you think we should wear for the wedding? Before you answer, did you see what Mrs. Soara wore yesterday?"

"To the party?"

"No," replied her friend with wicked humor. "To the funeral. What else would I be talking about?"

Maami was a couple of years older than Mrs. Banjo, but you would think it was the other way around.

Maami's eyes brightened. "Ehn, beeni. I remember now. That green foil lace is gorgeous. It must cost an eye."

Mrs. Banjo sneered. "We know it is beautiful, but is it the only decent dress in her wardrobe, eh?"

"Has she worn it before?"

"Rolake! You have eyes but cannot see!" chided her friend.

"She wore it to her father's birthday party last year, don't you remember? The same green foil lace to my cousin's housewarming party in February—and what a disaster that was—and she wore it again yesterday. Kilode?!"

"Ah! It has turned into a uniform."

"I think she has fallen on hard times after running her mouth about the contract her husband got from the government last year." She executed a loud, startling hiss. "Shior! Oya o'jare, tell me, which one are we wearing?"

Soon, both women were debating which gele had more presence. Maami liked the classy taffeta white brocade with ivory markings, but Mrs. Banjo felt the tomato red damask with serpentine embroidery would, well, paint the party red.

"If you had made up your mind about it, Iyabo, why did you ask my opinion n'gba yen?"

"I asked you so you won't say I didn't ask you."

Maami scoffed and tore open the first letter. She groaned and raised a hand to the heavens.

"Lord, come and save me!"

"Kilode?"

"The shares have depreciated again."

"Again?" I slipped a shrimp into my mouth. "For the third year running."

"You are still putting your retirement money into shares?" asked her friend in utter disbelief. "You will not learn! Why don't you kuku set up a bonfire in your backyard and burn the money?"

"What am I to do? It's all I have."

"Turn that little vegetable garden of yours into a block of flats with your money. This is Lagos, ma lo slow!"

"You know I can't do that, oremi—"

"He's dead, Rolake," Mrs. Banjo cut in, folding the fabrics. "He's not coming back. I have been telling you for years, but you are deaf to what I say. My mouth is smelly."

"He is not dead. I saw him."

"You think you saw him, stubborn woman. What you saw is someone who looked like him, abi what do you think, Deji? Talk to your mother."

I looked knowingly at Maami.

"If who you claim you saw is him, then you have started seeing things like that madman at the junction people tell me is good with baba ijebu. Is it true about what they say? Can he see winning numbers?"

I nodded. "Everyone around here says so."

"A pity he cannot see a cure for himself. So oremi—"

"I am not mad, Iyabo—"

"I didn't say you are mad." Mrs. Banjo snatched a couple of shrimps, threw them into her mouth, and chewed noisily. "But the madman doesn't think he's mad, too."

I was shaking my head when Mrs. Banjo eyed me and asked, "When were you going to tell me you and Sade were friends, abi you think I don't know?"

From the corner of my eye, I saw Maami's jaw drop.

"Iyabo?!" she cried. "How did you come about that knowledge?"

"I will pretend you did not ask me that question, Rolake." Mrs. Banjo looked truly insulted.

Maami shook her head like a reprimanded pupil.

"You know, there is nothing happening in this corner of the world I don't know about. I won't know about it only if I'm dead!"

Maami swallowed.

"I was suspicious when you started asking me questions, but when I saw the painting they sent to her family, I knew my painter was the painter!"

"You saw the painting?" asked Maami, wide-eyed. "Bawo lo'se se?"

"Stop looking so surprised, Rolake. It makes your face look old."

"Old is what I will get. I asked you how you saw the painting?"

"I went to her house. Her mother showed me. Nosy woman. I think she enjoyed the attention."

"Iyabo!"

"Stop shouting my name, jare. I don't want to go deaf." Mrs. Banjo adjusted her dress, clearly enjoying the attention. "I made sure I was part of the people who paid them a condolence visit some days ago."

There was a mischievous look on her face.

"What is the connection between you and the girl, Mr. Painter?" she asked me with a bit of seriousness now. "I hear things."

There was no point denying anything with Mrs. Banjo, so I gave her a watered-down account of how it all happened. She sighed after I had finished, looking genuinely affected. She also seemed interested in the idea of a covert sleuth and pledged her support. She even joked that it would enhance her street credibility as the local parrot.

"Fear not, my child." She beat her bosom. "I am behind you like the hump on the back of a cow."

"Ose oremi." Maami was grateful. "So do you know anything that can help?"

"I don't know too much," replied her friend, somewhat disappointed. "But, eh, when I was at her parents' house, that friend of hers with broomstick legs was there too—what do these girls eat nowadays, eh? Noodles? Anyway, that man she was going to marry—the drummer boy—was there too, and I can tell you, oremi, that something is going on between the two of them, and it is not after that girl died! Laye!"

"Ah!"

"Kini? Do you have a shrimp in your throat?" grunted Mrs. Banjo. "And will you open that second letter, abi? Why are you holding it like there is a bomb in it?"

She could not have put it better. It was, literally, a bomb. The air went out of the house when Maami opened the letter. A great cry escaped from her mouth. Mrs. Banjo panicked and fled to the garden. Maami, hysterical, collapsed. I picked up the letter, dated a month ago, and began to read.

Dearest Rolake,

I hope my letter finds you in good health. News has reached me that you are retired. How you loved to teach the children. I am so glad of the woman you became. You remain my idol. I also heard our son, Ayodeji, is a painter. Where did he get that talent from? I think it must be from you, my dearest. You were always the imaginative one.

I know my actions have caused you untold pain. Rolake, I think of you always. I always wanted to write, but every time I pick up a pen, I don't know what to say most of the time. I am just ashamed of myself.

I am in Kaduna, where I have been all these years, although I started out in Lokoja. I want you to know that no one in my family knows this. I swear it. My mother went to her grave believing I was dead. I also heard that Raimi, my best man, died in an accident some years back. What a conscientious man he was.

Rolake, why I chose to cut loose my old life remains to me a monumental mystery. Even as I write to you, I have often thought in my heart that I am cursed. Or possessed. But what I know as I reflect back to that time was that I was going through a period where I felt I might go mad. You didn't know this, of course, and it was never a fault of yours.

I spent the first few years on the streets of Kaduna. I did some jobs, odd ones at that. I even worked in a garment factory. Can you believe that? I didn't know what I was doing. At one point, I journeyed to Burkina Faso, where I spent about a year touring the towns and cities. I had no job and didn't even know how I survived. I cannot explain the compulsive desire to travel I felt, but somehow I was happy. I learned some French and moved briefly to the Ivory Coast. A man like me from Senegal, whom I met in Bobo Dioulasso, told me I might find the country inspiring. It didn't work out, and after about a year, I moved back to Kaduna.

Here, I met a woman, Anne, a librarian. She straightened me out, although I felt I wore her out in the process. We are not married but have two children together, Alice and Alexander.

Why didn't you move on with your life? Why?

Recently, everything has been eating me alive, and I don't want to die without letting you know or seeing you, for that matter. You have endured an ordeal no woman should be put through. I will write you again and hope someday I can see you again, and maybe then you will forgive my sins.

With love,
Olusoji Depiver

Along with the letter came a photo of him. It showed a white-haired man in a white kaftan, serious-eyed for the moment but clearly willing to break into a smile. A man with a shifting persona.

It was a photo that lifted the lid on repressed memories, and for an instant, I was transported back to when I was small. I recalled vividly that it was a Friday. Maami, who taught me in class, took me to the market after school to buy groceries to prepare dinner. Night came, and there was no sign of Father. It was the days of landlines, so she called his boss only to be told he had resigned a month before. This set off alarm bells because he hadn't told her anything and always dressed up for work. She began to call his friends to find out if he was over at theirs. No, they said. She began to panic. Where had he been going dressed for work every morning? His car, clothes, and other personal effects were still intact, so by the third day, she filed a missing person report, to no effect. Days grew into months and months grew into years, and ten years after he'd disappeared, his family declared him dead in absentia. Why, after all these years, was he suddenly alive?

Later that evening, even after the dust had settled and some normalcy returned, a thin fog of uncertainty still hung in the air. Maami had snapped out of her hysteria and was now served some vegetable soup concocted by her friend, who claimed it would calm her nerves.

"Now you see, Iyabo, when I tell you I am not mad abi o ri'nkan, bayi. It was him I saw the other day. This letter is proof."

"Just eat your vegetable soup."

Maami regarded the soup and murmured, "It looks like something the deity Oya would cook for the god of thunder, Sango."

"Sango ni good taste ni'gbayen. Eat the soup o'jare!"

She pushed it away.

"Oremi, you don't know how I feel. Why is he coming back into our lives now? Do you think he's outside watching the house?"

Mrs. Banjo sprang to her feet and looked around from the window.

"I don't think so. Don't frighten me, woman!"

The thought had occurred to me. The person Maami claimed to see must have been him, and he must have sent the letter ahead of coming.

"What could have been going on in his mind, eh? What kind of life is that?"

Mrs. Banjo bared her thoughts rather forcefully.

"He's right, Rolake. O'oto loso. He was cursed. Not many people liked your marriage with him, abi have you forgotten?"

"Are you saying someone charmed him away?" She took the bait.

Her friend tapped her palm with the outside of her other hand theatrically.

"Didn't you tell me his first lover, whom he courted for years, showed up at your wedding without an invitation? What did you even do with that present she gave to you?"

"I threw it away. You remember you asked me to?"

"It does not mean she didn't do something. It is very cheap to bewitch a person, but to undo it is expensive. I hear these things every day. Is she still alive?"

"I don't know." Maami looked helpless.

"Not only her gan," reasoned her friend. "Didn't you tell me your mother-in-law wanted him to take a second wife?"

"But shebi…"

I had heard enough and closed my eyes and shut my ears. I had read a book some time ago about meditation and thought now was a good time to practice it and calm the turmoil in my head. I let my mind drift into space and imagined a dark, quiet place devoid of past or future thoughts, as the book *Headspace* implored. Barely minutes into it, and wondering why meditation was such a hard thing, my mind wandered back in time for the second time today and replayed every detail of Father as I remembered it. Looking back now, he was a man of few words with a distant personality. Sometimes he didn't say more than a few words to me all day. Maami, now noticing my reticence, implored me to say something. I shook my head, still bereft of words.

"There is nothing to say, Maami. I don't understand any of this."

"You were too small to understand."

"I mean, even now, Maami. Ko ye mi rara."

She looked at the photo and said for the hundredth time, "You look so much like him."

"Baba e lobi. Who else will he look like?"

"I pray you are not like him."

"He is not like him."

"This headache," Maami complained after a moment of silence, touching her forehead. "It comes and goes like waist beads."

"Eat your soup, Rolake. You will feel better."

"*O ti tutu.*"

"Why won't it be cold, eh? Chu chu chu chu chu. Do you have medicine for headaches in this house for your mother?"

CHAPTER ELEVEN

I wanted to divest my mind from the curious case of Father's return from the dead, so I decided to do a little digging into what sent Sade in the other direction. What better time to start than the bright afternoon of the following day? I left home and arrived at rehearsal a little ahead of schedule. I saw a few choristers, but none of my persons of interest were present yet, so I sat down and observed, taking in the twittering of the barely familiar group. It was Thanksgiving next week, and they appeared very excited indeed. Soon, the known faces began to trickle in. First came Nike, hurriedly informing the group that the choirmaster had had an emergency and was going to be very late, possibly missing out altogether, but the good news was that she had been asked to preside at his behest. This drew some approving noises. Nike, a little embarrassed by the positive euphoria, soaked in the attention by giving a shy bow of the head. She noticed me in the process, and we exchanged warm pleasantries.

"Good to see you again."

"Have you come to join our choir?" she asked with a crooked smile. One could tell she tried desperately to hide her awful teeth.

I laughed. "I was wondering if you would come at all."

Nike looked surprised. "Thanksgiving is just next week. Why wouldn't I come? We have numbers to prepare for."

"It's just a feeling."

"So what are you doing here?"

"Erm, nothing really." I looked around. "Just hanging out here."

"It's about Sade, abi?"

I smiled. "You see far into the spirit."

"I understand." She nodded gravely. Then suddenly her eyes lit up. She drew closer to me and whispered, "There is something I remember about Sade, but I will tell you later. You are not going now, are you?"

"No. I'm around."

"Good." She turned to leave, but then asked, "Do you sing too?"

"Eh?"

She poked a finger at the sheet in my hand.

"No, no. I don't." I let out an embarrassed chuckle. "I picked this up somewhere. I think it's the numbers you did last week."

"That's too bad because you have a good voice. Don't let it go to waste."

"You are just saying that."

"No, I'm not. I can hear tenor." To buttress her point, she tapped a nearby chorister and asked for confirmation, which came readily. I allowed my eyes to bulge a bit. I wasn't really surprised at the flattery. I sometimes sing in the bathroom, and to my ears, I sound good.

"You think so?"

"Yes!"

She took the sheet away from me and gave me a new one from her bag. "That's the song we are practicing today. You will join us!" She was joking, of course, but I didn't protest.

"How is your husband?" I folded the sheet and slipped it into my pocket. "And have you changed those colors?"

It was as though someone had pressed a button remotely and changed her countenance because the smile disappeared from her face, replaced by a distant look. Someone chuckled behind me.

Nike hesitated, then replied impassively, "He's fine, thank you. No, we have not changed the colors. Excuse me." She disappeared into an unmarked room. I stood there dismayed. Had I said something wrong? I wondered.

Someone tapped me from behind. It was the lady who chuckled. "Next time," she whispered to me, "don't ask her about her husband, okay? She will think you're making fun of her."

Next came Richard and Lara, exactly one minute apart. My immediate thought was that they had come together but walked in separately to make it look like they hadn't come in together, but this, in my mind, was unlikely to stop tongues wagging. Richard saw me and waved before waltzing to the technical area. Lara saw me too, but pretended not to. Nike came out of the room, handed out sheets from her bag, and barked a few orders. They started with prayers and then voice training. They were all belting ha ha ha ha ha… in different notes. Almost as soon as they began properly, Modele clattered in.

"Sorry, I'm late." Her heels clapped loudly on the tiled floor. "Traffic is so…urgh! You know how it is. Wow, Nkem, I like your hair!" She greeted a few friends, hugged others, and when she saw me, exhibited mild hysteria, apparently in great delight at seeing me again. Modele loved attention. She was the showstopper.

"Modele, we were about to start rehearsal." Nike wanted to restore some decorum.

"Without me?" she laughed. "What kind of rehearsal will that be without me, eh, Nike? Where is Jimi?"

"He will be late," someone replied.

"Traffic!" muttered Modele, shaking her head. "The danfo I boarded nearly tore my dress! Someone better buy me a car o, before I vex!"

There were a few giggles. Lara, who was having none of Modele's antics, was whispering to a lady next to her, who in turn frowned and shook her head wildly.

"Is there a problem, Lara?" asked Nike, concerned.

"I still can't find it," Lara shrilled. "I still can't find the microphone Sade loved so much since the day she died."

"You are talking about the heavy cord one, abi?" Modele asked, heaving as she'd just run a mile. She dabbed a handkerchief over her heavily made-up face.

"What else would I be talking about?" Lara snapped, visibly annoyed. "Everyone knows Sade didn't use any other mic except the Lucky Mic!"

Modele shot back, "It's a nice mic if you can't sing very well." Then added with stinging sarcasm, "Every Mary and Martha sounds good on it."

Someone giggled.

"You know that's not true, Modele."

"Shut up, Bisi. I wasn't talking to you."

"Is there something you want to tell me?" Lara was asking Modele, who rolled her eyes. Lara had the face of thunder but managed to keep her voice cool. "I haven't seen it since. I asked about it last week, but nobody said anything. Where did it disappear to? What happened to it?"

"Take it easy, Lara. I'm sure we will find it." Nike, who still hadn't gotten a foothold on things, said, "We all liked to use the Lucky Mic."

"Especially you, Nike." Modele appeared to enjoy testing everybody's patience. "You liked it so much before it became Sade's toy."

"Maybe it was stolen?" asked a voice next to her. It was the dark and lovely lady who had spoken to me earlier about Nike's husband.

"Don't be silly, Rekia," said Modele, irritated. "It's a mic, not a piece of jewelry. Who would steal a common microphone?"

"It's not a common microphone!" Lara cried. "It meant a lot to Sade."

"It's possible it was stolen," said Nike thoughtfully. "Shebi, you remember last month Richard couldn't find the cymbals. We had to buy another set."

"And the month before," Rekia said, "we lost a few tambourines."

"This is different," Lara insisted. "This one is different."

Nike herself had become exasperated. "How? How is it different?"

"I am happy that you asked, Nike." Lara placed her hands on her hips. "Why was the mic stolen that same day she died? You were all here when she was upset and looking for it. Abi, have you all forgotten?"

"Hm," murmured Rekia, "and by the end of the service—"

"She was dead!" Lara completed. "Thank you, Rekia."

"Jesus!"

"Ah!"

"Na wa o."

"You see what I'm saying now, eh?"

"You are making a mountain out of a molehill," said Modele, putting the hanky back in her purse. "It may not be related at all."

A man had just come in, scratching his head. "Erm, now that you are talking about it, one of the cleaners found a torn cord somewhere last week, but there was no mic on it. I think it's from the Lucky Mic."

My interest piqued, I asked, "Did she say where she found it?"

"Who are you, please?"

I looked at Nike for help.

"He's a friend of my sister Sade."

Modele laughed. "You mean the guy trying to find her killer. You people like to sugarcoat things like kilode! Ah!" There were a few audible murmurs.

"You are welcome," replied the man. "To answer your question, I think she found it on the floor somewhere, but I don't know where. I saw her put it in the dustbin."

"Was it torn with force?" I asked. "Or maybe with a blade or scissors?"

He looked at me, puzzled. "Brother, how will I know something like that?"

Richard, who was next to him, appeared thoughtful. "But it was very long, so it must have been cut very close to the tail."

There was a long pause.

"Maybe it's not the Lucky Mic," Nike offered with a brittle smile.

"It's a blue cord," he added.

"It's the Lucky Mic!" Lara gasped. "It's the only one with a blue cord. Why?" she cried. "Who did this? Who hates her so much to do this?"

There was a moment of silence. I found myself thinking that there was more to this missing microphone than met the eye.

"Is it maybe a joke or something?" Modele asked. She laid her hand on my arm. "Do you think it's a joke? Like a prank?"

Before I could reply, Lara launched a scathing attack on her.

"Yes, it is a prank! A prank by you, Modele! Yes, you, Modele. It was you! Like the other day after rehearsal, you tore Sade's bag to shreds with a blade, or did you think we didn't know it was you?"

Modele pulled back, confused. "What are you talking about, Lara?"

"Don't pretend like you don't know what I'm talking about!"

She clapped her hands, furious. "It was you, Modele. Admit it! You hated her so much."

"Did the girl at the salon weave your hair too tight again, Lara?" Modele asked, dismayed. "Because I don't understand what you are saying. When did I do this thing you said I did?"

"Please, ladies, let's not fight," Nike pleaded. "Remember where we are."

"Let me finish, Nike! Let me finish!" Lara continued indignantly. "You hated her so much, Modele. I know it. I will not say why you hated her, but I know you did! You frightened her, tormented her, now she is dead, and you still torment her." Clouds of tears formed in her eyes. "Let her rest in peace, please. Pleeeeease, I beg you!"

Lara had spoken so exhaustively that she began to pant.

"Call your doctor as soon as possible, Lara," Modele sneered. "Your medications are not working!"

Then she walked out.

"Modele, wait!" Rekia ran after her.

Lara wiped her face and excused herself. Nike sighed audibly. When she said, "Shall we begin?" I slipped out quietly. Outside, Modele was talking animatedly with Rekia in a corner, but they did not see me.

I made the short walk from the annex to the main church building. There were a handful of worshippers scattered in the pews. As expected, the changing room was locked. I looked around in time to see the old caretaker coming along. Having bribed him earlier, he was coming to honor his end of the bargain. When he opened the door, we stepped in, and he pointed to another door on the right.

"That's the changing room?"

He nodded.

"What about these?" I pointed to the two doors that faced us.

"Toilet."

"Thank you, baba."

He departed, but not before carefully suggesting that I make it quick.

The room was not as I had imagined it would be. I had a mental picture of a vibrant space adorned with lights, bright walls, mirrors, and mahogany wardrobes similar to what you might find on a movie set; whatever put that idea into my head. What lay before me now was a dreary, claustrophobic space with a few religious insignias. I let my eyes travel around, searching the room with more than a cursory glance, disappointed. It was surprisingly bare, almost threadbare: a few wooden benches, a few wooden racks that held a few well-worn choir robes, a water dispenser that was out of order, nothing to suggest the exciting getaway that Nike and perhaps Modele had made me believe when I interviewed them.

I went to the window and took in the faint, musty smell that suggested an acute lack of use. Somto's theory, at least one of them, was that whoever killed Sade was a stranger who came in through the window. Right now, I could not see how. A section of it was occupied by a window air-conditioning unit, which, upon further examination, showed that it was firmly rooted in place. The other section was sealed shut with iron bars. I was more convinced now than ever that I had spoken to her killer over the last couple of weeks. It was only probable. But who exactly? I wondered. My eyes flickered around and came to rest on the crucifix, a memento mori that reflected the tragedy that occurred in this room. A shudder rippled through me. How much pain did she feel as her killer struck the blows? I wondered. Did she fight for her life? Did she panic and submit? Did she…

"Did you find anything?" I did not know Nike had crept in. "Sorry if I scared you."

I would be lying if I said I was not close to jumping out of my skin, but I said, "No, it's okay." I fixed my gaze on her and raised a brow.

"Jimi is not back yet, and I'm getting very tired." She looked exhausted. "I saw you come in here. Did you find anything?"

I shook my head. "I'm just looking around. I'm sure that if there is anything to be found, it would have been swept away by now. It's been a few weeks."

"I'm always afraid to come in here." She walked in slowly and stopped by a rack. "This is Sade's old robe…or is it? No, it's Lara's."

"You don't use this place anymore?"

"No. Nobody wants to. We don't keep our things here anymore."

"No wonder." It explained why the place looked stripped to bare bones. "So what is it you wanted to tell me?"

"What?"

"Earlier. You said you wanted to tell me something."

"Oh yes! I remember. Well, erm, did you… Did you know that Jimi and Sade were…?" She made an intimate gesture.

"So I was told, but I still need to ask him."

"You don't need to. It's true. And…" she added quietly, "she was even pregnant for him."

"I know all about that." I could scarcely hide my disappointment. "Is that all you wanted to tell me?"

She held her hands together. "You don't think it's important?"

"I don't know what to think right now, Nike. Who told you about her pregnancy?" Lara had told me only she knew about the secret, or at least led me to believe so. Had she confided in Nike too? I wondered.

"Modele," she said and looked away. She appeared uneasy. It struck me that she was anxious to convey the impression that we spoke in confidence.

I nodded. "Listen, about that man you saw." I watched as her face grew apprehensive. "Do you think maybe it was a woman?"

"You mean like Jimi's wife, abi? Major Kofo."

I was taken aback by her direct reply, but agreed with another nod. "Yes. Like her."

"I've thought about it too."

"So what do you think?"

"I don't know. Do you think it's possible?"

I shrugged.

"I didn't see any face."

"Can you walk me through what happened in here that day?"

Her eyes were wide and alert. "I don't want to think about it." She was shaking her head now, very frightened. "Where exactly were Jimi and Sade?"

For a moment, she did not speak but breathed heavily. Finally, she said, "There," pointing to a wooden bench that overlooked the door. It was almost opposite, but at an angle to the right. "They sat there talking."

"And where were you?"

"Here," she pointed to where she stood opposite the bench. "With Modele. We were talking about her shoes. I told you that before now."

"And where was Lara?"

"On the same bench with Sade," she replied and indicated that she had sat a little further from them. "She was playing with her phone."

"No one else was in here?"

"No."

"So they were not talking to her?"

"They were, sometimes. Jimi and Sade were the ones talking, but sometimes Lara would join them and say things like 'Really?' or 'You don't mean it.' Things like that."

"Sade was in the middle?"

"Yes."

"So what happened next?"

"I don't know. I didn't stay long. I left."

"Nike," I began carefully, "you are the only one who saw a strange man around this room. It was after you left here that you noticed him?"

A slow nod.

"But what if you didn't see any man at all?"

She looked bewildered. "Are you saying I'm crazy? That I don't know what I saw?"

"That's not what—"

"But you said it before, that it could be a woman like Jimi's wife. You said that just now."

"No, I never said that. What I'm trying to tell you is that—see," I pulled her close, "look at that window. Look at it. There is no way an intruder came in through there. It's burglar-proof! So I guess what I'm trying to say is that whoever killed Sade must be one of Jimi, Modele, or Lara!"

Her eyes widened in horror. "No…"

"That is the only explanation, Nike," I said with finality.

She shook her head, very anxious. "There must be another explanation. I can't imagine it!"

I stared at the flustered figure before me for a full minute. "You may be right." A slow reprieve crept into her eyes. "There must be another explanation."

Nike sighed. She held my hand and squeezed it warmly. "I'm so happy you think so, too. God has opened your eyes like Abraham's. Do you read the Bible?"

I shook my head.

Another sigh. "I'd better go back to them now. I can hear many of them going off-key."

I examined the room for another ten minutes or so and juggled it all in my head, but I was no closer to making sense of what happened here. Exhausted, I closed the door and left the building. It was around 6 p.m. I wanted to have another word with Modele, but she was still rehearsing, so I walked about the car park like a struck head until an arm suddenly pulled me. It was the choirmaster.

"Mr. Smart," I croaked. He was barely recognizable. He looked like he had been attacked. His left eye was swollen shut, and his upper lip was fat and split. "What happened to you?"

Quickly, he narrated to me that he had been in an argument with his wife. One thing led to another, and she landed blows on him.

"Sorry about that. Have you been to the hospital? It looks bad."

"I'm fine. I can't miss rehearsal. It will be gone by tomorrow."

It did not look like it would be gone by tomorrow, but I asked, "Is she hurt, too?"

"No!" he replied harshly, as though taking offense. "I will never lay my hands on a woman. Never."

"So she was beating you, and you just stood there?" It sounded improbable.

"I tried to stop her, but she was very angry. I ran out of the house. I've never seen her that angry before."

"What did you fight about that made her so angry?"

"That's part of the reason I want to talk to you. I am happy I found you here." He took me aside, next to a dirty white car, and said, grimacing, "Before I tell you, eh, there is something you should know. Something I couldn't tell you when you came to my home the other day."

"Is it about the affair with Sade? I know all about that."

He did not appear too surprised. "I wanted to marry her. I know you will not believe me, but it's the truth. I was going to leave Kofo for her. It was a risk I wanted to take."

I frowned. "I thought you and your wife were happy together. That was the impression I got."

"That's Kofo for you," he snorted. "She wants the world to believe we are the best couple around when, in fact, we are not. When people visit us, she is normal, even caring and protective, but when they are gone, she is the devil himself." He coughed and spat.

"So what caused your fight?"

"She found out Sade was pregnant. Someone told her!"

"She knew about the affair?"

"Yes."

I nodded, easily picturing the scenario. Major Kofo must have been irate. "Who told her?"

"I don't know. She was very angry and started throwing things around. Stools, knives, anything she could lay her hands on. I understand why she did that. We have been married for a long time now, and she has never been pregnant. I think that made her more angry."

"How long has she known? About the affair."

"Maybe two or three months now. We fought about it, but I promised her I would stop seeing her."

"But you didn't."

"I loved Sade. I was going to leave Kofo. Our marriage was a mistake. This is why I wanted to see you in private. I think Kofo killed Sade! In fact, I am sure of it. Kofo killed Sade."

"How did you know that?"

"I will tell you." A vengeful smile touched his lips. "Every Sunday we drive to church in my car. After service, I usually have a fifteen to twenty-minute meeting with the choir, and she waits for me. Except on the day Sade died. I didn't see her or my car. I had to follow a friend home. Do you see where I am going, eh? Do you see? She killed her, panicked, then ran home with the car. It didn't occur to me until today, when we were figh—when she was fighting me!"

This story corroborated what her maid had told me. There was a time gap where no one could account for Major Kofo's whereabouts. It was circumstantial but relevant.

"She has never gone home without you before?"

"Never! Kofo likes everyone to think we are the best couple in the church. Except this one time!"

"Hm," I mumbled, thinking. Was there some kind of hole in the changing room that only Major Kofo knew about? It was a preposterous idea, but I could not think of any other explanation. Jimi's eyes searched my face expressly for a reaction. He did not get any.

"I also remember something during the service."

I glared at him. He paused to think before continuing. "It happened before we went into that changing room. Kofo sat where she normally sat, and when I looked at her, there was this look on her face, as if she wanted to kill somebody. But when I looked at her again, I realized that she was actually looking at Sade."

Well, this one made sense, I said to myself. It was Major Kofo who frightened Sade that day.

"So it was her."

"Eh?"

"She frightened Sade."

"Yes! She did not know I was looking at her."

It was another compelling but circumstantial piece of evidence, and nothing yet put her in the changing room unless… unless she had someone else do it for her? My thoughts were suddenly interrupted by a startling cry.

"Brother Jimi! Brother Jimi!!" It was Modele running wildly toward us. "Nike was just telling me what happened, that you were robbed and assaulted! My God, look at your face!"

Jimi, who immediately looked like he would rather be elsewhere, said woodenly, "Thank you for your concern, Modele, but it's not as bad as it looks."

"It is swollen! I'm surprised you can even talk. Ah!" She examined him like a nurse would a patient. He resisted, but Modele was insistent. "Good for you that I know how to use first aid. Just wait for me and let me get the box."

He tried to dissuade her, but Modele would have none of it. She clattered away, arms out for balance as though walking on a tightrope.

"I don't know what to do about her," he said to me after she was out of earshot. "She will do anything to get my attention."

I didn't say anything.

"So what I'm saying is, Kofo killed Sade. Think about it. It had to be her."

Nike's high-pitched voice pierced through the gathering dark, reaching a feverish crescendo. A cloud of bats swarmed over our heads from a nearby tree as though on cue.

"Do you have a theory as to how she did it?"

"Very simple. Kofo entered the changing room somehow, and don't forget she is well-trained in stealth. She got into the room and struck her head with something hard. Could even be her fist, as you can see the damage it can do on my face. Nike told me she saw someone around the room at that time. I believe that person was my wife."

I nodded. "But how did she get out? Someone should have noticed something, an usher doing rounds, a chorister with a wandering eye, something should have gone wrong. Otherwise, this is the perfect crime."

"Why are you asking me?" he protested, looking like roadkill. "You are the investigative journalist. Investigate it. Write it in your column or whatever. You can bring it to people's attention. That is why I have come to you first and not the police." I ran my fingers over my head. He continued, "Kofo's family is well-connected. They can make things happen, but not if you first write and expose her in your column. Do you understand?"

Then I explained to him that I was not a journalist. He didn't express any disappointment like I thought he would. He merely laughed in a manner that made his wounded face look grotesque and sinister.

"Kofo said it," his voice broke. "She said you were not what you claimed to be. Ah, that woman is good."

He turned and walked away.

CHAPTER TWELVE

"He's gone, abi?" asked Modele when she returned. "Just left now." She dropped the first aid box and leaned on the car next to me.

I looked at my watch. It was a quarter to seven, but it was already dark. The lights were out, and the moon was just emerging. The car park was illuminated only by diffused light from the street lamps.

"I hope the robbers get him again. I hope they kill him this time," she muttered, tossing some pills to the ground. She stomped hard on them in a rash, hurried fit. Satisfied with the extent to which she had expressed her frustration, she examined the bottle of water in her hands, contemplated throwing it away, but instead unscrewed the cap and took a sip.

"It's unfair to like someone who doesn't like you in return. It's not fair at all."

I brought out my cellphone, checked for messages, and slipped it back into my pocket. "He's a married man, Modele. You cannot like a married man. You can like him, but not like that."

"Yen yen yen!" she snorted with laughter. "You sound like my mum."

"I'm just saying."

"You don't know the story. You don't know anything."

"Maybe I don't."

"It was not like this before, you know," she said after a while. "It wasn't. Our relationship was better than this. He came to me when he was down and needed a shoulder to cry on. We became friends, even when I knew it was wrong. I allowed it. We enjoyed each other's company. He's funny when he wants to be. I told him everything about my life, and he told me about his. That's how I knew about his marriage and how unhappy he was. I, too, was just getting out of a bad relationship, so I understood. He was very sweet and told me nice things, like how I was the exact opposite of his wife." She paused and took another sip. "That's how I knew the marriage would not last, and he was going to leave her, you know. I mean, why is he telling me all these things if he didn't have it in his mind to ask me to be the woman to replace her?" She sounded very hurt. "He said I was all he wanted in a woman. Everything his wife wasn't. He told me that with his mouth!" Then she began to laugh. "Then that Jezebel came and spoiled everything. He began to avoid me, but…" She laughed again, this time wildly. "…that is not even possible… it's… why am I even telling you this?"

"Somehow, I can relate to what you are saying. I've been in a situation like that before. A long time ago."

"Really? How did it end?"

"I had to let go."

She snickered. "Modele will not do that. Modele doesn't give up. Modele fights!"

I didn't say anything. My eyes stayed on one of the lamps that suddenly began to flicker.

"I saw Nike go into the changing room while you were there. What did she want?"

"She wanted to know if I found anything."

"You won't find anything there," she replied matter-of-factly. "We don't use the place anymore."

"I didn't find anything," I confirmed, looking in the direction of the church. The rehearsal had come to a close. I heard Lara shouting something at the top of her voice. I asked Modele if she had settled her differences with her.

"That witch," she spat. "Every time I hear her name, all I hear is drama, drama, drama. Rekia dem had to beg me; otherwise, it's bye-bye rehearsals, and they know how important I am. But thank God she realized her stupidity and apologized."

"So what was she really talking about?" I asked. "I mean about the mic."

"How should I know? It's just something stupid about the mic. It's the oldest around. Sometimes I use it just to spite her!"

"It's like bragging rights."

"Yes!"

"What do you think happened to it?"

"Lara is always crying wolf, but she's the devil in disguise. I think she hid it herself. I don't know why, but that's what I think."

The more I thought about the missing microphone, the more significant it became.

"You told me that you did not see any strange man around the changing room that day Sade died, abi?"

Her voice cracked. "Yes."

"But it's not true. Someone saw you speaking to a very dangerous-looking man in a red pullover shirt the very morning before Sade died." Something about her breathing told me that she was alarmed. Then suddenly, a laughter that sounded like a horse neighing escaped from her mouth. "Lara told you this, abi? Well, did she also tell you that she snatched Richard, her best friend's fiancé? Eh?"

I pretended this was news to me, folding my arms. "Really?"

She placed the bottle on the car's roof. "They are seeing each other. I'm not blind. Can you not see it?"

I shook my head.

"You should pay more attention."

"You still haven't told me about that strange man."

"There was no strange man," she snapped. "It was a man asking for directions. I just happened to be the one giving them. That is what Lara saw. I know she's the one who told you."

"Let us go over that day in the room again."

Modele cast a speculative look at me. "I don't think I remember anything anymore. I have many things to think about. Like, when am I going to get married?"

"As soon as you find the right man," I supplied. "Did you hear what it was Sade was telling Jimi at all?"

She shook her head, finally tossing the bottle. "Ask Lara. She sat close to them."

"I heard two things," I said, almost to myself, "but I don't know which she was actually telling him, because I don't think she was telling him both."

Modele was interested. "What did you hear?"

I tried to sound as confused as possible. "Was she telling him about the stolen tithe or that she was pregnant for him?"

"Sade was pregnant?" Modele asked, incredulous, but immediately composed herself. "Ah, look! Rehearsal is over. They are coming out now," she continued in a soft, conspiratorial whisper. "Do you see Richard? Look! He is the one walking by the flowers away from them. His back is to Lara. Can you see her? She's the one with Nike. The two of them are pretending nothing is going on between them, but they can't fool me. They can't fool Modele!"

"I think they are coming this way," I said and straightened my stance in anticipation of their arrival. Soon, we were joined by them.

"Modele, did you help Jimi tend to his face?" asked Nike kindly.

"Yes. He is better now. Abi, Deji?"

I looked at her and stuttered. "Oh, yes. Better."

Nike looked relieved. "Where is he now?"

"I called a taxi to take him home."

Lara said, "You didn't finish the rehearsal with us, Modele. Are you still angry with me?"

Modele feigned surprise. "I am not angry, Lara. In fact, eh, I was just telling Deji how in tune you were today. What will we do without you?" It was praise so faint as to be almost unconscious.

"Modele!" Lara showed all of her teeth in a big, frozen smile. "Who knew you could say that about me?"

"I can say anything I want, darl, as long as everyone knows I have no rival in this choir." She oscillated her head as if to buttress her point.

"Ah, Modele! We missed your small small wahala sha. Hope you will bring them to the next rehearsal?"

"Where else would she put them?" joked Nike, not unaware of the phony exchanges but understanding that an occasional chime-in wouldn't do any harm. "Modele will not be Modele without her wahala."

"Deji, you said you wanted to see me?" Lara suddenly turned to me.

I frowned. I didn't remember making such a request. Before I could open my mouth, she grabbed my hand and led me away.

"Sorry," she said, looking left and right to make sure we were alone. "I said that so we could talk in private."

I nodded and asked, "What's the matter?"

She burst into tears.

CHAPTER THIRTEEN

"**M**odele did it!" Lara cried with disconcerting fervor. "Modele killed Sade!"

I looked about. Modele and Nike were safely out of earshot.

"What made you say that?" I tried to hold her still, but Lara was agitated. "What did you see?"

"It's not what I saw!" Tears welled in her eyes. She broke free from my grip and circled around as though disoriented. "It's what I dreamt about! What the spirit told me."

I stared at her, irritated for a moment. I wanted to shake her like a ragged doll till her eyes popped out.

"A dream, eh?"

For some odd reason, I knew where this was likely headed, and Lara did not disappoint.

She nodded and wiped a tear.

"I don't dream a lot, but when I dream… it's usually a message."

"I see."

"My mother even used to call me a witch. Because of my dreams!"

Funny, I thought. Modele had used the exact same word to describe her only moments ago. To hear her repeat it herself was surreal, and as a result, I began to take a more relaxed view.

"Okay, that's fine," I said. After all, I have had a few of my own telling dreams. "What did you dream about?"

I was more inclined now than before to be open-minded when people express a hunch, gut feeling, or even an epiphany. Yesterday's letter from the cold was a good example that sometimes the ridiculous was, in fact, the reality.

Lara began, incoherent.

"We were here… rehearsing… everybody… Sade too. She was standing beside me. We were having fun… a lot of fun. Everything was normal. Then… then all of a sudden, I just saw her chasing Modele around the room with a microphone in her hand. In the changing room!"

She paused and tapped her chest, sucking in air.

"She was chasing her round and round and round… in circles. And she was still chasing her when I woke up."

"She was chasing her with a microphone?" It was comical, but I repeated what she had said, so I wasn't mistaken.

"Yes."

"The same lucky mic?"

"No," she replied. "It was a big microphone."

"What's a big microphone?" I asked. In my mind, I was thinking along the lines of a megaphone. Perhaps that's what she meant to say. What I heard next made my head spin.

"It was a mic as big as this." There was a shade of embarrassment in her voice as she made an expansive gesture. "As big as that thing we use to… pound yams."

"A pestle."

"Yes," she nodded slowly, realizing just how silly she sounded. "As big as that."

I couldn't stop a chuckle from escaping my throat. I have had one of those ludicrous dreams too. And who hasn't? I remembered one such delirious dream after a terrible bout of malaria, where I was trying to swallow a gigantic rock. So yes, this wasn't all that silly.

"I know you will laugh, but that's what I saw!" she protested. "It's not a joking matter, rara."

"Lara," I said conciliatorily, "you know, people sometimes say dreams are stupid."

"Not my dreams! I'm telling you it's a message. Sade is trying to tell me something."

"And you think what she's telling you is that Modele is responsible?"

"Yes!"

"Okay."

Modele and Nike were heading back to the church building. Modele was returning the first aid box. Richard ambled around, without a doubt in my mind, waiting for Lara.

"There's another thing I remember about that day," Lara continued. "It just came to me now. Modele went back into the changing room when I left. I think that's when she did it."

"Why are you just remembering that now?"

"Because it just came to my head!"

I looked at her.

"So you saw that she went back in a second time?"

An emphatic nod.

"But I wasn't concentrating. I just remember seeing her."

"Was it before or after Jimi came out?"

"I don't know," she appeared slightly confused. "But I'm sure Modele went back inside."

I called on Richard to join us. When he came, he had the look of surprise and refused to make eye contact with Lara. He attempted some chatter, but I was all business and asked right away:

"Listen, Lara is just telling me something now. Did you see Modele go back into the changing room after she came out that day?"

"Did you?" Lara echoed.

Richard frowned, considered it, then shook his head slowly. He didn't remember anything like that, but Lara was adamant.

"Okay," I said, looking in the direction of the church building. The lights had just come back on.

"So what are you going to do now?" she asked. "Are you going to ask her about it?"

"I don't know what I will do yet. Maybe I will."

"Because if you are going to confront her now, let me be on my way o. I don't want Modele's wahala. What time is it, Brother Richard?"

Richard checked his watch.

"It's eight o'clock, Sister Lara."

"It's late. I'm going."

Lara hurried off. An awkward Richard appeared to be caught, I could tell, in two minds. Should he follow his secret lover and raise even further an already raised eyebrow, or should he stay back and talk maybe a little bit more and keep his secret secret? Fortunately for him, I had other things in mind and put him out of his dilemma.

"I don't think I should take any more of your time. I need to talk to Modele again."

He appeared relieved.

"Thank you. Good night."

***

I slipped back to the church building and peered into the vestibule. Modele, Nike, and Rekia were talking. A reference to Sade had made me pause and eavesdrop. Although they were nearer to the altar, their voices carried through clearly.

Rekia was saying, "...and you are right too, Modele, because I have to say that I have been enjoying the choir more now. No more tantrums. Hallelujah, somebody!"

"I thought I was the only one," agreed Modele. "Nike, you must be so relieved to be the lead again."

I guessed Nike had suppressed a smile in typical fashion because the other two giggled like little girls in primary two.

"I don't feel any difference, my sisters," said Nike warmly. "Don't forget I was the lead before."

"That's what we are saying—"

"—until Sade turned his head—"

"—I'm sure Brother Jimi had his reasons for doing what he—"

"Since when did men reason, Nike?"

"Don't say things like that, Rekia," said Nike, dismayed.

"He was nice to give it back to you, sha," Rekia added. "I thought he was going to give it to someone else."

"Like who?" wondered Modele.

Rekia stuttered. "Er... like fat Aunty Bukky. But didn't you want to be the lead, too, Modele? Don't make it sound like you didn't want it too."

There was a pregnant pause.

"You know, Rekia," Modele rasped, "there are more important things in life than being the choir figurehead."

Nike made a hacking sound.

"O ga o," Rekia murmured with exaggerated condescension. "You kuku know me, Modele. I'm not well. I am not like Lara, whom you can bully as you like."

"Did I say anything to upset you?"

Nike said quickly, "Has anyone called Brother Jimi to know how he's doing? I didn't see his face, but someone told me it looked bad."

"I have to call a cab." Modele checked her watch. "I can't be attacked like that."

Nike was full of pity. "What did they even want from him, ehn? His phone? Wallet? All those are material things."

Rekia scoffed, then laughed. "Is that what he told you? That he was attacked?"

"Yes. Why?"

"Nothing."

"Rekiaaa," Modele hooted. "I know that look on your face when you are not telling me something."

"It's none of my business." Rekia was getting ready to leave. "I have been minding my business ever since I poked my nose in a friend's family matter and got the slap of my life! Since then, lailai! I stay in my lane."

Modele grabbed her arm and twisted it. "Talk, jor."

"Okay, okay, you big bully!" Rekia stomped her feet. "You know I pass his place whenever I'm coming to church, right?"

"Hm-hm."

"Yes," Nike chimed in. "And he sometimes gives you lifts to church."

"Not today. I heard noises from his house when I was coming. Like a fight."

"Ah!" Nike ejaculated.

"Are you saying he fought with his wife?" asked Modele. "And she beat him up like that?"

Rekia nodded. "They always fight, and she always wins the fights, my kind of girl! Everyone knows they are a public success and a private failure. Pass me the songbook, jare. I don't want to forget it today."

"What were they fighting about?" Modele passed her the book.

Rekia lowered her voice and said something inaudible.

"He is sleeping with the maid?!" Nike gasped, covering her mouth.

"Then what was he telling Deji outside?" Modele didn't look so surprised. "He can't be telling him his wife beat him up because she caught him sleeping with the maid."

Rekia shrugged, slipping the book into her purse.

"And they spent a lot of time talking too," Nike pointed out.

"What were you even talking to him about earlier in the changing room?" Modele was asking Nike now. "I saw you talking to him."

Nike gasped. "How did you see us talking, Modele?!"

"I dash the old caretaker's money. He tells me anything. Everything."

"Oh, okay." Nike cheered up a little. "Nothing really. He was looking around. I told him we don't use the room anymore, and he won't find anything useful in there."

Modele wasn't convinced. "I feel like you are not telling me everything, Nike."

"It's the truth. Why will I hold back?"

"I think my other robe is still there. The old one," said Rekia. "But I can't go in there all alone. It's too scary."

"Well," said Modele, clutching her purse, "we'd better be going, Rekia."

"See you later, Nike!"

At that moment, I walked in.

"Oh," blurted Modele, with a hint of disappointment. "You are still here."

"I thought you had left." Nike rose to her feet.

"I will soon be on my way," I said. "I didn't want to leave without telling you."

"Well," said Nike, spreading her arms, "I know everything was somehow today, but did you like our rehearsals?"

"I liked it a lot. Thanks."

She smiled.

"Dis one na sample," Modele enticed. "Don't miss Thanksgiving Sunday. It will be the bomb."

"I will miss it, unfortunately."

"Why?" Nike asked.

"I have an exhibition at the National Gallery of Modern Arts that very day."

"Art exhibition." Modele's eyes brightened. "Sounds like a place to meet a lot of rich Lagos and Abuja men."

"Are you a painter?" Rekia asked. "Like an artist?"

"Yes."

"Oh! So it was you who sent them that painting?"

I ignored her.

"Can I ask you a question, Modele?"

Modele looked doubtful.

"It's important."

"Let me come and be going then." Rekia jumped. "See you later!"

"No," said Modele quickly. "Wait for me, please. We have to go together." To me, she said, "Whatever you want to say, abeg make it quick."

"Can you take your mind back to that day for me, please?"

Modele flipped her hair. "It's there."

"Did you go back a second time?"

"Before nko? Of course, I went back in like everyone else. When Lara was screaming."

"I mean, before that."

She frowned and considered. "As a matter of fact, yes. But I did not go into the changing room. I went to the toilet in there to, you know, but it was…"

There was a loud crash. Nike immediately dropped to the floor.

"Sorry," she scrambled around. "I dropped my phone."

"Is it broken?" snapped Modele.

"It's scattered everywhere," said Rekia, helping to pick up the pieces.

"Are you alright?" I asked Nike, who suddenly looked ill.

"You don't look well, Nike," observed Modele.

Nike mumbled some words.

"What are you saying?"

"I think I'm sick." She was visibly shaking.

"Maybe you need to go home," I said. "You've had a long day."

"Let me help you to the gate and get a taxi." Rekia helped her to her feet.

"We'll meet you at the gate," I said as Rekia led her away.

Nike nodded, and I thought I caught a hint of hesitation in her manner, as though she would have liked to stay a little longer.

It was a minute or two before Modele said, "When I went back in, I went to the toilet, but it was locked. Someone was using it."

"Did you look in the room?"

"I didn't look, but they were still talking."

"Sade and Jimi?"

She nodded.

It bothered me a little that she always seemed to have an answer for every question.

"You didn't see him attacking her or anything like that?"

Modele hesitated, then shook her head.

"What else do you want to ask?"

I shook my head.
"I'm free to go?"
"Yes. I will walk you to the gate."

CHAPTER FOURTEEN

"What I think, my friend, is that we may never solve this case. Nothing about it really makes sense." We sat under the solitary tree in the garden. Power had been out for days now, and the high humidity meant it was uncomfortable to stay indoors.

"Oh, okay," muttered Somto, picking his teeth. He had been doing that since he came around, and I had no idea why. "So it's we now, eh? No be so?"

"Should I have said I?"

"It won't make any difference, but I like the sound of 'we' better."

"What I'm saying is, I can only think of one scenario that actually makes sense."

"And that is?"

"They all committed this crime and covered it up to confuse everyone."

I expected a sudden reaction from him, like it had happened to me when the idea first crossed my mind yesterday. I had been working in the studio on an old painting that needed retouching—one of the ones I would be exhibiting at the gallery—and my mind wandered to the events at the rehearsal, and the idea reared its head.

I had dropped my paintbrush at that very moment and stared into space for a minute or two, wondering if I could prove the theory.

Somto merely worked the pick further into his mouth with the indifference of a cat served fruit. "That's your theory, abi na hypothesis, get one problem," he said. "Two women cannot keep a secret, let alone three."

Funny how, in your mind, you are convinced of something, and boom—you hear it from another angle, and suddenly you look like a complete idiot. "I see your logic there."

"You can't swear women to secrecy! You can't!"

"But that's the point. What if all the accusations and counteraccusations were just to throw us off?"

"Who is accusing whom?"

I began to recount the events of that day. After I had told him everything, I said, "Let us look at Lara, for instance—"

"Josephine."

"Jo—who's Josephine?"

"What's the name of that dreamer in the Bible?"

"Joseph."

"Joseph. Josephine. Same thing. Lara is Josephine."

"That's neat. Okay, Josephine. So what do you make of her dream?"

"I believe in dreams," Somto said, "especially ones that are symbolic."

"She implied, even before she told me about the dream, that Modele was responsible for her death. That Sade was upset and looking for that mic on the morning of her death, and later she was dead."

"And the mic appeared in Lara's dream."

"Not the missing mic."

"I know," he cut in. "It's a mic. That's the symbol I'm talking about."

"I know the mic is related to her death somehow, but that's *how* I don't know."

"Dat girl Lara fit be ogbanje, you know, a familial spirit." Somto said with a thoughtful pause. "But why is the microphone so important?"

"I don't know." I patted Rocky on the head after he licked my feet a few times. "What I know is what I have told you. It's Sade's favorite, hers to use by right, but sometimes others use it just to spite her. What bothers me is why it went missing that same day she died." We didn't say anything for a minute or two. A strong breeze swept across, upsetting a couple of birds in the tree. Rocky darted away, uttering a few barks.

"One thing is," I said to him finally, "anyone can claim to dream about something like that, but we can't verify the dream, can we?"

"Dreams are stupid."

"Exactly what I told her, but she insisted her dreams always meant something. Don't forget Richard already told us how upset Sade was about the missing mic."

"But Lara and Richard are in bed together now. Their story will match."

"You are right."

"You didn't tell me anything about Richard."

"He was surprisingly quiet that Saturday. I still haven't asked them about the affair, but it's so obvious that I don't need to ask at all." Somto shrugged and got busy again with the pick. "Then," I added, "there is that accusation Lara made about Modele tearing Sade's bag to pieces during rehearsal. Don't you think that paints a picture of… derangement? I wonder how I'd depict something like that in a painting."

"Modele?"

"Yes."

"Easy," Somto whistled. "Just paint a formless woman screaming and pulling her hair out. You will get derangement."

I imagined it in my head, and it looked good. "Your mind is dark."

"Creative, biko," he grinned. "Give me credit."

"If Modele did that, then she's capable of anything. Plus, she has that love-hate relationship with the choirmaster. I tell you, there is something sinister about her. And—damn!" I paused and tapped my forehead.

"What is it?"

"There's something that has been bothering me about my conversation with Modele. She said something that caused a revolt in my head. If only I could just remember what it was she said that set off the alarm in my head!"

"You think it's important?"

"It must be. Otherwise, why is it eating at me so hard?" I cast my mind back again. Modele had said something, whether by accident or design, that made me realize, in that instant, I had been… misled.

"So what about the choirmaster and his wife?"

"I'm surprised at his desperation to pin it on his wife."

"You are now excluding her from the crime?"

I thought long and hard. "Yes."

"Why?"

"I cannot answer your question because I don't know why I feel like that. I mean, she looks like someone who can kill without trouble, just look at the blows she dealt her husband. But I can't get past the fact that she couldn't have entered that room unnoticed and slipped out unnoticed!"

"And it's not like she's one tiny person who can fit into a traveling box."

"She's bigger than you! I am also curious to know where she went before the service ended. That is a suspicious disappearance."

"And you say it had never happened before?"

"No. Both her husband and the maid said so."

Somto shifted his weight.

"What?"

"Where did the woman go?!"

I shook my head desperately. "I don't believe she somehow snuck her way into the changing room, killed Sade, crept out, and drove off without being seen. It's not possible!"

"It doesn't make sense to ask you if there's a secret door?"

"No, there's none. I checked. Whoever entered must use the main door near the choir stand."

"You don't think she used a professional mercenary?"

"The mercenary will still have to gain entry, wouldn't he?"

Somto sighed. "Dis one pass me. How do detectives do it? I have headache just trying to think it through."

"I will have to find a way to ask her where she disappeared to," I said. "But how do you ask a major a question like that without incurring her wrath? She already knows I lied about being a journalist."

"I'm just happy I'm not you."

"Urgh!"

"But why does the husband think his wife did it if, as you have said, it is almost impossible?"

"He's just tired of the marriage. She beats him."

Somto laughed. "Yeye man. How does your wife beat you up?"

"I wonder if anybody saw Lara go into the changing room when she found Sade's body, and how long it was before that great cry," I said.

Somto was nodding slowly. "Because this will tell us if she stayed in there long enough to kill her friend, or if her cry was instantaneous, like she entered and met the shock of her life."

Somto frowned. "So who do you think could be her witness?"

"My guess would be her lover, Richard. He had the advantage of that vantage point. He could see everywhere."

He seemed to consider it. "What if Richard had something to do with her death?"

I blinked. "What makes you say that?"

"What if he actually killed her?"

I chuckled. "And how will he do that?"

"What if he actually left his seat and went into that room and killed her?"

"He didn't leave his seat. He was in my view."

"Yes, during the service. But was the guy in his seat when you all closed your eyes to say the closing prayer? Did you not close your eyes to say the grace? Abi you be devil pikin wey no de close eye for church?"

I considered. "Are you saying he went in there, killed his fiancée, and crept out without being seen? All in maybe under a minute?"

"He will need a lot of luck," admitted Somto.

"He will need to be a professional assassin!"

"Look at it this way," he said earnestly. "Jimi and Sade were the last people in that room, abi? We don't know how long they stayed back, but if my woman is in any room alone with another man, kata kata go burst-o."

I reflected on this. "So you think it's a crime of passion?"

"You get it."

This theory is k-legged, I thought.

"The church is always noisy until the last worshipper comot. No one will hear her cry as dem de knack am for head."

This new angle made me uncomfortable. Could Richard be the one? Did he ever leave his seat that fateful day? I wondered. I let out a sigh and swallowed. From across the street, Kabiru's taxi revved hesitantly. I heard him curse.

"Anyway, na guesswork."

"Exactly," I nodded. "Just one of many possible scenarios."

"But who stands to gain the most by her death?" asked my friend after a minute or two of thoughtful silence. "Lara abi Modele?"

"I can't see how Modele gains, except for the wishful thinking that Jimi will look her way. But then," I shrugged, "people have killed for less."

"So Lara?"

"Love is a strong motive for murder."

"What about Nike?" Somto asked after a couple of minutes. "She's useless as a suspect. Useless as a witness, too."

I chuckled. "You say that because she left the changing room quickly. Because we cannot suspect her too much since she didn't stay long enough."

"Yes. It makes her a weak suspect. That, and because she no get wahala with the victim."

"That is not necessarily true, Somto," I said. "Nike was the choir lead before Jimi shuffled the cards. Nike may still hold a grudge."

"Still weak."

"But the way she crept up on me when I was looking around the changing room is…" I slowly shook my head, lost for a word to describe it.

"Suspicious?"

"You could say that," I agreed reluctantly. Suspicious didn't quite describe it. "I had a feeling like she had been watching me for at least a full minute before she made her presence known."

"Spying?"

"Something like that, creepy. Creepy is what I wanted to say."

"I hate it when people spy on me."

"It felt like she had been there longer."

"Do you think she knows something?"

I frowned. "She doesn't believe anyone from the choir did it."

"Or maybe she knows something but is protecting the choir."

"I have thought of that. It sounds like something she would do." For some odd reason, that niggling portion of Modele's conversation played in my head again, only to get stuck at that juncture I'd been trying to remember. I closed my eyes and tapped my head lightly.

"Any information on that man she saw?"

"No."

"Maybe there's no man."

I nodded, the thought having occurred to me too. The fact that there was no other witness to corroborate her story made me believe that perhaps Nike fabricated it to protect the church.

"What time is it?"

"Quarter past two."

He rose to his feet. "I am going to borrow the newspaper and read at home. Maybe I will find something."

"This coming Sunday is the art exhibition."

"It's a year already? Do you even have enough work?"

I nodded. "Will you come around and help me?"

"Are you going to pay me?"

I looked at him.

"Fine. I'll bring along my camera. Take good pictures."

When he left, I took a nap. I had been feeling listless somewhere in the middle of our conversation. Just over an hour later, I woke up feeling better. I continued retouching the painting from where I had left off before Somto came around.

I was still painting when my mind strayed to Lara's ludicrous dream. I smiled. It recalled, again, dreams I had when I was a child: nightmares of endless chases, dreamscapes of riding unicorns. Dreams are a land of stupidity.

I stopped painting suddenly when an idea dropped into my mind like a bag of cement.

As I thought deeper and deeper, transported into a miasmic place of blood and sonic psychedelia, a bizarre scenario unfolded behind my eyes. An epiphany of sorts.

The microphone!

It was the ringing motif of the rehearsal and… and… could it be?… unless… unless!

I was interrupted by the sneaky presence of Kabiru, more so by the offensive smell of cannabis that followed him in.

Quickly, he told me what he wanted, and he had an interesting story to tell.

He had dropped off a passenger, a talkative elderly man who wanted to visit his wife's grave. They chatted and ended up talking about the lottery. The man was an avid punter and a lucky one, too. He had never won the jackpot, of course, but was a regular winner of two-sure and three-directs.

He drew inspiration from a lot of things, but nothing was quite as useful as the dates of his dead wife's anniversary. It had worked in the past, so why shouldn't it work this time again?

The secret was to place the bets a day after the anniversary.

Kabiru wanted all of the money I owed him to stake on the numbers the man had given him. I didn't have enough, but I gave him most of it.

I looked at the time on the wall clock. It was a quarter to six, but it was already getting dark.

"Can you take me to the church now?" It was Thursday, and rehearsal should still be ongoing.

Five minutes later, we were on our way.

CHAPTER FIFTEEN

No sooner had I arrived than it finished. It was seven sharp on a moonless night. A few choristers were making their way out of the door as I entered. Others were in small pockets, enmeshed in frenetic conversations. A quick scan assured me that all of the players were still present. None of them had departed yet. But if any one of them saw me, they did not show it. The atmosphere, as I approached the center, felt tingly, exacerbated by the funky melody coming from the keyboard.

"You didn't sing those notes well-o," Lara, who appeared jaded, was telling Rekia. "And Thanksgiving is this Sunday, ah! What do you think, Nike?"

Nike, seated quietly, offered a tight smile and busied herself with the contents of her purse.

"Last year," continued Lara, "when Sade sang the coda of this same song—so amazing—you remember now, don't you, Nike? I had goosebumps all over my body. But the way you are singing it now, Rekia…" She let out a weary sigh and shook her head. "I don't know, sha. Maybe we will see another you on Sunday."

Rekia rested her head lazily in her hands and gave Lara a death stare.

"Don't mind her, Rekia darling," Modele said, unclasping her legs and rising. "I think you did it the best way you could. Jimi thinks it's nice, and that is what matters. Besides, you cannot please everyone. You are not jollof rice."

Jimi was in the technical area and, upon hearing his name, looked over his shoulder but appeared too knackered to care.

"I'm just saying," Lara went on, careful now, "that she could do better now that she is taking Sade's place in almost all the songs. Sade was always in tune."

Modele snorted.

Last Thursday's embers still crackled between these two, I thought to myself, and walked to Richard, who was packing some equipment into a duffel bag. Jimi saw me coming and steered away. His wounds had healed, I said to myself. Only a dark patch under his eye remained from the fight with his wife. Richard was warm and cordial and appeared surprised to see me.

"What brings you around again?" he asked after we exchanged pleasantries.

I went about my approach in a roundabout manner. "I'm just curious about something," I said and paused, looking at Lara's animated movements.

"What are you curious about?"

"I don't know. What about that lucky mic you told me about? Do you have one that looks like it here?"

Richard appeared confused and dug into the duffel bag. "It's a cord mic. Just like this one." He handed me a black mic with a black cord.

"Oh…" I was surprised at the weight, having never held one before. "It's a bit heavy."

He smiled. "The missing one is even heavier than this one. One of those old vintage mics. What do you want it for?"

"I don't want it for anything. I'm just wondering," I said loudly for the benefit of everyone, and, thinking to myself that it was the only logical message from Lara's dream, added, "if Sade was struck with it."

The building went so quiet you could hear a pin drop.

Lara clattered to where I stood. "I'm not sure I heard what you said," she said to me, wide-eyed.

"I think we all heard what he said," Modele said, approaching with uncanny poise. Rekia cowered behind her like a flustered pullet. "What do you mean, Deji?"

Lara cupped her mouth with her hands. "Is it true? Is that what really happened?"

"That's what I think," I said, looking at the mic in my hand. "I mean, what else could have happened to the mic? They didn't find the weapon. The mic is missing. So the mic could be the missing weapon."

Modele gave me a look, the kind you might give an insistent beggar. "Listen to yourself," her voice laden with disdain. "Do you think with your feet?"

A vain chuckle escaped Nike's mouth. "It's… not possible."

Is it? I asked myself and proceeded to do a little demonstration. I drew in a long breath and raised the microphone in my hand, and in one swift motion swung it down on the table that held the keyboard. Gboa! There was a small indentation at the point of impact.

"Have you lost your mind?" cried Jimi, snatching the mic from me.

"We got that mic as a gift!" moaned Richard.

"It's broken now!"

"Sorry," I apologized, looking at the small depression on the table. "I just wanted to know if I'm not mad, if what I think happened is possible."

"And it is!" said a woman I didn't recognize.

"Yes," I agreed, feeling justified. "It can crack a skull even."

"My God!" cried Lara, shocked. Rekia squealed. Richard covered his face with his hands.

An indeterminate sound escaped from Modele. "And here we are," she said, rolling her eyes like a possessed doll, "thinking it must have been a rock or something."

"A baton," Nike said in a surprised breath. "I remember telling the inspector it must be a baton."

"Baton," Modele muttered, staring at Jimi. "I wonder who can get a baton."

"Well, it's not!" Lara cried. "It's not a baton or a rock. Now I know why I had that dream. My God!"

"What dream?" snapped Modele.

Lara looked at me. "Don't ask me. I won't say!"

Modele turned up her nose.

"So what are we going to do now?" asked Nike, composed.

"Where do you think it is, Deji?" Lara was bristling.

"Whoever is with it killed Sade!" said a young lady.

"Do you think it's buried somewhere?" asked a deep voice.

"It is evidence, abi?"

"I think we are missing the point here," I said. An icy spark shot through me. "What I think we should be asking ourselves is who had the mic before it disappeared."

Silence.

Now it gave way to lugubrious murmurs as they began to cast curious, speculative glances at each other, each regarding the next with cold suspicion. Nike's eyes were fixed on me as though in a trance. I felt uneasy but ignored it and shifted my focus to Richard. He was isolated now and had a beleaguered look on his face. Like Nike, he appeared suspended in space, unaware of the everywhereness. I made a mental note to ask him later if he ever left his seat that day.

"Rekia." Nike finally snapped out of her daydream and said with certainty, "I last saw the microphone with you, Rekia."

"I was just about to say that," said the lady next to her.

Every open eye came to rest on the figure behind Modele. The cream gown on her now looked like an oversized sack. She stepped forward after a moment's hesitation, wild-eyed. Then, with venom, she exploded: "If any one of you thinks I had anything to do with Sade's death, you are insane!" The choir reacted with collective gasps and dismay. "Insane!" she repeated.

"Rekia!" Nike's tone was admonishing. "Don't say things like that in the house of God."

"Be mindful of your utterances," Jimi said, looking annoyed.

"I will say what I want!"

"Rekia, dear," Modele soothed. "No one is accusing you of anything, yet."

"Shut up, Modele," she snapped and turned to Nike, jabbing her finger at her. "You were there, weren't you? Or have you forgotten? Was it not you, Nike?"

"Me?" Nike was mystified.

"Yes, you, Nike. Did you not tell me you wanted to use the mic that morning when I was helping George set up?"

"But you didn't give it to me!" she protested.

"I didn't because I couldn't find you. I just put it by George's keyboard on my way to the changing room to get my robe."

"I remember seeing you," Modele offered.

"You remember, abi? Thank you."

"You didn't put it back in the bag where you took it from?" Lara asked.

Rekia raged. "What's the point? Someone will want to use it."

"No wonder Sade couldn't find it that morning," Lara hummed. "She looked everywhere for it."

"Rekia, are you sure you kept it by the keyboard?" Nike asked.

Rekia, incensed, tried to keep a straight face. "I am not a baby, Nike. I know where I put it."

"I'm just asking—"

"And I've answered you."

"Who is George, please?" I asked.

"He is our keyboardist," said Jimi. "He is not here today."

"He called in sick," said Nike. "Malaria."

"I wonder if he saw the mic around his keyboard," I thought aloud.

"I think…" Rekia's words trailed off.

"What are you thinking, Rekia?" asked Modele. Rekia waved a be quiet hand. "I'm trying to remember something."

We waited.

"Brother Richard," said Rekia finally. Richard's stare was chilling. "Shebi, I heard you telling Sade something about the mic? I must have walked around and overheard. I think it was just before the service started."

For what seemed like the entirety of a minute, there was an awful chorus of groans stemming, I believe, not from surprise or shock, but from the tantalizing unexpected twist. They were enjoying the drama. Eyes probed inquiringly at Richard. He had not uttered more than a few words since I arrived, and it struck me now as worrying that he had made a conscious effort to stay in the background.

"I was telling her that day," said Richard tiredly, as though lacking the will to protest, "that I saw the microphone under one of the chairs in the choir stand." Someone let out a sudden laugh.

"Not on the keyboard where Rekia said she left it?" I asked.

"Not there."

"How did it get there?" wondered Rekia.

"That's exactly what I wanted to ask," said a lady who seemed adept at door-to-door gossip.

Richard shook his head.

"Maybe it fell on the floor," Modele offered.

Lara glared at her.

"Why didn't you tell us this before?" I asked.

"Because I thought Sade kept it there herself."

"Why would she keep it there?"

"Is it not obvious?" asked Modele in a mocking tone. "She didn't want anybody to use it."

"She has done it before," agreed a vague voice.

"I thought maybe she forgot where she hid it," added Richard.

"But did she hide it there herself?" I asked.

Richard shook his head. "Now that I'm thinking about it, someone must have put it there. Hid it there."

Modele shifted her weight onto her other leg.

"So who put it there?" asked Nike.

"Someone was hiding it from Sade!" Lara cried. "So she wouldn't see it. To upset her."

"Can you just hear yourself?" Modele hissed. "Why would anyone hide it from her?"

"Was I talking to you, Modele? Is your conscience worrying you? The truth will soon come out. You will see!"

"Do you remember whose seat it was?" I asked Richard.

"No. I don't remember."

"When did this happen?"

He looked at Rekia. "Just like she said, before the service started."

"Can I ask you something?" I looked around, wondering if it was polite to do so.

Richard shrugged his shoulders.

"Okay. Erm… did you, at any point during the service… leave your seat?"

A hurt look touched his face. He shook his head. "Did you not mean to ask if I left my seat in the middle of the service to kill my betrothed?" I chewed on my lip. That was exactly what I had meant to ask, if only he were a little more patient.

He sighed. "I never leave my seat. People here can testify to that."

"That's true," Lara said quickly in his defense. "He never leaves his seat. Jimi! Say something. Richard never leaves his seat, abi?"

Jimi could only shrug. I had a feeling Jimi and Richard were not particularly fond of each other, and why should they be?

"I didn't mean to imply that you had anything to do with Sade's death."

"But you did. I could see it in your eyes that you did." Richard dropped his drumsticks and faced me. "I didn't leave my seat. I didn't do that to her. Do you hear me?" His words were knives that cut tiny lacerations on my flesh. "Maybe if I did, Sade would still be alive today, but I didn't. So leave me alone." He walked out into the dark.

There was a brief moment of silence where everyone looked at me.

Nike cleared her throat. "It's late, people. We should all be going home now."

"Please don't go home alone," Jimi added. "Go with a friend."

There was a collective reluctance to leave, but eventually they began to trickle out. Modele and Rekia were first out the door. Nike came to me and led me outside. "Do you really think one of us did it?" Her countenance was a mixture of surprise and dogged disbelief that made her face look even more distorted.

I nodded. "Nike, I can't see any other explanation."

"But who, eh?" Those buck teeth seemed larger than I remembered.

"I don't know yet. But I will find out. Mark my words."

"Sometimes I wish I had not left the room when I did. Maybe I would have seen or noticed more."

My gaze had traveled from my vantage point through the window to the other side of the building and came to rest on Richard, who had been joined by a figure. The area was poorly lit, but I saw clearly who it was—Lara. I could not, of course, hear what they were saying, but there appeared to be some sort of discord. Lara spoke animatedly, and Richard, when he wasn't speaking, paced about, occasionally throwing his hands in the air. I was interested to know what the fuss was about—if only I could get close and eavesdrop. Nike was still speaking, saying something along the lines of an intruder must have done it.

"Yes, yes," I cut her short. "I understand you, but I want to stay behind for a few things." She looked startled at first but dismissed me with a quick nod and joined the exodus. I tiptoed my way around the wall to the other side and was just in time to see Richard pull Lara further into an area of thick shrubbery and disappear from view. I quickly decided that I must drop to my knees and crawl through the muddied area of yellow bushes and crown-of-thorns that demarcated the property to get close to them. I was so consumed by curiosity that I didn't mind the indignity at all. I had barely gotten down on my knees when a voice behind me stopped me cold.

"I thought you had left."

I spun around to see a dark figure—Jimi. He stood in the dark, behind the sliver of light that permeated from one of the church windows, his hands ominously out of sight behind him.

"I'm still around." I swallowed, feeling my mouth go dry. Had he tiptoed behind me without my noticing? I wondered and stepped forward a little, thinking he would do the same and come into the ray of light, but Jimi remained stationary in the shadows. My heart raced.

"Are you following them?" He nudged his head in the direction where Richard and Lara had disappeared. So he is aware that I'm following them.

"I—I'm just waiting for them," I croaked, shaking my head. Even to my ears, I didn't sound convincing.

"The bush is not as deep as it looks," he said casually, "but there is a swamp behind it." I quickly looked in that direction and agreed with a nod. The croaks of frogs grew louder, as though in acknowledgment of the fact.

"Does the church have a plan for it?" It reminded me of Maami's garden and seemed like such a waste.

An ominous fraction of a second passed. "Yes. A burial ground."

"Oh."

Did I detect an odd ring in the way he said "burial," or was it all just in my head? And why was there something dramatic about the way he was carrying on this conversation that felt deliberate? Like he was enjoying it. Plus, why were his hands still behind him? I took a step back.

"What do you think they are doing inside the bush, eh?"

"I wish I knew." It was an awkward question to answer. "But what I know is that they are not having an intercessory prayer session in there."

I shook my head. "I don't think so."

"That's not where we do that." His tone was amused. "But some prayer warriors like to do deliverance for people there. Exorcise demons from them. Have you seen an exorcism before?"

"No." My heart was not only racing now—it was pounding.

"I have seen a few."

"I just hope there are no poisonous snakes there."

"It's a swampy area," he muttered. "There will be poisonous snakes." For a minute or two, we just stared at each other, his eyes gleaming in the dark like an owl's. "You know what's going on between the two of them, abi?"

"No, I don't. What's going on between them?"

He laughed. "You are not stupid. I'm sure you know."

"I wonder why you say that now."

"Look, Deji, I want to tell you something, but you are too stubborn—too smart for your own good. You know, eh, what you are looking for in Sokoto is inside your sokoto, but," he hissed regretfully, "you are too blind to see it, and it is a pity!" I resisted the urge to actually put my hands inside my sokoto because, with the oddity of this conversation, you just never know.

"Kofo has disappeared." The announcement was so unexpected that I let out a gasp.

"What happened?" I asked. "How do you mean disappeared?" I saw his shoulders rise and fall in a shrug, but his dark silhouette remained without emotion—like an undertaker.

"I've not seen her since last Sunday after church."

"That's four days now." I made a quick mental calculation. "Did you fight again?"

"It's not about the fight," he moaned. "It's about the guilt that is eating her. The guilt she's feeling. Because why would she run away? I told her I knew what she did to Sade. I told her that the night before."

"Where do you think she's gone to?"

"Only God knows."

"Have you told the police?"

"No. I called her family, but they don't know where she is either."

"But you should inform the police."

"Her family doesn't want me to. They don't think she is missing."

There was a faint rustle behind me. I looked sharply in time to see Lara duck among the yellow bushes. She was alone and trying to navigate her way toward the back door. She must have forgotten something, I said to myself. When I looked back at Jimi, a sudden sense of claustrophobia enveloped me. He had moved closer into the light, his hands now in his pockets. A paralyzing fear spread through my body like icy liquid metal. My legs twitched, fighting the impulse to whirl around and sprint up the damp, shadowed corridor to the gate.

His voice had neither warmth nor concern. "You look like you have seen the devil, Deji."

"I think I forgot something back in there," I fumbled.

"What did you forget?" I was so incapacitated by fear that I just stared at him, numb. "Hurry up then. Before the caretaker locks up."

I fled into the building, heaving a sigh of relief. There were five people left, including Lara, who had just successfully dispatched a haughty elderly woman and now seized her bag, ready to leave.

I walked up to her.

"Ha-ha! You are still around?" she feigned surprise.

"Yes. I was waiting for you."

"Really? I have been here praying, and now I am tired and hungry." She let out a fake yawn that epitomized her poor theatrical performance. "I just want to go home."

"I thought I saw you outside a few minutes ago in the bush by the swamp."

Lara laughed.

"I have not left this place since I came in the afternoon. Maybe you saw Sister Caroline. People say she walks like me. Where is she, sef?" She giraffed her neck around. So brazen was the lie that I didn't bother to dignify it with a response.

I paused for a minute before whispering, "Did Richard know Jimi was having an affair with Sade?"

Lara fidgeted with her purse and looked uncomfortable. The caretaker came in and rang a bell.

"Will you tell him I told you anything?" She sounded really frightened.

"I won't say anything if you don't want me to."

"He suspected it."

"You told him?"

"Yes!"

"What about you and Richard? Hmm?"

"Brother Richard has gone home."

"I'm talking about your affair."

Lara looked about like a startled hen.

"How could you do that to your friend?"

"I can't talk about that here. Please understand."

"You betrayed her."

"You don't understand," she whispered. "Sade stole Richard from me."

"Another lie. No one will believe you. I don't even believe anything that comes out of your mouth."

"But it's the truth." It looked like Lara would cry again. "I found Richard first. She took him from me, and I didn't complain because she was my friend." I wanted to scream and rip my hair out. What a complex loop this was turning out to be. I watched her clutch her bag under her arm and begin to moan. A sudden idea occurred to me.

I said, "When you found Sade's body that day, did you go in there with a bag?"

"Like a handbag?"

"Yes."

She stared at me, teary-eyed. "Yes. Why?"

I shrugged.

She removed her bag from under her arm. "In fact, it was this same bag I carried that day. How could I ever forget?"

I nodded, thinking how easily she could have slipped the mic into the bag before people rushed in, or how else would you explain why no one found anything at the scene?

"Why do you ask?" She wiped her face.

"It's a nice bag."

She looked at me. "Don't you want to know how Richard and I met?"

Unsure whether this was going to be another concocted nonsense, and unwilling to complicate what already looked like a flimsy trail of clues in my now throbbing head, I said, "It's late. I should be going. Have a nice Thanksgiving on Sunday."

As I walked out of the building, my legs wobbled. I didn't look back, but I felt Lara's unflinching eyes watching me all the way to the gate.

CHAPTER SIXTEEN

For much of the trip to the National Arts Theatre in Iganmu, Somto poked fun at Kabiru. As it turned out, the lotto numbers the cheerful old man had given him were not very useful. In fact, they were not even close. He had bragged around the neighborhood that he would soon become a millionaire and even shared the numbers with a few neighbors, some of whom were so convinced that they staked large sums. Somto himself punted a few thousand.

When the news broke out yesterday evening that they had lost, they made their displeasure felt. Rocks were hurled at his house, which kept him awake all night, and this morning, his already deplorable taxi was missing a side mirror. I felt pity for him, not because he had lost money again, but because the expectation of a miracle had been quashed.

The National Gallery of Modern Art was located below the cavernous auditorium of the National Theatre. Dated in appearance, it still managed to exude an eclectic, somewhat academic aura. The whole place reverberated with activity: artisans, enthusiasts, collectors, all in varying degrees of engagement.

The fat curator expressed delight at my paintings.

"I see a lot of improvement over last year, Depiver," he remarked. "The detailing is up there with the best around here."

"They are no Picasso or Van Gogh, Dr. Woods."

"Who is talking about Picasso, eh? Who can paint like Picasso?"

"I'm glad you like them."

"I like them. Not all of them, but most. Your mind is becoming more artistic. More audacious. At this rate, you will become popular."

"Thank you."

Having agreed with him that this year's exhibition featured more impressionism than urban art, I excused myself and went about the business of exhibiting my works.

Somto roamed about, took photographs, managed to annoy a few people, and even argued with an official who insisted on a new policy of no flash photography, before disappearing to the modern sculpture section.

By late morning, a pair of collectors had agreed on fees to purchase a couple of my works. Things reached a climax by midday. Somto behaved like a nomad, coming and going, not staying in one place for long.

An overweight white man dressed in mocha shorts and a gaudy Hawaiian shirt came around to my corner. I had just disengaged from a middle-aged woman who wanted to hire me to do a portrait of her.

"What a remarkable painting," I heard him expel forcibly. "Extraordinary!"

I immediately knew the object of his attention, having already heard an earful of plaudits: *Sade Nightingale on the Beach.*

"Extraordinary!" he muttered again, placing his hands on his barrel waist. "The background… vivid realism. Top-notch art."

"Thank you, sir," I said and went around to him. "My finest work, people tell me."

"Well, it should be!" he belted. "Don't you think so, honey?"

A flamboyant, fair-headed girl half his age giggled.

"Yes, sugar pie. I totally love it!"

"Remarkably similar to a painting I bought a couple of years ago in Hong Kong. *The Girl on the Island*, that one is called. Same motif."

"Art is mysterious."

"Indeed, indeed it is. The girl in the painting was naturally a chink, hahaha, but my word—you could have painted it."

I laughed. "Except I didn't."

"Of course not. Unless your name is Sue Wong. I'll take it. I'm a collector. I must have it at once."

My stomach flipped.

"Er… it's not for sale, sir," I stammered. "I can't—can never sell it. I've never even considered it."

"Artisans!" he erupted in a belly laugh. "Always trying to drive a hard bargain—I give you that. Name your price! I've got a good feeling about this one."

I shook my head.

"This painting means too much to me, sir. I can't let it go."

The man frowned, stroking his mustache, his face a study in bemusement.

"You serious?"

I nodded.

"But," I said quickly, pointing to my other works, "I am open to any one of these. Can I bring your attention to this one I call *Carousel*? It's one of my early forays into abstract—"

The man and the girl had already walked away.

Well, good riddance, I thought. I wasn't going to sell my last good memory of her, not for all the money in America. Her memory is immortalized in that painting. I briefly wondered if my infatuation with her was even healthy.

A prominent politician came in rather loudly with his lavish entourage. The gallery officials immediately lost all sense of organization and acted as though the Queen of England had made a surprise visit, trying hard to please him. The curator even halted the exhibition to announce his presence.

After about a quarter of an hour of chaos, the politician left for the culture section, and things returned to normal.

It was then that I noticed that I had company.

The lady, very dark-skinned with small, delicate features, was dressed in white iro and buba and looked distinctly out of place. She stood in front of *Sade Nightingale on the Beach* and appeared to have been there for some time.

I drew closer to her, but she did not seem to notice my presence.

I cleared my throat.

She turned to face me slowly, serious-eyed, and then returned her gaze to the painting.

She looked like Arugba, I said to myself. Arugba is the chosen maiden of the Osun-Osogbo sacred grove. She oozed piety too.

"Are you transfixed by the artwork?"

Silence—as though she hadn't heard me, but I suspected otherwise. She simply folded her arms and stared on.

At that moment, Dr. Woods' voice came on, urging artists and the audience to watch an essential audiovisual presentation that would only take two minutes. After it finished, I turned back to her.

"You are the artist, abi?" she said finally, in a guttural, semi-literate, mildly affected accent. It made me think she didn't grow up in Lagos.

"People say it's enchanting. That's what the last critic said."

"She's a beautiful woman," she agreed with a rapid nod. "But that's not why I am looking at her, Mr. Man."

Her white teeth dazzled in stark contrast to her dark, full lips.

Slightly puzzled, I stepped out of the way to allow a group of enthusiasts to pass.

"Okay," I said with a bit of mirth. "Will you tell me why you are staring at her?"

"What she's saying to me," she replied and angled her head obliquely. Her earrings of cowrie shells dangled like puppets on strings.

"Well," I said with a quick shrug, "art has its own language. What she says to you is a matter of interpretation. It's subjective. It may be entirely different from what the artist intended. No two people can have the same interpretation of any work."

"You speak too much English," she snapped. "That's not what I am saying."

"So what are you saying?"

"Sssh!" she hushed me and leaned toward the painting, her hands cupped around her ears.

"What are you doing?"

"Listen to her."

"Excuse me?"

"Please don't speak!"

I looked to see if anyone was paying attention to what was beginning to look like a farce, but then again, art seems to find a way of attracting interesting people. After a few seconds, she retreated with a feeling of mild annoyance.

"I can't hear her now. Maybe I touch her…"

"No!" I said, with enough emphasis to startle her. "You cannot touch the painting."

"Sorry-o."

"Who are you?"

She hesitated and looked around worriedly, as though not wanting to draw attention to us.

"I… I see things—hear things that are not clear a'times, and they may mean more to you than to me. And if you help, I can help you listen to what she's telling me."

I thought it might be rude to ask if she was a witch, but with what she had just said, and the cowrie shells around her ears and neck, she left me with no choice.

"Rara-o," she shook her head with an understanding smile. "I jus' see an' hear things ord'nary people can't."

A medium. I am talking to a medium.

Wave after wave of apprehension poured through me. I drew close to her.

"So what are you hearing? What is she saying?"

"Not clear."

She touched her ear again, pulling at the cowrie as though it held the switch that enabled her to hear from it.

"Is it because of the noise? Can we go someplace quiet?"

"I don't know." She looked doubtful. "I don't know if she will speak to me again if I lif here."

"So what are we going to do now? Can she hear me?"

"Be patient!"

"I can't be patient." I was excited. "What has she been telling you before?"

She paused as though weighing how much to say.

"She is not happy not to be living with us."

"How did you know that?" I almost screamed.

Her smile was somber.

"I can only hear things from people who are in the great beyond."

She spoke now in Yoruba.

"She died violently?"

"Yes."

A sad shake of the head.

"That is why I see red things around her."

"What else did you see?"

Could she tell me who killed her? I wondered. Is that even possible?

"I see a white thing on her head."

"White thing? What does it look like?"

"It's a cloth. Like a headband. She was a nurse?"

"Yes!"

"No wonder!"

A small, indeterminate sound escaped from her mouth. She took a deep breath and closed her eyes.

Wait… is this really happening?

"What do you see?" I was anxious now. "Is there anything she wants to tell me?"

"I don't know. But I can help you to know."

"Please."

After a minute or two, she opened her eyes.

"Give me your hand. No, your left hand."

She held my palm open.

I looked around. It was still fairly busy, but no one paid attention to us.

This is unreal. Is this really happening, or am I in a dream? Somto, where are you?

"I can hear something now," she whispered almost immediately, her brows drawn together. "She is telling me something. She's happy about something… something you are doing for her."

The lady began to roll her eyes unnaturally.

"I can't understand what she's saying now… she's talking fast… angry…"

"At me?"

"No… I see another person now. Someone like her. Does she have a twin?"

"No. She's an only child."

"I see someone just like her."

"Well, she has a friend, Lara, who looks like her."

"Yes, her. She's angry now… angry at her… I see them running… running… her, away."

Then, quite suddenly, the mysterious lady let go of my hand, doubled over, and began to gasp for breath.

"Water… I need some water."

"Be right back."

I went to a nearby dispenser. When I returned, she was gone.

Perplexed, I looked around, checking all the half-dozen dispensers in the gallery in the hope that she had gone to one herself, but I didn't see a woman in a white iro and buba. I searched around and even went to the other sections. It was as though she had vanished into thin air.

I was still trying to make heads or tails of the unexpected encounter when Somto's voice punctuated my thoughts. He rambled on about something that excited him, but I listened with half an ear.

When he realized he was only talking to himself, he asked, "Wetin happen? Why is your face like that of a rotten tomato?"

I told him about the encounter with the medium.

"Chineke!" he whistled, hanging the camera around his neck. "Just when I thought I had heard it all. Do you believe in psychic people?"

"It is not about what I believe now. It is about everything she said."

"Strange."

Someone yelled profanities that briefly drew our attention. A clumsy woman had dropped a canvas.

Somto said to me after the woman had apologized, "I wonder what it feels like to have that kain special ability."

"I've heard of people like that, but never would I imagine I would see one in the flesh, or interact with one. I don't even know her name. Will I ever see her again?"

"I doubt it. Encounters like dat be like belly buttons."

He took the camera off his neck, doubled up, and took a shot of me.

"What does that mean?"

"It means you only get one. Smile."

"I don't want another photo."

We ruminated further and became none the wiser. At some point, we considered the possibility of a reincarnation. How had she vanished?

The exhibition was reaching a close now. The curator was getting ready to give a speech.

"Anyway," I said to my friend, exhausted, "she indicated that Sade was angry with Lara."

"Is Lara our girl?"

"I don't know. She's been very suspicious lately."

"You saw her again."

I nodded.

"Another thing is bothering me about this woman in white. I had a sense of déjà vu talking to her."

"You met her before?"

"Not her," I said, looking at Carousel. "But I've seen a woman dressed like her before."

"Where?"

"In a painting. A painting I saw in Modele's house."

"Hian!"

I hope I don't go mad with all of these bits and pieces.

CHAPTER SEVENTEEN

Ilistened for the crickets that starry night when I opened the gates, which was my custom whenever I returned home late. I found the melody of their chirping therapeutic. Tonight, they were silent. This was not unusual, but there was an eerie quality to their collective silence. An impish connivance. Looking back, it was a foretelling of what lay inside the house.

I opened the garage door and instantly knew that we had company. Mrs. Banjo's screechy voice tore through the silent night. She was saying something to Maami forcefully.

Gently, I unwrapped the foil I had kept *Sade Nightingale on the Beach* in and hung it back in place. I would return to the gallery tomorrow to retrieve my other works, but I didn't feel comfortable leaving this one there after I had turned down more offers to sell it. I had a terrible feeling it might be stolen.

I looked at it now and thought about the strange episode. While the message from the medium was straightforward, I couldn't shake off the feeling of... of what? I asked myself. Unease? Circumspection? Fear?

Ha!

Whatever it was, it didn't feel right.

Exasperated, I looked around my cluttered lair. The past couple of days leading up to the exhibition had been chaotic. Brushes, paint cans, crumpled drawing sheets, broken frames, palettes, and a few other pieces of gear were strewn everywhere. I made a mental note to ask Somto for help clearing it up tomorrow.

"Is that you, my son? Are you back?" I heard Maami ask from the kitchen.

I moved the easel out of the way and replied that I was.

"He walks well," said Mrs. Banjo with a throaty laugh. "Just when supper is ready, his legs are good."

There was a noise from the sitting room like the scraping of a chair. A cough followed, and Mrs. Banjo said something unclear. It was then that I realized there was another person in the house.

"I'm fine, Iyabo. Thank you."

I froze.

I recognized the baritone voice. It immediately transported me back to childhood—faint echoes of fleeting, tenuous memories like half-forgotten dreams. A voice I thought was lost in my innermost thoughts and would never hear again.

My heart stopped cold.

"Let me get you some water." I heard Mrs. Banjo's footsteps and the fridge open.

This cannot be real, I said to myself. It cannot be true.

I stepped out of the garage and went into the sitting room. It was dim and hazy from frying oil. Seated quietly was the man whose photo I had seen two weeks ago. His head was bent over, and from where I stood, I could hear his breathing.

Light from the dining area fell on one side of him.

For a moment, I thought I had been sucked into a vortex of unconsciousness. A maelstrom of mirage and uncertainty; a teasing, desperate dream. His presence had been so unexpected that I looked around and wondered if I had entered the right house.

Dressed in light colors, his beard appeared whiter than in the photo, giving him a somewhat angelic appearance.

He felt my presence and looked up, first with hope and relief, then with sadness and regret.

Mrs. Banjo returned. After he accepted the cup and drank, she asked almost casually,

"Have you greeted your father?"

My head throbbed with confusion and fatigue.

"Junior."

The name registered like a well-struck chord, sending waves of emotion sweeping through me. That was his pet name for me. No one had called me that in a long time. In fact, no one had called me that since he disappeared.

I looked at him now, numb and uncertain how to reply or even react. I wanted to say "Daddy," as I remembered I used to say, but now it didn't feel natural or appropriate, or earned.

I just stood there, rooted to the spot, and stared.

He got up and spread his arms in anticipation of an embrace.

"You won't greet your father?" Mrs. Banjo wondered.

I shook my head and left the room without uttering a word.

I went outside into the backyard and tried to shut my mind off.

What really is going on, ke?

I had had too much these past few weeks, and it was suffocating. I wanted to pretend nothing had happened and that he still didn't exist.

I strolled around the compound. Everywhere was silent. Usually, at this time of night, you would hear the loud television from the next house or the slurred voice of a drunken character stumbling down the street, but I heard none of those now.

It was as if the neighborhood was aware of the strange occurrence at the Depiver house and was keen to hear the faintest detail.

Or was I imagining it?

Rocky patrolled the compound.

Rocky is quiet too, I observed as I sat on the bench under the tree.

It was a strange night on the back of a strange day. A very dark, oppressive night.

A strong breeze came and brought a small reprieve. I closed my eyes and felt it touch my face. I allowed my mind to drift and blocked out every unwanted thought.

Maami's voice called out my name. I answered and told her where I was.

When she came, she sat next to me and placed her head on my shoulder. I listened to her gentle breathing for a minute or two, expecting her to say something, but she didn't.

A bat zipped past.

"How do you feel, my husband?" she finally spoke. "You are my husband, abi you don't know?"

"I don't know who that man is, Maami."

A bitter chuckle.

"That's what I said a few days ago when I saw him at the door."

"He has been coming?"

I felt her slow nod against my shoulder.

"This is the third time he is visiting. We didn't want to upset you yet. I cried and cried. He cried too."

"He cried?"

"Like a baby."

"Why did he cry when he did this to himself, to us?"

Maami let out a soft, sibilant sigh and wrapped a wrapper around herself to deter mosquitoes.

"If only we could enter everybody's head and see what is going on in there. Let me tell you what I think."

Maami began by saying how he was like a prodigal son who had lost his way and come back home even after all those years. Would you reject him?

She told me how, by his second visit, which was only yesterday, she had decided to forgive him in her heart. They talked on and on as though he had only been away for a few days, as if nothing had happened.

For the next ten minutes, Maami convinced me to give it time and, at least for now, let bygones be bygones. If you do not forgive those who have hurt us and forget the past, we would not have people to call our own.

"Is that why you are now calling me your husband?" I asked after feeling a weight lift off my shoulders. "So I won't feel bad about his presence?"

She laughed.

"I call you my husband because you are my son. Don't you hear mothers call their sons like that?"

"But you never called me that before."

"You will be jealous–o!"

"So what is he to you?"

"The father of my son."

"Ah, okay."

"Kini? Oya, let us go inside before these mosquitoes eat me alive."

Inside, after finally acknowledging Father's presence, to which he appeared privately grateful, I helped Maami set the table for supper. The success of our little meeting outside was not lost on Mrs.

Banjo, who began serving hot topics and amusements that everyone enjoyed. Twice, she nearly choked on her food.

No reference was made to the past or anything related to it, and I watched in admiration at the sprightliness of these two women who were determined to put a positive spin on this unusual situation. They made it look as though he had only been gone a fortnight. When they spoke to him, he often replied shyly.

"Eh-ehn, Iyabo!" Maami exclaimed suddenly. "I remember you said you wanted to tell us something when my son arrived. He is here now. *Kilo fe so*?"

Mrs. Banjo frowned before quickly saying, "Eh, beeni. It's about that fine choirmaster, Jimi, abi what do they call him."

"That's his name. What happened to him?"

"You remember my friend Yeside?"

"Which Yeside?"

Mrs. Banjo allowed a morsel down her throat, then regarded her friend.

"Yeside, the one I told you hasn't stepped a foot in Mecca but has a gold tooth and calls herself Alhaja… that Yeside."

"I know her!" Maami hooted with a rapid nod. "Kilo shele? What did she say?"

"It's not what she said," Mrs. Banjo said, looking slightly irritated. "It's what her brother-in-law's friend said about Jimi at their grandfather's burial last Friday. The party was good, but I will tell you about that later."

"What did he say?"

"He told me that he knew Jimi when they were neighbors many years ago in Ikeja."

"What a coincidence."

"Small world," she nodded. "He said Jimi had a woman he wanted to marry then, but she died suddenly."

"Eeeeeeh," Maami reacted with sadness. "Kilo shele? How did it happen?"

Mrs. Banjo drank some water and burped.

"Jimi said she died in her sleep, but his neighbors didn't believe him from here to there. They say he gave her rat poison so he could continue with another rich woman he met in Ikoyi."

"Ah! *Lobatan!*"

"Was he arrested?" I asked, wondering if this was the reason he refused to go to the police with his convictions about his wife, knowing there had been a cloud of suspicion over him in an earlier case.

Wait a minute!

His wife, Kofo, has also disappeared, according to him.

Did he poison her too? I wondered.

Mrs. Banjo shook her head.

"But people didn't believe him, jare. How can you die in your sleep at twenty-two, eh?"

"Hmm!" muttered Maami somberly. "The slithering snake must surely have inner hands!"

"Ose, oremi," her friend nodded appreciatively. "What you have said is exactly what I said to him too."

"Do you want more soup?" Maami asked Father, who shook his head.

"Poor girl. Does he think Jimi killed Sade too?"

"Who knows?" growled Mrs. Banjo. "But if the witch confessed yesterday and the child died today, who doesn't know it is the witch who killed the child?"

Father had a grim line across his mouth. I could tell by the look on his face that he was wondering how a simple chatter at dinner had suddenly turned macabre. Maami read his mind and told him about Sade's murder. On one or two occasions, Mrs. Banjo helped fill in some details.

He listened attentively, giving the occasional nod but saying nothing.

He doesn't want to upset me.

"Isn't that how it happened?"

I nodded. "Yes."

"They were friends," she continued. "He wants to find out who killed her. Oya, tell us, do you think it is the choirmaster?"

"I don't know, Maami. But something happened at the gallery today."

I told them about the encounter with the medium. Mrs. Banjo stopped eating and laughed so hard she choked again.

"What is funny, Iyabo?"

"Those charlatans!" Mrs. Banjo was now in full gist mode. "I see them under and around Oshodi Bridge. Jobless women! Some as old as me and some as young as secondary school girls! They have white beads on their necks and legs, on their waists too, if your eyes are sharp like my own! They jiggle small bells and claim they can see my star. My own star! I kuku let them say what they want to say, and when they say they want to pray for me, I let them pray for my family and me. Who doesn't need prayers, eh, Rolake? In this Nigeria that we live in?

"But when they finish praying, they think I, Iyabo, will put my hand in my bag and give them one hundred naira or small change? Olorun maje! I just bend my knees a little for them and thank them and say, *aje* a wa o!' More blessings!"

"Aje a bugba je!" Maami roared with laughter. "Heavy blessings!"

Father chuckled too.

I told Mrs. Banjo I didn't think anyone could successfully con fifty naira out of her.

"They will have to kill me first!"

"But," I said, a bit more serious now, "she didn't ask me for money. That is the strange thing about her."

"This woman," Maami said gravely, "is not like those hungry ones under the bridge. Abi ki lo ni mo wi? What do you think?"

Mrs. Banjo considered this but continued in the same vein.

"Where are people like that when you need them, eh, Rolake? I will want someone like that to speak to my dead aunt, Abeni. Remember, I told you she died without telling us where she kept those silver jewels and gold chains."

Maami dismissed her friend with a hiss.

"This situation is like muddy water," she said, now with remorse. "Only God in heaven knows what is really going on, or God Himself is telling us something. Because if the witch is saying that her friend Lara is the one, what will—"

Maami let out a scream that ran my blood cold.

"Kilode, Maami?" I sprang to my feet.

"The window!" she gasped, terrified. "There is someone at the window!"

My eyes shot across in time to see a disappearing figure.

"Someone is there!"

Father shot to his feet.

Instinctively, I reached for the switch and turned off the lights. The room went dark except for diffuse light permeating from the kitchen.

"Tani?" a visibly shaken Mrs. Banjo whispered. "Do you know the person?"

"I didn't see his face," Maami said, her voice laden with horror. "But he was looking inside."

"Find something," Father ordered. "Find a weapon!"

We fled in different directions and looked for possible weapons. Father grabbed a rake. I seized a cutlass while Maami snatched a turning stick from the dish basket. Mrs. Banjo returned with her shoe.

We huddled together and went out into the dark.

The night was silent and a bit chilly. A light rain had fallen without our knowing it. We went around the compound in search of the intruder but found nothing out of the ordinary. Nothing appeared to have been disturbed.

Rocky was at the gate, wagging its tail.

Useless dog, I thought.

The gate was unlocked, and I thought I remembered locking it. So who was it at the window?

I locked the gate, and we returned to the house and discussed what had happened.

Father wondered if it was a stranger who had come to the wrong house.

Mrs. Banjo, a bag of nerves, said, "It must be a burglar."

"But why didn't that dog bark?"

"It is useless, Baba Deji. Rolake, give it to the Calabar people to eat!"

Maami looked worried.

"Don't you think this is connected to the murdered girl?" she finally spoke. "Because this has never happened before."

She had read my mind perfectly. I had been thinking just that.

Mrs. Banjo screamed and let loose her gele.

"If this is true," continued Maami, "it means you have scared someone. You must be close to the truth."

Inasmuch as what Maami said was logical, I couldn't help but wonder whose feathers I had ruffled exactly.

Nike?

Modele?

Jimi?

Lara?

We couldn't go back to dinner because we had all lost our appetites. Mrs. Banjo cleared the table. Too afraid to drive home alone, she called her family and said she would be spending the night with us.

Father, whose sleeping arrangement had come to light, decided against going back to the motel nearby, at least for the night. He would sleep in his old room, which Maami had kept clean periodically.

After they had all managed to go to bed, I slipped outside again and patrolled the compound. I didn't know what to expect, but I felt the need to protect my family.

Nothing lay disturbed, and everything appeared fine, so I went to the garage and lay on the recliner. As I lay there in the dark, listening for sounds, I let my mind wander to the events of the past fourteen hours or so, sidestepping any thoughts of Father.

If the mystery intruder was connected to Sade's murder, how close was I to unmasking her killer?

Outside, the crickets had begun to chirp again.

CHAPTER EIGHTEEN

I got a call from Nike very early the following morning. She was curt and wanted me to meet her at her house, and no, it could not wait.

I found Kabiru in the taxi. He had slept in it. Risi had locked him out. Eager to get his mind off his problems, we arrived at the isolated property in about forty minutes.

Like the last time I was there, the dwarf opened the door. He seemed shorter than I remembered, but was genial as ever and let me in. We exchanged pleasantries, and he showed me into the sitting room.

Nike and a rustic-looking woman sat waiting. She stifled a smile when she saw me and rose.

"This is Sister Ronke. She lives close by," Nike began after we greeted each other. "She is in the choir. She was there when you were telling us about the microphone the other day. She has something to tell you. Sister Ronke, oya."

The woman hesitated.

"It's okay. Tell him what you told me," Nike said.

"Good morning, sir," she greeted demurely.

"Good morning, madam," I replied. I sat down and sensed reluctance in her manner. "You can tell me anything."

She looked at Nike, who held her hand and gave a reassuring nod.

"That day you came, I could not say anything because I was afraid. The choir are my people. But what is not good is not good. Sir, I saw Brother Richard give the microphone to Sister Lara that day Sister Sade died."

I heard a loud bang in my head.

It made sense. Perfect sense.

It would explain Richard's incoherence when asked who he had given the microphone to. Of course, it was Lara. Little wonder they had what looked like an emergency meeting in the shrubbery by the swamp.

What baffled me, however, was why Lara drew so much attention to herself in such a reckless manner. Surely her incessant harping about the missing microphone was bound to backfire at some point and trigger a recollection from someone.

"Richard lied," said Nike sternly. "And all liars shall go to hell!"

"Are you sure about this?"

"With my two korokoro eyes, sir, I saw him give it to her."

"Did you see anything else?"

She shook her head so wildly I thought it might snap.

"That is why I called you," Nike said. "I can't say something like that on the phone. That's not all, abi, Sister Ronke?"

Another wild shake of the head.

"Sister Lara has been looking at me with evil eyes. She did it at rehearsal on Thursday and then yesterday at Thanksgiving."

"I think she suspects Sister Ronke knows about the microphone," Nike said to me. "She is scaring her."

"I am not afraid of her," Sister Ronke said with a timid smile. "I jus' don't like the way she has been looking at me."

"It's the same thing," Nike laughed a little. "Anyway, thank you, Sister Ronke. You can take your children to school now. Greet your husband for me–o."

"Wan gbo."

The woman departed.

"I wanted you to know about it," Nike said.

"I'm glad you told me."

"What do you think, ehn? I know something is going on between Richard and Lara."

"Do you think Lara killed her friend?"

She hesitated.

"I don't know about that. It's the reason I called you. Lara had that microphone all along, and just look at the way she kept accusing Modele… ah!"

"Can I ask you about something?" I asked after a thoughtful pause.

"Anything," Nike said, raising her shoulders. "I want to help."

"It's about Modele."

She shifted.

"Have you ever been to her home before?"

"Yes." There was an animated look of surprise on her face. "She has been here too. We try to visit and encourage each other. Everyone in the choir."

"Then you know about her roommate."

Nike frowned, picking at a fat pimple on her chin.

"She lives alone."

"I know. But she had a roommate before. She told me that."

"Ah, yes. Dorcas. What's wrong?"

"Nothing. Do you know what happened to her?"

Nike hesitated.

"I think she left."

"To where? Do you know where she lives?"

She shook her head.

"But I know where her salon is. I retouch my hair there sometimes."

I collected the address, thanked her, and fifteen minutes later, we were in front of a small roadside shop.

Dorcas was a small, fair woman with a hawk-like face and a no-nonsense attitude. She was cleaning and just beginning her day. A customer was already waiting, so she was in no mood for small talk. When I mentioned Modele, she went berserk.

After managing to assure her that I meant her no harm, she let her guard down.

"Clean your shoes on the mat outside–o," she said and waved me in finally.

I obeyed and entered the cramped but tidy salon. I waited until she began to shampoo her customer's hair before engaging her.

Soon, I navigated to her relationship with Modele, and she began to tell me her ordeal at the hands of her former roommate.

Everything seemed normal about her at first, she began. They lived happily together, no wahala. But things took a strange turn toward the end of last year when Modele began to lose her mind.

She could not be sure what it was, but she thought Modele was in love with someone who did not love her back. Modele did not confide in her, but she was certain it was a man from her church.

She began to have episodes and tried to make it look like it was Dorcas who was going mad, and imagining things.

"She's evil. Na wetin she be."

"She told me you left the house because of some domestic accidents."

"Domestic ko, international ni," Dorcas snorted. "She's a big liar, that girl Modele. If you catch a penis inside her skirt, she will tell you it's a corncob!"

The customer, now drying her hair with a towel, cachinnated, but Dorcas remained deadpan.

"She burn my food on purpose. Put salt and locust beans in my pap—"

"Ah ah!" exclaimed the customer.

"—She even pushed me in the bathroom one night and did like she was sleeping in the room."

"Is she possessed?"

"Thank you, o, my sister. She is mad. Kiakia, I spoke to my feet and left the house for her before they come and carry my dead body."

"Na wa o!"

"Wetin she do?" she asked as I was about to leave.

Hesitant, I said, "Nothing serious, but thank you for your time."

"If you think Modele do something bad," called Dorcas behind me, "then she do something bad!"

***

It was not until I got home that afternoon, after a stop at the gallery, that the absurdity of Father's return from the dead really hit home.

There were a few neighbors in the house, those who had been around at the time of his disappearance, and you could tell by the looks on their faces the perplexity of the situation. Beneath the exterior of relieved camaraderie was a private air of shock and disbelief.

Maami went about with poise, serving slices of watermelon from her garden. At one point, everyone laughed when she joked that he had aged better than she had, which was false, of course, but people laughed nonetheless.

I think there was an unspoken agreement to move on from this fiasco, much like the way you treat a schizophrenic who is suddenly getting better and has no idea how much trauma he caused his family. Father gave little away by way of explanation, and no one was prepared to probe, but they all seemed genuinely happy to see him.

I did not hang around the sitting room for long. I went into the studio after I greeted Somto's father and flicked on the light above the easel. I was suddenly full of thoughts and pictures.

I looked around and found an old canvas from which I had removed the paint. I placed it on the easel. Next, I opened the wooden chest and retrieved a box of watercolors I had not used since I began using oils.

I checked it and saw that it was still good, and added a little water from a leftover bottle. I dipped the brush into the red paint, took a step back, and assumed a comfortable position. Then, in a quick whipping motion, I swung my arm upward, tainting the canvas and creating a splattered effect.

Then I began to work it in haphazard horizontal strokes. I continued doing this and added more red paint. Satisfied that it looked wild enough, I picked up another brush and dipped it into the blue watercolor and flicked it onto the canvas. I used soft scumbling.

I watched as it turned purple in parts.

Then, with a plastic spoon, I scooped yellow paint, turned it toward the canvas, and with my other hand pulled the top of it and let go, slinging the paint onto the canvas. I repeated this with other colors: orange, green, black. It produced a nice, delirious mix.

I was suddenly filled with memories of Sade.

I knew I was onto something, but a few things were still unclear. What was clear to me was that I would be having another chat with Lara if recent developments were anything to go by.

But who, who was that at the window that frightened Maami?

I continued working until evening and started on a second canvas. I had a preposterous idea to create an exact replica.

By now, the house had gone quiet. The neighbors had left. I heard Maami saying something about going to the market.

There was a soft knock on the door, and Father peered in.

"Can I come in?"

I hesitated, then shrugged my shoulders.

"This garage feels so small now," he said, almost to himself, stepping in.

He walked about deliberately, his head held up keenly to examine every canvas. He put on his glasses and examined them one by one.

"They are nice," he murmured. "It must take a lot of effort."

Our eyes locked briefly. I nodded.

Satisfied he'd fed his eyes enough, he came around and stood next to me. He looked intently at what I was doing.

"What is this you are painting?"

"My feelings," I replied and continued with the mindless swirls.

Father waited. I could tell he could not comprehend it and perhaps expected me to elaborate, but I did not.

"They are nice."

The garage was open, and a light breeze drifted in. The sun had dropped on the horizon, leaving a reddish-orange tinge.

Father walked slowly out into the compound with his hands behind his back, an introspective habit of his, I recalled.

When he returned, he spoke animatedly about how he did not expect to find his old Peugeot around. The car was from the '80s and had a few rust spots here and there, but nothing out of the ordinary.

"Maami kept it for you," I said, examining the splash painting. It looked nothing like the first one and embodied what I was feeling:

a cacophony of emotions. I made a mental note to donate it to a nearby school tomorrow. It was no use having it around for too long.

"She said you would come back."

After a period of silence, he said with a rueful smile, "I don't think you will remember how you enjoyed following me out in that car?"

"I remember."

Father's eyes grew behind his spectacles. He sat on the recliner and laughed abashedly.

"You still remember?"

"Yes, Daddy."

Wait, did I just call him Daddy?

I was immediately transported in my head to times we had together: my fifth birthday at the park, the trip to the zoo in Ibadan at Christmas, and him teaching me a dance for the end-of-year party at school.

There was a part of me that instantly felt free, liberated. I did not resent him anymore. I was just glad I had a father to talk to.

It felt so dramatic, to the point of questioning myself, but I soon realized I liked how I felt now more than I did yesterday.

I stopped painting and went to the chest and opened it. Beneath a pile of broken frames and canvases was a neatly wrapped painting.

I pulled it out and gave it to him.

"I did not think a day like this would come," I said, and sat next to him. "Open it."

Father had been on the verge of tears, but it was the painting that finally caused them to flow.

It showed him standing in the sunshine with his tall afro, carrying me in his arms. The blue Peugeot was in the background. He was happy and showed all his teeth.

In the painting, I looked like his spitting image, without the afro.

"It's one of the first paintings I did when I was just testing my skills."

He was nodding his head, but the tears continued to flow.

"I remember this photo," he said finally in a low voice. "Your first birthday."

He went over a few details of that day with a smile and thanked me for the painting.

It was then that I asked him what I had been dying to ask.

***

"He wanted a fresh start?" Somto was incredulous.

"That's what he said. He wanted a new life away from his old friends and family."

We were out on the street along with a handful of angry men. A woman had falsely raised an alarm that her toddler had been kidnapped by ritualists, only for her to find later that her baby had crawled under the bed the whole time. As we dispersed, Somto and I did some catching up.

"Is that reasonable?"

"I'm just telling you what he said."

"Well," said Somto, "if you look at it with another eye, you will understand what he did. It's nothing new."

I stopped walking and looked at him.

"Are you trying to justify it?"

"Let me tell you something, Deji," said my friend tersely. "I have thought about doing that before. Things hard, man."

"What?"

"I mean, look at me. Thirty-plus, no job... still living with my parents... no job... wouldn't it be better if I just disappear from Lagos and go to some place, maybe Toronto in Canada, and start afresh? Maybe even have an oyinbo wife. Born fine yellow pikin?"

"What about the pain it will cause your family, eh? Them not knowing what happened to you?"

The morning was bright, and the birds sang beautifully. A school nearby was agog with pupils singing: the day is bright, it's bright and fair…

"So wetin be him reason for absconding for two decades plus?"

"I thought I just told it to you."

"What you told me was the excuse. What caused the excuse?"

"Dunno. I don't think he has any. What I know is that it's not a good enough excuse to vanish just to take flight from one's own existence."

"It's sad, sha."

"He said he wanted to take me with him, but he felt it would kill Maami."

"Does it make you feel better?"

"That he wanted to take me?"

"Yes."

"I don't know," I said, opening the gate. "I've not thought about it. Don't you want to come inside and greet him?"

CHAPTER NINETEEN

When Nike called me a few days later, she had disturbing news. No one had seen Lara since yesterday. She had not turned up for rehearsal, and her cellphone was out of reach.

Had I seen her? Had she run away? Was she feeling guilty because everyone knew about the microphone?

Nike barked off these questions, questions I had no answers to, but I assured her I would go to Lara's house to find out what was going on. I had wanted to go anyway. I had questions of my own to ask her.

I took stock of the studio and decided I needed more canvas. Since the market was not far from Lara's house, I wanted to kill two birds with one stone.

Kabiru was out on an errand, so I took the bus. When I got to the area, I took an okada that brought me to the decrepit house. A woman was washing her clothes by the scum-filled gutter. I greeted her and climbed the stairs.

I knocked on Lara's door.

Silence.

I knocked again, this time firmer.

"Lara?"

A door opened behind me, and a pot-bellied man in a well-worn singlet and dirty towel came out. He appeared to have just come out of bed.

"Good afternoon," I greeted the man.

"Good afternoon," he said, rubbing his eyes. "I tink say na my door you dey knock."

"I'm looking for Lara. Do you know where I can find her?"

The man shook his head.

"I never see her since yesterday morning. My wife has been looking for her too. Hope no problem?"

I shook my head, held the handle, and pushed. To my surprise, it opened.

"The door dey open sef," the man yawned.

I went inside the tiny room. Nothing appeared to be out of place. The air smelled normal. The soft hum that came from the fridge was normal. The bed was made.

A half-eaten plate of noodles and eggs sat on the table.

I went over to it, smelled it, and quickly determined that it was yesterday's meal.

I felt a slight panic tug at my chest.

I began to retreat, unsteady from the barrage of thoughts flying through my mind.

At the door, the man had been joined by his wife, a disheveled woman who did not particularly like my intrusion.

"Wetin happen, oga?"

"Something has happened here. Do you know any of her family?"

She nodded, very concerned.

"Call them immediately," I said, heading for the stairs. "Tell them she's missing."

* * *

At the market, I was beset by a great sense of foreboding. As I walked past shops, makeshift sheds, and umbrellas that lined the sides of the road around the market complex, an inexplicable uneasiness enveloped me. Although the day was hot, I felt cold. I stopped and looked behind me.

The market was fairly busy. I did not see anything or anyone that stood out.

I detoured to my left onto a small path that looked like a dead end. I paused, frowned, and looked back again. Then I continued walking for several yards, moving past a chain of retail stores, and came onto a wider road where canvas merchants sold their merchandise.

Fifteen minutes later, I had the canvases in a polythene bag.

As I made my way back to the bus stop, I sensed for the third time that I was being followed.

It seemed a ridiculous idea since it was a market and you were always going to be trailed by someone, but something just felt off.

When I looked back again, there he was, just a few yards behind.

He, too, had stopped cold.

I had surprised him.

He was a big, burly man with a jagged scar that ran across his face. The corneas of his eyes were red like Kabiru's.

They glared at me, cold as ice.

My mouth felt dry.

I quickened my pace and meandered through traders selling used clothes around a train track.

When I saw that he was still tailing me, I darted off, knocking into bodies.

"You don drink ogogoro abi? Foolish man!" yelled a woman hawking ointments and herbal remedies.

"E no go better for you o!" cried another, pregnant.

At first, I continued running along the length of the track, but soon realized he was the better athlete. I veered off the track into a maze of shacks and stalls, pungent with urine and decay, and lost sight of him.

I paused to catch my breath by a woman selling akara.

What was that about?! I wondered.

More importantly, who was he, and why was he after me?

I had only begun to ask people how to navigate back to the bus stop when I saw him again, charging at me.

He was yelling:

"Ole! Ole!! Thief!"

Determined not to get caught by my unknown adversary, I took to my heels again and ran into a shop that sold women's wear when I thought I had lost sight of him.

To the dismayed shopkeeper, I held a finger to my mouth and hid behind the door.

The teenage boy recognized that I was in danger and went about fluffing the brassieres as though I was not even there.

"Na dat shop e dey!" someone gave me away.

Soon, I heard the man at the door.

My heart pounded against my rib cage like a gangan drum beating a eulogy.

The boy stopped fluffing and froze.

"Where e dey?!" barked the man.

I watched as the boy began to urinate in his shorts.

It's now or never, I told myself.

In one swift movement, I seized a stump wedged behind the door, kicked the door away from me, and swung it with all my might.

It crashed tamely across his torso.

Livid, my assailant brushed off the impact and struck me across the face with a backhand.

Crashing to the floor like a sack of onions, and for a minute or two, I died.

***

"Give me your head."

Major Kofoworola Kosile-Smart collected the ice pack from the big, burly man and held it against my temple.

"Adamu thought you were a common criminal. I only told him to ask you to come to me!"

"Sorry, oga, no vex," the man apologized with an oafish smile. The deadly set to his face had been replaced by clownish meekness. "Kai, walahi, very, very sorry."

Major Kofo had been in Yaba on some unofficial business and saw me get down from the bus. Eager to speak with me, she ordered the overzealous hand to get me by any means necessary.

"You only hear go! Adamu," she said to him with deliberate sarcasm. "You are deaf to come!"

There was a different look about her today. She was still butch, her crop-top hair looked better on her than on most men, but she was less aggressive.

The drugstore owner smiled and examined my face again.

"You go dey fine, oga. Na small swelling. By tomorrow or next, you no go see am again."

We were at the bus stop, so a few busybodies gathered around us. The sergeant dispersed them forcibly.

Major Kofo gave me the ice pack and sat on the bench next to me, her broad body shrinking my space.

After a couple of minutes, I asked with considerable pain, "What did you want to speak to me about?"

Forcing a shallow breath out through her mouth, she looked at her subordinate, who immediately retreated.

"I have been hearing some things."

"What kind of things?"

"My husband," she said in a whisper. "He has been jumping around saying bad things about me… abi?"

"Can you be specific?"

"Don't pretend you don't know what I'm talking about." Her face grew cold. "I know he has been talking to you. Is he not telling people that I killed that girl?"

I did not react. My face was going numb. I put the ice away and felt my temple.

"Answer me!"

"He thinks so, yes."

"Foolish man."

She let out a bitter laugh.

"I know what he is trying to do. But I have his secret in my hand. By the time I'm through with him, he will understand that khaki and leather are not the same thing. How did he say I did it? Tell me."

I sighed.

"He did not say how, but I think he believes you killed her that day and ran away with the car. Something like that."

"I am not surprised!" she bellowed. "What will he say before?"

"Why did you leave with the car that day? He said it never happened before."

For the next couple of minutes, I soaked in Major Kofo's furious narration. She was very angry that day. She believed Sade was flirting with her husband in the church.

When she had had enough of him disgracing her, she decided to leave him stranded.

"I was watching them," she continued indignantly. "She was laughing with him… touching him… talking in his ear… what do you call that, eh? He promised me it was over… that we would repair our marriage."

I paused to think.

I remembered that day like it was yesterday. Sade was next to Jimi, and yes, they communicated, but I did not recall any forbidden overture.

A scorned wife would interpret things differently, something whispered to me.

"I saw how they went into that room, how the other women left them there. And they were there alone. I saw everything!"

I switched the ice to the other hand and continued with the cold compress.

I stared around, immersing myself in the disorderliness of the busy Yaba road: commuters cursing, drivers barking, horns blaring, traders shouting, the everyday madness of the city.

"They say you are looking for a microphone?"

"Yes." I frowned. "Did your husband tell you?"

She shook her head with firm avidity.

"And you think it's what killed her, eh? Microphone?"

I answered mechanically that I thought so.

"Microphone is not like a baton," she muttered. "It's a hunch."

"When I heard about it, I laughed. I thought, mumu! You must be stupid. But when I started thinking about it…"

I looked at her.

There was a wretched quality in her voice.

She placed a firm hand on my thigh.

"That's why I wanted to see you."

I raised a brow, wondering if there was any sort of subtlety about this woman.

"There's one microphone in his room," she announced very dramatically, as though she had prepared very well to deliver that simple line.

I felt a shudder down my spine.

"And this microphone has been in his room since around the time that girl was killed. I remember very, very well."

Flustered at this revelation, I instinctively looked behind me at the drugstore owner. He was busy counting the mostly dirty bills.

"Do you think he killed her?"

"Is he not the last person to see her alive?"

Her lips curled in contempt.

"But why would he want to kill her?"

"It's not my business to know," she snapped. "You are the journalist, have you forgotten?"

I winced at the sudden disdain in her eyes.

"I know you are not a journalist. I know. I know what you are doing. We hear things. You cannot hide everything. I want to help you."

"How are you going to help me?"

"I have left my house for some time now. I am not going back to him. Of course, I will take the house from him, but that is a matter for another day. Leave him poorer than I met him. If you want the evidence, you will have to get it yourself. You are the investigative somebody," she chuckled. "Go and investigate it yourself."

A low exclamation came out of my mouth.

"How will I even do that?"

"I will give you the keys."

Her face darkened.

"Just go there and see for yourself what my husband is hiding in the house."

I regarded her.

"Don't be afraid. I will tell you when you won't meet him at home."

"You want me to get evidence that will incriminate your husband?"

Major Kofo gave me a long, hard look before saying, "Yes. That's what I want you to do."

As piqued as my interest was, an open invitation to break into her home set off an alarm.

"Okay," I said quickly, not wanting to upset or antagonize her, but trap, trap, trap kept ringing in my ears.

As soon as she saw that she had secured my consent, she began describing the layout of the house and where his room was.

"You better go tomorrow afternoon," she added, "around three… he will be at his friend's house playing draught, birds of a feather. If not, go on Thursday evening when he is in church for rehearsal."

"What about your housemaid? Is she not home?"

"I sent her away. He was sleeping with her."

"Sorry about that."

"Why are you sorry? It's what you men do."

There was a pause.

I thought I caught a glimpse of something, vexation in her eyes.

"Is there a reason why you want me to do this?"

"I know you would ask."

She rose to her feet, her voice a weak surprise.

"But this is for both of us."

"How?"

"You will be solving my problem, and I will be solving your problem," she replied briskly. "You understand where I'm going?"

I gave a tame nod.

"How is your head now?"

I shrugged my shoulders, wondering if I had been manipulated.

***

When I got home that evening, Maami fussed about the bump above my eye. I did not want to upset her further after the episode about the mystery man at the window, so I told her a flailing arm had caught me on the bus. She boiled some water and insisted on a hot compress. I wanted one anyway, so I did not object.

She gave a lengthy monologue about helping Father reach out to some of his remaining family for much of the day.

"Ah, before I forget," she said, placing the hot towel on my forehead, "one fine lady came looking for you this morning."

"When?"

"Just after you left."

"Who is she?"

"She didn't say."

"Ah ah."

"Strange woman, o… like she had just woken up from sleep. She was standing at the door and said she wanted to speak with you. I said you were not around. That's all I said, and she turned back and walked away. Hold your head still, jare!"

"She didn't tell you her name?"

"No. I asked, but she kept on walking… as if something is wrong with her. She was saying things that I couldn't hear."

"What did she look like, Maami?" I was tense now.

"Fair and lovely."

That could be any woman from Ikoyi to Ikotun.

"What has been bothering my mind since morning," she continued thoughtfully, "is how familiar she looked to me. Like I have seen her before."

"Maybe she's a customer."

She considered, then shook her head.

"I don't think so. She didn't even carry a bag. What woman doesn't carry at least a purse?"

"Some women don't carry bags."

"Not even a small purse? Rara-o."

I sighed. "Maybe she will come back."

Maami looked doubtful.

That evening, I drifted in and out of sleep and woke up an hour or so later, sweating. My head throbbed, and my mind wandered amid the internal tumult.

Before I slept, I had debated whether or not to do what Major Kofo had asked me to do. If indeed the weapon was in her house, why did she not go to the police herself? I wondered.

After a cold bath, I felt slightly better. When I went to the garage, I pulled out the canvases I had bought at the market and set one up on the easel. I had no plans to paint, but I wanted to get my mind off everything, do something besides think.

Luckily, Somto came around and announced that he would be having an interview with a manufacturing company tomorrow.

"That's great," I said, glad for him.

"Thanks. Been reading tips all day. Dis one sweet my bodi no be small."

"I just hope the position on offer is not that of a doorman, you know, like the last time."

"God forbid! If na play, stop am o."

"I'm only joking. Lightning won't strike twice."

We talked some more, and he soon revealed he had printed some photographs from the exhibition and thought I might want some.

I did.

In one of the photographs, I saw the medium. She appeared in a hurry to leave the gallery. She was looking back over her shoulder, and I caught something sinister in her eyes.

"You must have taken this when I went to get some water. I don't see her trying to get some water to drink."

"That's what I thought. She didn't look uncomfortable there, did she?"

I shook my head.

"It looks like she's trying to get away."

"Running away."

"Exactly. Any thoughts?"

He shook his head.

"At least we now know she didn't vanish into thin air."

I nodded.

"But each time I remember this woman, my mind keeps going back to that painting in Modele's house!"

He departed when night fell.

Bored stiff, I decided to do a few sketches instead. I grabbed my pencil and began to work.

As my hand went through the monotonous motions of strokes, my mind circled the dark, obscure shadow insinuating itself into a shape behind the mask of murder, teasing into form before exploding into a revelation of nothingness.

God, I'm losing it.

I tried to get her out of my mind, but it kept straying to our meeting at Freedom Park.

On the sketchpad, I had drawn an indeterminate thing. It looked neither like a fruit nor a place. I shook my head vigorously, trying to dislodge the sounds of mockery I was hearing.

Suddenly, the door flew open and Maami, half-dressed, darted in.

She was hysterical and pointing madly at the wall.

"It's her!" Her chest heaved with emotion. "It's her!"

I jumped.

"Who, Maami?"

"The lady! It's her!"

She was pointing to *Sade Nightingale on the Beach.*

"Sade?"

"Beeni!" she cried. "I saw a ghost! I saw a ghost! Egbami-o."

Oh.

It suddenly clicked in my head.

"You didn't see a ghost, Maami." I held her still. "What you saw was Lara, her friend. I'm sure of it. They look alike."

Maami turned limp. She let out a long, embarrassed hiss.

"Look at me, almost going mad. Kilofe? What does she want?"

"I don't know. It was her house I went to this morning, but she wasn't there."

"Eh ehn?! But she came almost as soon as you left. Does she live nearby?"

I frowned.

"It means she did not come here because she heard I came looking for her. It takes like an hour to get to her place. Even longer if you are returning."

"So what is happening, o'jare? I am confused."

"Nike thought something had happened to her. That's why I went over there."

"She did not lie." Maami nodded, tying her wrapper close to her chest. "She could not have put it better. That girl did not look normal. She looked lost."

She was almost leaving when my cellphone rang.

I recognized the caller.

"Hello, Nike."

"Hello? Is that you, Deji?"

A pointless question since who else could it be?

"What is it?"

Nike was breathless. The call lasted a minute. I listened attentively and made an exclamation or two.

When she hung up, I said to Maami, who was looking at me wide-eyed, "That's Nike."

"Is she not one of them?"

"Yes. She's at the hospital with some choir people. Lara tried to kill herself."

Maami gasped.

"How?"

"She ate a cup of salt."

CHAPTER TWENTY

The first thing that came to mind the following day was that Major Kofo had planted the microphone in her husband's bedroom to set him up—or how else would you explain her invitation to break into her own home? Yes, it was far-fetched that she would do that and rely on chance to find and convince me to do the job, but stranger things have happened. It didn't take much to convince Kabiru to join in on the act, given his past. Breaking into homes was an old pastime for him, but I asked him to stay in the car and be the lookout.

We arrived a little early and parked a few houses away. After about a quarter of an hour, I set out. Walking casually into another man's property without attracting unwanted attention is a notoriously difficult thing to do, especially under the glare of the sun, but the street was so quiet that I didn't feel afraid. At the gate, I found the keys where she said I would—in a pot of red acalypha— and let myself in. I walked to the front porch and unlocked the door, half expecting an alarm to go off and a team of agents to come out of nowhere. It was eerily quiet.

The duplex was cozy and tasteful. It looked smaller inside than it did from the street and had a soft allure to it. I didn't waste time admiring it, though. I climbed the stairs and found Jimi's room. It was large and airy, with subdued tones and a distinct machismo smell. Across the gray wall where the bed sat were silhouettes of pigeons in flight. On the bedside stand was a collection of perfumes and pomades. In one corner was a bookshelf containing books on unimportant topics.

It was when I looked around that I realized I didn't know where in his room I might find the microphone. Major Kofo had indicated it was there, but omitted where. An honest mistake or a deliberate oversight? I wondered, feeling a slight panic build. I listened for sounds. Satisfied that I was still alone, I began to probe the space around me, starting with the drawers and sifting through the usual—pills, pens, cuffs, watches, stuff like that. The wardrobe was filled with clothes, expensive suits, and ties—nothing out of the ordinary. I checked under the bed and found a few magazines, disused items, and a black earthenware pot holding odd bits and fetishes that scared me to death—but no microphone.

Confused, I went back to the wardrobe and went over it with a fine-tooth comb. Then I checked the space above it, using a chair as a makeshift ladder, and found a few forgotten items—old wallets, shoes, pedicure kits, and essential oils. Further back was a stack of stationery, and shifting it out of the way revealed a folded brown envelope. I snatched it, half expecting it to contain bills and documents, but quickly realized that it held what looked like a microphone.

Aha!

I sat down and opened it. It was a microphone, all right, but it wasn't the microphone. It was wireless and battery-powered and did not have any severed ends. No telltale blue stump—just a smooth end. In fact, it looked like a new microphone.

Na wa o, I murmured, disappointed, and returned the microphone to where I had found it before leaving the room, as I had found it.

There is a sense of adventure you get when you are alone in people's homes—something that urges you to explore. I found Major Kofo's room and immediately understood why Jimi might want a room to himself. It was a bird's nest. Clothes, shoes, and military paraphernalia were strewn everywhere, and although you could tell it hadn't been lived in for some days, it retained an air of chaos.

I had barely opened the army-green drawer when the gate opened, and I heard a car pull up in the driveway. I froze for a moment, an avalanche of thoughts flooding my mind. From across the window, I saw Jimi step out of the car.

Oluwa o!

A forceful, visceral fear gripped my body. I fled down the stairs and hid in the kitchen. The door opened; my feet trembled.

"Kofo?" I could hear the hesitation in his voice. "Is that you, Kofo?"

The soft hum from the fridge sounded like bulldozers in my ears and threatened to give away my position. Jimi muttered something unintelligible. I heard his soft footsteps in the sitting room.

"Kofo, are you up in my room?"

My fingers curled into fists in a bid to stop myself from shaking. Each second felt like forever as I stood perfectly still. Then I heard him climb the stairs, muttering something about the absence of her car. I saw my chance. When he was out of earshot, I tiptoed into the sitting room and fled the house.

I found Kabiru slumbering in the car.

"Start the car!" I shook him and yelled, "Go, go, go!"

***

I paid Modele a second visit to her home the following day. That painting on her wall and its resemblance to the woman at the gallery had cost me a few nights' sleep. I could not help but wonder if there was any significance to it.

Modele, however, wasn't as welcoming as the first time.

"Whatever it is," she snapped as I entered the house, "please make it quick. I'm going out."

"I won't take much of your time."

At the wall that held the painting, I stood motionless, examining it.

This cannot be a coincidence, I thought. There must be a connection.

"How did you say you got this artwork again?"

"I thought I told you."

"Can you tell me again?"

"Modele doesn't repeat herself," she snapped. "What is this about?"

"I spoke to a strange woman at the gallery who was dressed exactly like this painting—the beads, the cowrie earrings, the white iro and buba… everything."

"So?"

"She said some things." I searched her eyes for any signs, but Modele was expressionless. "Did you know her?"

"You are crazy! I don't know any woman. I don't know what you are talking about."

I tried and failed to probe further and establish a link. Modele held firm like a brick wall and was quick to point out that she would rather be elsewhere.

At the door, I said, "I met Dorcas, your former roommate."

She stiffened. "How is she?"

"Very well," I said. "She asked me to greet you."

As I made my way out of the compound, I asked myself why Modele had looked as though she had seen a ghost.

***

By the start of the following week, Father had begun to spend more time in the house and less at the motel.

"He is getting more comfortable with us now," Maami posited from the window as he cleaned the old Peugeot, "and that can only be a good thing, abi?"

We still didn't know his mission, and there were still a lot of bridges to cross—and we might never cross them all—but I was glad we were at least starting to try. He was really smitten with the Peugeot and wanted to bring it back to life. Maami liked the idea. It justified her belief that he would have wanted her to keep it.

One bright afternoon, we set out to find a mechanic. Kabiru recommended an old pal whose workshop was nearby, so we trekked there and caught up on a few unimportant things. A few people greeted us, smiling. We were like friends, not father and son.

Funny old man he is, too—I was starting to realize. He is like a two-faced individual: quiet and reserved sometimes, then lively and loquacious at other times. I suppose I take after him.

We found the mechanic, who didn't seem keen on the idea at first but immediately agreed when he recognized who Father was. His own late father had worked on the Peugeot before.

We returned with him to the house, and I immediately went to the studio. I still wasn't any closer to figuring out who the murderer was, but somewhat out of the blue, an idea occurred to me: to make a drawing of the four suspects and Sade in the changing room. I wanted to take a fresh look. Perhaps I had missed something—an important clue that had enabled the killer to remain undetected. I needed to connect the dots, so I began to sketch, caricaturing them.

Twenty minutes later, I looked at my progress and hummed with a nod. It was exactly as I had pictured it. I continued honing the details, and when I was done, I examined the sketch. I had drawn the changing room from a bird's-eye view in such a way that I could see the door and the small passageway that led to the opening into the main auditorium.

It's like I'm looking at them like God, watching their every move from above. Omnipresent.

I looked at the characters, beginning with Sade at the end of the bench, in an uncertain mood. *She didn't know it was going to be her last day on earth, did she? Jimi was in the middle, somewhat cautious in manner. Jimi. That was close the last time out, wasn't it? What if I didn't get the opportunity to get out of his house, nko? Hmm.*

My eyes shifted to Lara at the other end of the bench, toying with her phone. *Lara, I thought to myself, has been discharged from the hospital for some days now, but she's still avoiding me. Well, not for long. You cannot claim to be too traumatized to talk forever. You will still have to talk about the microphone.*

Opposite them were Nike and Modele. *Nike is always keen to help—perhaps too keen—and Modele is, well, Modele.*

Father entered and interrupted my thoughts. He was excited.

The mechanic would begin the restoration process immediately.

"What is that you are looking at?" he asked after a while.

"It's a sketch of the crime scene." I passed it to him. "I told you yesterday that I still don't know who did it."

He took it with immediate interest. "Maybe it needs a fresh pair of eyes," he said, examining it like an architect would examine a building plan. "Hmm," he added after some time, "they look like ordinary people."

"Except one of them is not ordinary. It's like a puzzle."

He nodded. "An interesting one. Which of them is Lara?"

"This one." I pointed her out with the pencil.

"Is that a gun in her hand?"

"It's a cellphone." I laughed. "Is my drawing that bad?"

"Where is the army woman?"

"She's not there. I know she has a strong motive for murder, but there is nothing to suggest she ever went into that room—or even Richard, for that matter."

"And Richard is not here, either."

"He's not there."

From the view that overlooked the door and the passageway, you could see a small section of the choir in the auditorium. Unless they all managed to doze off at once, someone should have noticed them going in. I explained this further to him.

"So it must be one of these ones in the room."

"Yes."

"Is there another exit?"

"Like a hidden door?"

"Yes."

"No. There is only one entry door."

"What about this door before the entrance?"

"That's the toilet. There are two of them—male and female."

"Does it have an exit?"

"Like a door inside the toilet?" He nodded, doubtful.

"I don't think so."

"You know," he said, "I'm not good at these things, but the killer could have hidden in the toilet after he killed her. Maybe that's how he got away. Did anyone check the toilet?"

I could almost hear the snap in my mind. I snatched the sheet from him and looked at the small passageway. It was there, and then the veil dropped from my face and hit me like a blast of cold wind. Everything became clear as day. I crashed into the recliner.

"Oluwa o!"

"What's wrong, son?" Father was alarmed.

I replied, almost in a trance, "Daddy, I think I know exactly what happened."

***

Kabiru parked the taxi at exactly 6:45 p.m. that evening. I got out and approached the elderly caretaker. He was upset about something and didn't want to listen to any request, so he trudged off. I looked around, contemplating a plan.

I need to get in there.

The church doors were open. A Bible class was going on. Only a handful of members were present.

"I'm a little late, ma," I said conversationally, sitting next to a pudgy elderly woman.

"No one is late before God, my dear," she said, handing me a tract. "Everyone is welcome at any time. Where is your Bible?"

I looked at her, unable to respond.

"Hmm!" she eyed me affectionately. "You are one of those young people who read the Bible from their phones, abi?" I smiled sheepishly. "You are lucky I always carry two." She pulled out an old, dog-eared copy from her bag and gave it to me. "That's the New King James Version. I prefer the old. Is it funny that the copy in your hands is old and tattered, and this one in my hand is new, but is the old version?"

"Ironic." I thanked her and pretended to look through it. For the next ten minutes, I barely heard what the teacher was saying. I looked around, unsure how to get the keys to the room. An idea came to me, and I clutched my stomach.

"Kilode? Are you all right, my dear?"

"It must be something I ate, ma. I think I need to go to the restroom."

"There is one at the back—"

"What about this one here?" I pointed to the changing room.

She frowned. "I don't know if it's open, my dear, but I saw some workmen there this afternoon. I think they want to convert it into an office, you know, because of what happened there. Check if it is open."

I got up quickly, clutching my stomach. The door was unlocked. I slipped in. Two doors faced me. The one next to the changing room was marked "Female." I opened it. The toilet was relatively clean, except for some dust and cobwebs here and there.

I entered, wondering if I should have come alone. What if I'm wrong?

I looked around and didn't see any obvious place to hide anything. Then I went to the cistern and lifted the lid. Inside it, partly submerged, was a microphone.

My heart raced.

I set the lid on the toilet bowl, pushed down the lever to flush, and when all the water was gone, I wound some toilet paper around my hand and lifted the mic, which had begun to show early signs of rust. It was weighty, and on the head was a streak of what I suspected was dried blood.

Someone cleared their throat behind me. I almost dropped the mic.

It was Reverend Brown, dressed in a burgundy clerical shirt and dark pants.

"I don't mean to disturb your peace, sir," he began, almost comically, "but you are in the ladies' toilet. It's clearly indicated on the door. Did you miss it?"

"Oh no, Reverend," I said apologetically. "You don't understand. Let me explain myself."

"I heard about you," he said after I'd finished. "I don't approve, of course. It's a police matter, and that is how it should be. What is that in your hand?"

"The murder weapon."

"Father in heaven!" Reverend Brown cried, immediately looking sick.

I examined the exhibit again, noting the blue stump where the cord had been severed.

"I am going to call that inspector now—"

"No!" I blurted out. "Don't call him, sir. Please."

"Why?"

"Because I know who did it, and I can prove—"

"I'm sure it's no one here," Reverend Brown interjected, then paused. When I didn't reply immediately, his mouth began to drop.

"It's someone here, Reverend," I said finally. "I know who killed her, but I can't tell you now. I have a plan, and it's good."

He regarded me for a minute or two before giving me the benefit of the doubt with a slow, conniving nod.

"How long has that been there?"

"Since the day she was killed."

The water had stopped flowing into the cistern now. I placed the mic where I'd found it, then covered it with the lid.

"It has been here all along. I want you to do something for me, sir. I want you to lock this place."

"Till when? I want to remodel this room."

"Until tomorrow."

He sighed, relieved.

"So what is your plan?" he asked after he'd locked the room. The class had just finished.

In great detail, I told him.

***

On our way back home, I dialed Jimi's number.

"Hello?"

"Hello, Mr. Smart. Deji Depiver on the line."

"Oh, Deji. Evening."

"Good evening. I need you to do something for me."

"What do you want me to do for you?"

"I need all four of you at the church tomorrow afternoon—and Richard too. I think I know who killed Sade."

A long pause.

"Hello?"

"I'm here. You say?"

"I said I think I know who killed your lover."

"It's not Kofo?" I could almost hear his heart beating.

"It's not your wife. I told the reverend about it, too, and he agreed we could use the church, so please call them. Let's make it 4 p.m."

"What are we going to—"

"Please contact the others." I hung up.

Tomorrow, I thought, feeling the gentle night breeze on my face. Everything will be over tomorrow.

CHAPTER TWENTY-ONE

Modele arrived shortly after I got to the church, and predictably, her mood was sour.

"What's so important, eh?" her querulous voice came floating up the aisle, interrupting my thoughts on my best line of approach. "What's so important that I had to cancel a lunch date? What is so important?"

"Take it easy, Modele," Rekia tried to keep pace. "I'm sure Jimi has a good reason for asking you to come."

"I am so angry, and I don't know why!"

"You are angry because he asked you to come."

"No. I was angry before that. Why didn't he ask you to come too?"

"I don't know."

"Maybe that's why I'm angry," Modele hissed. "Whatever it is, he owes me a very expensive lunch. At Tefrosia's Place. Not just any roadside dump."

"That's where your date is?"

"What do you think? Right now, I feel like slapping someone."

"Ah, take it easy. Calm down."

They came up to me.

"Hello, Deji," said Modele, surprised by my presence. "What are you doing here?"

"Good afternoon, Modele. Actually, I called this meeting. I asked Jimi to arrange it."

"Why am I not surprised?" Her anger grew. "What's so important?"

"Don't you want to sit down first?"

"I like standing."

"That's why we are a choir," agreed Rekia. "We stand all the time."

Modele nodded, mild curiosity still in her eyes. I scratched my head, a bit unsure how to put it to her. She lifted an indifferent brow.

"So why am I here?"

"Just a little demonstration. You will see."

"A demonstration?" Her nose twitched. "What are we demonstrating?"

"I want to prove to you, to everyone, that I know who killed Sade."

Modele was taken aback. She blinked rapidly as though a speck had entered her eyes. Rekia laughed rather foolishly.

"Well, who?"

"I didn't ask you to come, Rekia," I said with a tight smile.

The laughter vanished from her face.

"We are together," Modele said tersely. "I asked her to follow me."

"Modele, maybe I should come and be going now—"

"Don't go," I said. "You are already here. I think you will be useful too."

"Useful?" asked Rekia, perplexed.

"That's so rude!" Modele's annoyance went up a gear. "Who do you think you are?"

"I didn't mean it that way. I'm sorry."

"What do you mean, useful?"

"See, everyone will play a role—their original role," I explained. "But since we don't have Sade, you will play her part."

Rekia looked at me as though I had lost my mind, then turned to her friend, whose face registered rude surprise.

"What is he talking about?"

"I don't know," Modele said, her voice quavering.

"What I'm saying," I continued, "is that everyone from that day will play their roles now, and you, Rekia, will be Sade, for today!"

Rekia broke into mirthless laughter and leaned on a pew for support.

"I'm sick and tired of this," Modele boomed. "You are rude and arrogant. Yes! You think you can just call people as you like because you are… You are what exactly?"

"Mr. Depiver, you are so funny," Rekia said, still convulsed with laughter. "Hahaha… oh my God… you have killed me o. Are we like theater people now?" she burbled, casting a bewitching glance at me.

"You will see. It's not a stupid idea."

"This is not funny–o." She stopped laughing and wore a serious expression. "I wasn't even there when she died. I wasn't in that room, so how can I play her? See me see wahala o. Why did I even follow you, Modele? I think I should be going."

"You don't really need to do anything special, Rekia. Just play along. It's like a reenactment of sorts."

She seemed to consider this for an instant, then shrugged nonchalantly. "Maybe you are right, sha. People tell me I would make a good actress anyway. Like Omotola Jalade. A friend told me I do look like her, even. What do you think, Modele?"

"I think you are mad."

"Chill. It's not my fault he thinks I'm good and look good for the part. Sade was pretty, you know."

"You are not seriously considering this."

"It will be fun!" said Rekia, like a child. "Are you not innocent?"

Modele hesitated, then blinked. "I am innocent—"

"You didn't do anything. That's what you told me."

"It's the truth!" Modele was visibly upset. "I don't like this. I'm going home, Rekia. You can stay if you want."

She turned to leave. Rekia looked desperately at me.

"Wait!" she said, scurrying after her friend. "What will everybody say? Think about it."

"That's right, Modele," I called. "What will people say?"

"They will say things," Rekia cajoled. "Bad things. And you are innocent."

"I have nothing to hide!" Modele yelled back, but then stopped cold a few meters from the door in a sudden change of heart. Slowly, she began to retreat.

"I will stay," she announced tightly, "so they won't say it's Modele's fault. Everything is always Modele's fault! Sade's death is Modele's fault! I have nothing to hide, okay? Nothing!"

"No one can say you are responsible for it," Rekia comforted her as they sat. "What a stupid idea."

She gave a vague smile and said, "Am I the only one around?"

"Jimi is around," I said. "He is in the reverend's office."

"Reverend Benson is here?"

"Yes. I told him about it, and he gave his blessing."

"Will he be watching?" asked Rekia, bright-eyed.

"As a matter of fact, yes."

She clapped excitedly. She opened her bag and, in a showy manner, began to apply some makeup, adjusting the mirror to a convenient angle. Modele looked at her.

Rekia laughed.

"What are they doing there?" Modele asked me.

"I don't know," I said, checking my watch. "They have been there for twenty minutes now."

"I wonder what they are talking about," said Rekia, putting the kit away.

"Look!" Modele whispered suddenly. "The witch of Endor is here."

I glanced up to see Lara coming in. There was a look of desolation about her. She walked laboriously, as though pulling a cart.

"You will see now," Modele was telling her friend. "Richard will come within a minute. They are so predictable. Gosh!"

"They are still doing that?" Rekia whispered. "What do they think we are, babies?"

"Just watch!"

"Good afternoon, Deji," Lara greeted me. She looked like she hadn't slept for days. Her eyes were bloodshot and ringed with dark circles. "Hello, Rekia. Modele."

"Welcome, Lara," said Rekia. "You look sick. What's wrong?"

"I am sick."

"We heard you were at the hospital."

Lara hesitated, thought about saying something, then decided against it.

"How are you holding up now?"

She shrugged.

"Your hair is lovely, by the way," said Modele, insincerely. "Cornrows are made for you."

Lara rolled her eyes. "I have new growth, Modele. It's overdue."

"Is this about Sade?" she asked me. Her voice was so low, I had to strain to hear it.

"Yes," I replied.

Lara nodded quickly, breaking off my gaze. Just for a moment, she looked suspicious and afraid. She went to sit at a distance from us.

Then Richard walked in. Modele and Rekia exchanged looks. He seemed to wander around a bit, unsure what was going on, before coming to me, doing his best not to look at the women. We exchanged greetings.

"Did Jimi ask you to come too?"

"In a way, yes."

"Ah. So this is about Sade?"

"Yes."

"She is right then."

"Who is right?"

"Lara."

An awkward silence.

"Can I talk to you privately?"

I nodded. He led me all the way to the front door.

"You know she tried to kill herself."

"Lara?"

"Yes."

"I heard. I feel sorry for her."

"She feels bad about something," he said, and quickly added, "But she did not kill her best friend. You have to believe me."

I let out an audible sigh. "Is this the reason why she wanted to commit suicide?"

He nodded. "It's eating her alive. She wasn't thinking properly."

I looked behind me. Lara's sad, defeated gaze was on us.

The day of reckoning…

We returned to our original positions after the brief private meeting, and as soon as we did so, Nike walked in. She approached gracefully with a brittle smile. She greeted everybody in her usual warm fashion.

"I didn't know you would be here too," she said to me, looking around. "Where is Jimi?"

"He is in Reverend Benson's office," Rekia answered.

Modele hissed.

"Oh, okay. Why are we here?" wondered Nike.

"You don't know?" said Rekia, still with the attitude of a child. "We are here because Deji wants to demonstrate to us who killed Sade. He has proof!"

"Proof?" Lara, who was away from everybody, spoke suddenly, as though jolted by a minor electric shock.

"Take it or leave it, Nike," Rekia went on theatrically. "We are now actors. I will be playing Sade in this drama. What's the title, Deji? Does it have one?"

"So it's not an emergency rehearsal?" A frozen smile broke on Nike's face. Her voice carried distinct disbelief.

"Emergency rehearsal, ke?" scoffed Rekia with a wave of her hand. "What will we be rehearsing for? You are too serious, Nike. That's your problem."

Nike began to sweat. She fanned herself with her hand. "Don't blame me. It's what came to my mind."

"Better remove it." A lazy smile crossed Rekia's lips. "We are actors now. Why are you carrying an umbrella?"

"I think it will rain. I felt it when I was coming, so I went back for it, just to be safe."

"Ah!" Rekia got up and walked to the windows. "Did it not rain that day Sade died?"

"Yes," Nike replied after a moment's hesitation. "It's a bit hot here."

"I don't feel hot," said Rekia, coming back. "I don't know why I'm wild today, but what if it were to rain again while I'm here? Would that not be… scary?"

"It will rain," Lara foretold. From where she sat, she looked like a mannequin.

A puzzled Rekia exchanged looks with Modele, who immediately let out another loud hiss.

"What is this proof you are talking about?" Nike sat down.

"That's what I'm thinking too," Modele said. "It's a waste of time. There is no proof."

Rekia laughed suddenly, as though a phantom had whispered a joke in her ear. "Is this about the lucky mic, Deji? Have you found it?"

I didn't say anything. I wanted to slap her to keep her mouth shut.

"You found it!"

Modele looked at me with curious interest. Nike stopped fanning herself. Lara said something rather faint. A strange, labored breathing came from her, followed by a muffled crash.

Lara had collapsed in the pew, her arms sprawled wildly.

I sprang forward. "Lara! Lara!!"

"What's wrong?"

"She's fainted!"

Nike gave a cry.

***

"Do you feel better now?" Richard gave her some water to drink. Lara, lying on the pew, mumbled; a kind of staring dread spread across her face.

"How did this happen?" Reverend Benson wondered. "Is she sick?"

"Is she, Richard?" Rekia asked. "We just heard her say something, and then she fell…" Rekia threw herself into Modele, mimicking the fall. "Like this."

"What did she say?" asked the reverend, breathing hard. He was fanning her.

"She didn't say anything," Richard said curtly.

"But she said something, Richard," Nike chirped. "I think she said 'microphone.' Is that not what you said, Lara dear?"

Lara barely responded.

"That's what I heard too," Modele agreed, fixing a knowing gaze on me.

"It's true," I said. "Richard, how come you didn't hear it? You were the closest to her."

"I didn't hear anything!"

Lara mumbled again.

Nike dropped to her knees. "What did you say, Lara?"

She mumbled again, like a toddler.

"She is confused," said Nike. "Call a taxi, Richard. I will take her home."

"I don't think she is that sick," Modele said, examining her.

"How can you know that?" wondered Nike.

"Look at her eyes."

"Can't it wait?" asked Rekia. Then, to me, she said, "What about the proof?"

"It can wait, Rekia. Lara is not feeling well. Help me, Richard!"

"It can't wait," I said. "We must do it now. Reverend?"

The cleric gave me a skeptical look. "If she is sick—"

"Lara is fine. She is just lightheaded."

"We can do this later," said Richard.

I shook my head. "Lara, can you hear me? Lara?"

Slowly, she nodded her head, and after a moment's hesitation, she said, "Put me down, Richard."

"Are you better now?"

She nodded and took some more water. There was an audible sigh of relief from the reverend, and everyone appeared more relaxed.

"It has started raining now," observed Rekia after a bit of normalcy. "Does that mean we can start with the demonstration you talked about?"

"We don't need the rain to do that," I said, and looked at Reverend Benson, who gave a nod of approval.

I paced about, thinking how best to begin.

"That day Sade died…" I began. "You all went into that room, abi?" I pointed to the changing room.

"Not me," Rekia said. "I was here."

"Who went in first?"

"How is that important?" asked Modele with a bit of scorn. "You have asked this same question before."

"No," I waved a critical finger, "that's not true. What I asked before was who left first, and everyone said it was you, Nike."

"It's true," agreed Rekia with a nod.

"What does it matter?" said Modele, disinterested. "We just went inside, jare."

"All of you at once?"

Silence. Everyone looked thoughtful.

"Sade went in first," Lara sniffed. She still had the appearance of a hen with a broken egg inside her. "She was upset about something."

"Upset, eh?" I said.

"Oh, yes, I remember," said Rekia brightly. "She passed me. How can I ever forget that lemon perfume she wears? I think you followed her too," she said, pointing to the choirmaster.

"I did not," Jimi denied. "Nike was coming out when I went in."

"Oh…" Rekia's voice trailed off. "Then you went in next, Nike."

"Did I?" Nike quavered. "I don't remember."

I let a full minute pass before I asked, "What was Sade upset about, Nike?"

"Why are you asking me? I didn't know she was upset about anything in the first place." Her mouth fixed into a hard line.

"A lot of things upset her," said Modele with distaste. "If her hair was not perfect, she would be upset. If anyone was late to rehearsal by just one minute, she would be upset. If she didn't like the song we picked, she would be upset!"

Rekia gave a hysterical laugh that quickly died out under the reproachful glare of Reverend Benson.

"Maybe Jimi can tell us what upset her?" I said.

Jimi immediately looked frazzled and uncertain. "Go on," I encouraged. "Tell us."

He opened his mouth to speak, but couldn't form the words.

"Say it, Jimi!" Richard yelled. "Say it! Tell us how you took my fiancée. Let the whole world know what you did."

Everyone watched in stunned silence as Richard continued his intense upbraiding and only stopped when Reverend Benson begged him to.

"You must not be too emotional, Richard." He put a fatherly arm around his shoulder and patted him. "He has told me everything," the reverend went on. "He confessed everything in my office, and I have told him there will be consequences."

"That is not even what I'm talking about," I said. "What I'm talking about is what upset her before going into the room."

"Are you still talking about the microphone?" asked Modele.

"It's not just the microphone," I said, a little irritated. "It cannot be just that."

"I remember she was upset about something that day," said Rekia after a thoughtful pause. "Someone was singing loudly in the background, and we couldn't even hear Sade well. You know how that makes her feel."

"Hmm," Lara sighed audibly.

"Was it not you, Modele?" asked Nike.

Modele cringed. "I have never sung off-key before."

"I didn't say off—"

"Loud… off-key… they are the same!"

Rekia seemed to cogitate on the matter. "I actually thought it was you, Nike."

"Me?" Nike tittered. "My voice was normal. I don't sing loudly."

My gaze instinctively shifted to Lara, who was looking at Nike. She, too, appeared to be thinking about something.

"Well, maybe it wasn't you then. But I remember thinking someone was trying to annoy Sade with their loud voice."

"You mean the background voice was trying to drown hers?"

"Yes. And Sade hates that."

I went to the door and opened it.

"How did she appear to you, Jimi, when Nike was first coming out?"

"Upset," he replied. "I thought maybe Nike had done something to upset her."

"I only went in there to change my shoes," Nike spoke in a harsh whisper. "They were tight and painful. I didn't even notice her."

"Who went in next?"

"Me," said Lara.

"Lara," agreed Jimi.

"Nike and I went last," Modele said finally.

"Okay. Lara, did Richard ask you to spy on Sade for him?"

"No." Her voice was oddly hesitant. "I went in there because I thought my friend was upset about something. Why would I even do that?"

"I don't know." I shrugged. "Maybe because you want Richard for yourself?"

She eyed me fiercely. Reverend Benson looked at me quizzically. I shifted my attention to Nike and Modele.

"So the two of you went in last, together?"

"That's what I said," Modele snapped. "I wanted to show Nike my shoe."

"That means you went in twice, Nike?"

"Yes."

"First to change your shoe and second to check out Modele's shoe?"

She hesitated, then nodded. Reverend Benson scowled.

"Okay. Rekia, please come."

I pushed the door open and saw that everything in the changing room was where it should be.

"Are we starting now?" Rekia brightened.

"Please sit on that bench."

When she was seated, I asked Jimi to come in and show me exactly where he sat on that fateful day. He sat next to Rekia, who was all shades of excited. She was the only one enjoying this.

"Lara?"

Lara walked in somberly and sat at the end of the bench.

"Is that where you sat?" I asked.

"Yes."

"You were closer than that, Lara," said Jimi.

She ignored him.

When the last two walked in, Modele reiterated, "This is stupid. Are we really doing this?"

"Relax, Modele," Rekia cooed. "Are you not curious? You didn't do anything, remember?"

"Where am I going to stay?" asked Richard when Reverend Benson joined in.

"Stay outside," I said. "No, not in front of the toilet. Out in the auditorium. You are the most important witness."

CHAPTER TWENTY-TWO

"**O**kay," Nike murmured, looking at me with bright eyes. "So what do we do now?"

The rain outside added an air of mystery to the already tense atmosphere. Reverend Benson folded his arms and watched.

"Start," I said. "Recreate how it all happened. Let us all see."

"This is stupid," Modele moaned again. "It's like I'm having a dream. Somebody pinch me!"

"Better pinch yourself, Modele," said Rekia, tongue-in-cheek. "You are so dramatic. This is one play you are acting in. No escape," she added whimsically. "Does it have a title, Mr. Depiver?"

"You are enjoying this, Rekia," said Nike with a hint of disbelief.

"How can you be enjoying this, eh?" asked Modele. "It's annoying."

"It's fun," Rekia said with a cheerful shrug. "As long as your conscience is not bothering you, like mine is not."

"I hope he pours it all on your head," Modele said angrily. "I hope he says you are the killer, Rekia."

"Me? How?" Rekia looked at Reverend Benson, expecting reproach or condemnation. When she didn't get any reaction, she countered, "Oh, you are just bitter, Modele. I didn't do anything to her. This is your problem, not mine. None of you really liked her, but I have nothing against her. Nothing! What's wrong, Nike?"

"What?"

"Why are you hugging yourself like that?"

"I feel a bit cold."

"You were feeling hot before; now you are feeling cold. Are you possessed? I'm just joking, o. What's wrong with me today?!"

"I will just use this." Nike plucked a robe hanging on the wall.

"Eww." Rekia recoiled. "Do you know how long it has been there?"

"It doesn't matter. I just need it to help with the cold."

"Funny enough," Rekia squinted, "that robe belonged to Sade."

Lara also looked at it closely and agreed with a nod. "That's Sade's old robe."

Nike suddenly looked uncomfortable. She fumbled out of it. "Maybe I should just put it back."

"Why?" Rekia giggled. "Are you afraid of ghosts?"

"Use it," Lara encouraged. Reverend Benson did as well.

"So what are we doing now?" Modele blinked several times rapidly. "Who are we waiting for?"

By the way they looked at me, expectant of a cue, I realized the flaw in my plan. They could not just act it out as it happened. I had to walk them through it, step by step.

I said to Jimi, "So you sat down with her, eh? What happened next?"

"I asked her what was wrong with her."

"Other than what she already wanted to talk about?"

He nodded. "Her mood had changed. After we finished praising, I could sense it in her. She was... grumpy. You know the way women are sometimes."

"This happened when Nike and Modele were already here?"

"No. Only Lara was here then. Not long after, they came in."

"Modele and Nike."

"Yes."

"What did she tell you?"

"Nothing."

"She said nothing?"

He hesitated. "Yes. But I know she didn't mean it. I noticed that when they came in, she was looking at them."

"You mean at Modele and Nike?"

"Yes."

"How did she look?"

"Angry. Like she was angry with them."

"Both of them?"

"I don't know. I'm just saying. That's what I saw."

"Do you know why she was angry?"

"No."

I nodded. I walked a few paces and stood in the middle of the room.

"Did she arrange for you to meet here to have any talk beforehand?"

"Yes." He paused. "We couldn't see each other after service or just anywhere because... er..."

"Because you would be seen by other people," I finished for him.

Jimi let out a sigh and continued. "So she said we should meet here, like we sometimes did."

Reverend Benson shook his head.

This place is not exactly private, I thought to myself, but secret lovers have been known to do dafter things.

"So what happened after?"

"We talked. That's when she told me she was pregnant."

Modele spread her hands expressively. "I was not even here when they were saying all this."

"You were eavesdropping on them?" I asked. "Otherwise, how could you have heard what they were saying?"

A faint chuckle came from Rekia.

Modele quavered. "It's not a very big room. I thought you'd notice that by now."

"Can I say something?" Lara raised her hand.

"Yes, Lara."

"Sade wasn't pregnant."

It was a clear, succinct statement that reverberated across the room.

"What?"

"Ah ah."

Lara's gaze dropped. "She just wanted to know if he would leave his wife for her."

"She tricked him?"

Jimi's eyes opened wide, a mixture of horror and betrayal in them. Reverend Benson clapped his hands three times, dismayed. Everyone in the room but Lara herself was shocked.

"Women!" muttered Rekia finally after an uncomfortable period of silence. "Why do we like to do that?"

"Let us move on," I said, not wanting to derail the progress we had made so far. "So you talked about her pregnancy..."

Jimi nodded.

"Then, when did she tell you about Lara stealing the tithe? Or did she mention it in between telling you she was carrying your child?"

"I lied about that," he said, his head dropping. "She wasn't the one who told me. That was Modele. I told you it was Sade so that I could have a good excuse for our conversation."

Modele, while restrained, appeared to be quietly seething. "I didn't tell you anything," she denied.

"I don't know how she knew about it, but I believed her," Jimi continued, his voice grave. "Modele is always trying to get close to me by any means possible. She thought that by telling me things like that, we could get close."

"When did you have this conversation?"

"That was some days before she died. I think it was Thursday, just after rehearsal. Sade had gone home. I asked how she came to know about it, and she said Sade told her. I didn't believe her at all. Sade, too, was surprised when I tried to ask her. Modele later confessed to me that she lied about Sade telling it to her. I think she just wanted to come between us. I lie, Modele?"

It was quite a revelation, and Jimi looked relieved to find that Modele didn't show any sign of flying out at him over it. Instead, she frowned and folded her arms, petulant.

"Lara is here, and she's not denying it!"

Lara, we didn't know, had begun to sob.

"I just have one question to ask you, Modele," she dabbed at her wet eyes and whimpered. "How did you know if Sade did not tell you? Who told you?"

Modele shot a quick glance at Nike, who wrapped the robe tightly around her body. Their telepathic communication was, at least to me, apparent.

"Secrets!" she snarled, throwing her hands in the air. "Secrets to the grave!"

"You want to say something, Rekia?" asked Reverend Benson.

Rekia hesitated. "It's nothing, Reverend."

"Ah, for God's sake, Rekia, speak!" yelled Modele. "Why are you afraid, eh? What are you afraid of?"

"I'm not afraid. I wanted to say—"

Modele's voice quickly drowned hers. "Did you not take your best friend's man, eh? Did she not, Rekia? And you are here shedding fake tears. Where were the tears when you snatched Richard from your friend, eh? Or you think we don't know? We know that you snatched him, and don't tell us it was after she died that it all started because it's not true." She coughed and patted her chest from her exertions. "Abi, Rekia?"

Rekia nodded effusively, and Lara wailed even more.

"I heard my name."

Richard was at the door, his presence restoring instant decorum. Nike shuffled her feet and looked uncomfortable. Modele let out another grievous hiss. Rekia laughed a little.

At this point, I was uncertain what to do next. I had had a preconceived idea about the progression, but I began to realize now that I had underestimated the passion of a large cast, especially one with wayward characters like Modele and Rekia.

"Ah!" I muttered, somewhat pretentiously. "I was just about to ask Lara when the two of you began seeing each other."

Richard paused, unsure how to respond. "I was wondering when you would get to that part," he said finally, walking in.

"I am happy you have been listening."

Richard went to Lara and patted her until she stopped crying.

"I don't know how to tell you this, but… it just happened."

His frankness came as a surprise.

Not quite sure what to say next, and wishing he hadn't been so open, I asked, "So you were not exacting revenge?"

Richard hesitated. "I've known Lara even before I knew Sade. We were good friends. She introduced us. She introduced Sade to me. I liked her as my fiancée's friend, but then when Sade and I began to fight sometimes, and… and…"

His words trailed off.

"He knew she was seeing Jimi behind his back," said Lara, quietly but firmly. "We talked about it. He was unhappy. I think from there, we became closer."

"It just happened," said Richard. "We fit each other…"

"And Sade was in the way," I said, my tone accusatory. "Anyway, what you told me before was that Sade snatched Richard from you."

Lara looked a little taken aback. She coughed. "Did I say that?"

"Those were your exact words."

"Ah," Rekia muttered after Lara began to stutter. "Maybe she meant it in a different way. Sometimes what we want to say is not what we end up saying."

"I didn't mean to say that," Lara finally said. "What I meant was that I met Richard first, as a friend."

"How convenient," said Modele dryly, with a dramatic one-hundred-and-eighty-degree turn of the head.

"Did you ever talk to her about the affair?" I asked Richard. "I'm talking about Sade."

He nodded. "She said he was only being friendly with her. Making her a better singer."

"Did you believe her?"

He shook his head. "After she died," Richard continued, "I… we thought… why not just be together, you know."

"So you admit you had been secretly going out with Lara even when Sade was still alive?"

"I didn't say that."

"It looks like that."

"What do you want me to say now?"

"Did she know?"

"Sade? I didn't think so. Although Lara thinks she knew."

"Did she know?" I asked Lara.

"I don't know," she sighed. "I think… maybe she suspected."

"But you are not sure."

She shook her head.

I nodded, thinking how best to steer the conversation toward the microphone without sounding forced or contrived. Modele offered the perfect opportunity.

"You are not sure now, abi?" She gave a sound like an angry laugh. "But you were so sure before one of us took the lucky mic away from Sade. We know it was you, Lara. Tell us what you did with it. Shay, I lie, Rekia?"

Rekia sighed. "Sister Ronke saw you, Lara. You took it, and you lied about it."

Reverend Benson looked at me wide-eyed. He bent before her. "It was you, Omolara?"

Lara buried her face in her hands and nodded vigorously. Richard, who was still by her side, remained stone-faced. Reverend Benson consoled her.

"I took it, Reverend," Lara said tearfully. "But it's not what you think. I swear by the Bible, it's not."

Then she told a barely believable story. Her mood had been sour that Sunday: vengeful. She had heard Sade looking for the microphone and found it before her, by the keyboard. She proceeded to hide it from her friend. That was the last she saw of the microphone.

She doesn't want to implicate Richard, I thought, by excluding him.

"Ah-ah!" Modele flung an incredulous glance at Nike, who herself had the appearance of a cheerless graduand. "We believe you, Lara, we believe you. Continue with the lies you hear. Lies after lies after lies! When does it stop?"

Nike shook her head, doubtful.

"Why did you hide the mic?" I asked.

"Because I wanted to punish her!" she wailed miserably. "I wanted to punish her."

"I thought you were friends?" wondered Rekia.

"Shut up, Rekia!" Lara exploded. "Please tell her to stop talking to me. Stop talking to me, Rekia."

Rekia, surprised by the outburst, cupped her mouth with her hands and hastily looked away.

"Take this, dear," said Nike, extending some paper towels, which Reverend Benson took from her and gave to Lara, who cleaned her face with them.

"I feel so ashamed of myself," she continued, wiping her face. "I don't know what came over me, but I know I felt betrayed. Sade knew I took the money. I took the tithe. I told her myself. So when I overheard what Modele said to Jimi that Thursday night after rehearsal, something came over me."

"You overheard them?"

She nodded. "I was just by the door."

"Hmm!" muttered Modele angrily, shaking her head.

"Even if she had to tell someone," Lara continued bitterly, "I couldn't believe she told Modele of all people. Modele! How could she share a secret like that?"

"But Sade did not tell it to Modele," I said. Rekia, under a self-imposed gag order, nodded as though I had taken the words right out of her mouth. "She said it herself."

"I didn't know that until now!" cried Lara. "That's why I've been crying. It's not what I thought."

"Is that why you came to my house? Because you felt guilty?"

She gave a soft nod.

"You tried to kill yourself."

Lara looked exceedingly sad. "I knew whoever took that mic had something to do with it. It's the reason I was shouting my head off, wanting to know what happened to it."

"I don't believe one word you are saying," said Modele, icily cool. "I'm not stupid, even if everybody is. Sorry, Reverend!"

"How did you make that connection?" I asked.

"I just knew it in my spirit," she replied. "I felt it. And when you said you thought she had been killed with it, I was afraid. I... I... who would not think that I did it, eh?"

There was something in the way she said this that rang true.

Reverend Benson ran his hand over his bald head. He seemed unsure where this was going. I could tell by his anxious disposition. It seemed he had had the answer moments ago, but now things were taking another direction.

"Where did you hide it?"

"There," she replied, pointing to a locker near Modele. "That must have been when Sister Ronke saw me. I was going to take it home after service and throw it away."

"You were that angry with her."

"Yes."

"She actually saw Richard give it to you." I went to the locker and opened it. It was empty. "What did you keep here?"

"Bits and things," replied Nike. "We don't keep anything useful in it."

"There were old drumsticks in it when I put the mic there," Lara said, wiping her eyes again. "I just wanted to teach her a lesson. To upset her a little."

"Can you see the auditorium from where you are sitting, Rekia?" I asked.

She frowned and made an effort. "No."

"That means Sade couldn't have seen it, either," I said. "Can you?" I asked Jimi, who shook his head.

"Lara?"

Lara looked at me as though I had lost my mind. "If Rekia can't see it, then how can I see it from here?"

"Exactly," I said.

"What's your point?" asked Nike.

"You will see," I replied, then drew Richard aside. I whispered something in his ear. He nodded and left the room.

"What's going on?" asked Modele, suspicious. "Why didn't you ask me if I could see the auditorium?"

"Because your back is against the wall. Same thing for you, Nike."

"I know that," said Nike.

Modele whined some more. "I know what you will say. I know you will say I did it! You want to pin it on me, abi? You have no proof, you hear me? You have no proof!"

I turned to Jimi. "So you left her in here after you talked. Correct?"

"Yes," he replied. "We didn't... want to come out together."

I nodded and clasped my hands. "All of you left Sade in here. What we are going to do is reenact just that: how you all left here one by one. Now, starting with you, Jimi."

Modele's chin shot up. "But that's not how it happened."

"I was the first person to leave," Nike protested. "Everyone saw me leave first."

"I know that, Nike," I said. "But we won't do it that way. We will do it in reverse order, from Jimi, from last to first. You will see why. Don't worry yourself, okay?"

Nike bit her lip.

Jimi was agitated. He tapped his feet on the floor. Modele rolled her eyes, arms akimbo. Lara swallowed uncomfortably. Rekia looked on with a mixture of bewilderment and mild mirth.

"Ready?" I called out for the benefit of Richard, who replied dutifully, "I am ready!"

CHAPTER TWENTY-THREE

When Jimi eased himself out into the auditorium, I called to Richard, "How far?" I could scarcely mask the excitement in my voice. The end was near. I stood at the doorway from a vantage point that afforded me a two-way view.

"Yes! Positive!" he enthused from behind the drum kit. I had asked him to sit there exactly as he did on the day of her murder.

"Please stay there," I said politely to a perplexed Jimi. He was a few feet away and had his hands tucked behind his back like a frightened pupil.

"What's positive?" I heard Rekia giggle, stretching her neck to steal a curious, bemused glance at me. "What's he doing?"

"Lara?" I called. "You are next."

Lara didn't respond immediately, but at the urging of Reverend Benson, she ambled into view.

"Yes?"

I raised my hand in inquiry as her stale but delicate fragrance wafted across, and I got a rapid nod of affirmation from Richard.

"Okay," I said, snapping my fingers quickly. "It's your turn, Modele. Modele?"

"This is all nonsense!" she blasted, brushing past me. "I don't have time for this. It's like we are children again. I have had enough.

Enough is enough! Kilode?! I'm going, and nobody should stop me."

I signaled to Richard, who was already nodding his head.

Affirmative.

"Good."

Before I could call on her, Nike was already at the door.

"It's my turn?" Her tone was concerned. Rekia, behind her, was as loquacious as ever.

"It's your turn," I confirmed.

Nike cleared her throat and walked stiffly into the auditorium. My eyes shifted to Richard, and what I saw did not come as a surprise. I expected it. His gaze met mine, first with thoughtful hesitation, then a slow, damning shake of the head.

Everything fell silent. Even Modele's rant froze mid-sentence.

Nike turned to face me, her eyes worried. "Why is Richard shaking his head?" An affable yet wide-eyed smile followed. "Is something wrong?"

Richard had been right all along, and I should have seen it the first time he mentioned it when Somto and I visited his place.

"Richard, how were you that day?" I asked. He had left his place behind the drums and was now with us. He stuttered and appeared at sea as to what I meant by the question.

"I don't understand you."

"Were you… maybe not feeling well?"

His gaze went blank. "Like I'm sick?"

"That's not what I'm trying to say," I said. "What I mean is, were you all right? Were you in a good state of mind? Nothing to cloud your judgment or impair your reasoning, or your vision?"

He shook his head. "I felt very good that day."

"So you know exactly what you saw, eh?" I said, then added humorously, "You were not seeing double?"

"I know what I saw," he affirmed. "I am not a baby."

"Good. Did you see Nike come out of there?"

"I told you before, I didn't see her. Nike, I didn't see you."

Nike uttered a little cry. Her dark, greasy face looked shocked.

"That's funny," she chuckled uneasily, regaining a bit of composure. "Everyone saw me. Didn't you see me, Modele?"

Modele blinked doubtfully, sensing impending trouble. "Well…"

She turned to Lara. "Lara, you saw me, didn't you?"

Lara made a small face. She looked lost in thought, perhaps trying to recollect everything.

"Lara?"

"I remember you left," she replied, somewhat confused.

"Thank you."

"But I didn't see you come out of there," Richard said, very matter-of-factly. "You didn't come out."

"Were you even looking?" Nike laughed, looking like a trapped rabbit. "You were drumming. How can you see anything when you are drumming?"

There was a sudden silence that quickly broke apart with Richard's grating voice.

"I watched every one of you." As he said that, his eyes were on Jimi. "My attention was not divided!"

"And you didn't see me?" she asked, now clearly afraid.

Richard made an angry snorting noise. The atmosphere was thick with tension. "You think I won't remember something like that?"

"I know what you are saying, Richard," I said. "It makes sense to me now. What he's trying to say is that Jimi and Sade, his fiancée, were in the same room together, so he was watching closely from where he sat."

Richard nodded, grateful for the clarity.

Nike's eyes shifted. "This is a mistake. Modele, you saw me. Everyone saw me!"

"Everyone saw you leave the changing room, Nike," I said, "but no one saw you come out of it."

She lifted her shoulders and gave a small laugh. "What does that even mean?"

"Come."

I grabbed her hand and led her to the narrow passageway and opened the female toilet. A dozen feet scrambled behind us. I lifted the cistern lid, reached in, and pulled out the innocuous weapon. You could have heard a pin drop in the silence that followed.

"Is that a lucky mic?" Nike asked, very composed. I could tell she was trying hard not to breathe, not to give anything away, not to show any emotion.

"Don't you recognize it?"

"That's the mic o!" exclaimed Rekia. "How did it get there?"

"Yes, how did it get in there, Sister Nike?"

"I don't know!" Nike blustered. "I never touched it. Did you put it there, Lara?"

"I did not!" Lara screamed. "I only put it in the locker."

"Let me tell you what I think happened, Nike." I stepped back into the passage. "You left the room first, that is true, but you didn't go into the auditorium. You did not. Instead, you came in here and waited, and when Jimi left, you went back in and killed her. It's over, Nike. We have a witness who saw you."

Of course, there was no witness, but added pressure like that is usually effective.

For a moment or two, she stared at me. Then her resolve came apart like a cheap dress at the seams, and she fell to the floor and wept.

"I don't know what came over me," she cried. "But I couldn't take it anymore. The abuse was too much, and I… I became mad!"

Nike buried her face in her hands and practically rolled on the floor. Reverend Benson, also saddened, fought back tears of his own. He had not expected this.

Urged by us all, Nike told the story, which I have put here in my own words.

The murder itself was not an isolated event. It was the result of a series of long-standing feuds between the two of them, something Nike had done well to hide. You see, Nike and Sade, despite the façade of camaraderie, were mortal rivals. Both were great vocalists, perhaps even more so, Nike, but there can be only one queen.

Sade had a lot going for her: ebullience, a good nursing career, a beauty that turned heads, and a choice of men. But Nike had only one thing, her voice. She was everything that Sade was not. A stark contrast. She was not pretty and did not make many friends, but as the longest-serving member of the choir, she had been rightfully installed as the choir lead, a privilege that crowned her efforts and brought her joy.

Leading a choir as big as Mount Sinai's had always been her dream. Everything was going according to plan until meddling Sade came along. She, too, was ambitious and liked to make her presence felt. She would not take a back seat to anyone, especially someone she perceived as lacking and unworthy of the position. She was never afraid to make her feelings known, often challenging Nike's authority and undermining her position.

One afternoon, after being a little too critical of her input, Sade was offended by the open vilification. She met with Nike privately and swore to take the lead role from her. It seemed like an empty threat, and Nike did not take her seriously, and why should she? Sade might be talented too, but she had only been around for a couple of years. Besides, the position was never political, but Sade had other ideas.

She befriended the choirmaster, and things escalated quickly. A couple of months later, Jimi announced a major reshuffle. Sade was replacing Nike as the choir lead, just like that. Sade had made good on her promise.

It was a cruel blow to Nike's ambition and ego. Not only had Sade managed to carry out the seemingly improbable, but she had achieved it in a matter of months, and she rubbed it in Nike's face at every opportunity.

"She came to me here after rehearsal one evening and started laughing for no reason. She laughed and laughed until she left the room," Nike explained. She was humiliated but tried her best to make peace with the situation.

Having grown an unhealthy fondness for the microphone, Nike asked, as a reprieve, to continue using it. In her mind, it made her still the de facto choir lead. Sade refused, insisting that by right it belonged to her. After all, every choir lead before her had used the sentimental relic. Jimi somehow disagreed, and Nike was allowed to use it. It was a small victory that lasted only a few weeks. Her adversary waved her magic wand again, and Jimi rescinded his decision.

Nike fell apart inside. Sade had stolen her dreams and had not even made much of an effort at it. As if that were not enough, Sade completely overlooked her when assigning numbers for the upcoming Thanksgiving. Having overseen a few of those herself, it was a bitter pill to swallow. She had become her nemesis.

"If you are not happy about it," Sade had told her when she complained, "go and complain to Jimi… if he will listen to you."

The silent feud continued until Nike had had enough.

On the day of the murder, Nike had set out to fight back, to win back some pride, to cause Sade some misery too. *If I cannot have the lucky mic, then nobody will.*

The first thing she did that morning was to locate the microphone, but it had disappeared from the closet where the choir equipment was kept. Covertly, she asked around and finally got to Rekia, who admitted to seeing it and keeping it in the technical area.

When Nike got there, it had already been moved. Eventually, she spotted it on Lara, who, rather bizarrely, was smuggling it into the changing room. Having recovered it from where it was stashed, Nike grew cold feet and was unable to bring herself to do anything with it, given how upset Sade had been that morning when she could not find it. She later wound the microphone cord around her neck and covered it with her stole.

Sade, already incensed by Nike's backing voice trying to upstage hers, suspected the microphone had been withheld by her predecessor. After the final rendition, just before the end of service, she demanded it back when they were alone for the first time in the changing room. A mild altercation ensued. Nike tried to exercise restraint, but Sade poked fun at her, mocked her buck teeth, and said she was too ugly to be the queen.

When Nike returned a second time to the changing room with Modele, Sade curled her lips at her like a buck on the trail of a nanny in heat, in reference to her deformed dentition whenever their eyes met. Body-shamed and embarrassed, Nike quickly departed for the toilet.

It was there, in fury and self-hate, that she yanked off the cord from the microphone. Her anger was such that she burst into tears. She remained there for a while to cool off. Thinking that everyone had left the changing room, she returned to hide what was left of the microphone.

The problem was that Sade had stayed back.

Nike was caught red-handed, flat-footed.

Sade hurled another round of verbal abuse at her. What finally caused Nike to snap was when Sade called her the wife of a dwarf. It was as if someone had turned off the lights in her head. She charged at her in blind rage and struck her repeatedly on the side of the face until Sade went limp and collapsed on the floor.

It was at that moment that Reverend Benson announced the end of the service.

Panic-stricken, Nike slipped back into the toilet and waited for the unconscious Sade to be discovered. Only when the room was filled with sufficient sympathizers did she slip out undetected.

As she concluded her story, I felt deep sympathy for her. Sade was not around to corroborate it, but there was a ring of truth to everything she had said. Besides, the scenario fit my idea that the murder was spontaneous, on a whim, not premeditated.

"Well," I said finally, after acknowledging her confession with kind words, "there is still one thing I want to know. There was a lady I met at the art gallery. She claimed to be a psychic and tried to imply Lara might have been responsible for her friend's death." I watched her demeanor now, and it looked restrained. "You do know her, don't you?"

When she nodded, it was a wistful one. "I was afraid you would soon find out about the microphone. I had to do something. So when you said you would be at the theater for the exhibition, I thought of my friend Monisola. She works there with a theater troupe."

"And then you asked her for help?"

She nodded. "I explained everything to her, and she said she would take care of it."

"I think you put the idea to her. She did a believable job, I should say."

Reverend Benson paced about, animated. I felt pity for him. The business of murder in a church was bad enough, but a murderous member made it quite the scandal.

I went to meet him. He was upset, did not know what to do, and was barely coherent. I was about to speak when Lara cried out:

"Nike is running away!"

Out the window, I saw Nike's sprinting figure in the rain, disappearing fast. Paralyzed, I think, by the brazenness or absurdity of the act, no one moved.

"Let her run," I said finally, and to no one in particular, "Call the police."

CHAPTER TWENTY-FOUR

"**I** don't want her to be found!" cried Maami with the effect of a spontaneous explosion. "Ugly ones are beautiful too, but beautiful people are blind to see it because they are beautiful!"

Somto and I exchanged looks. It had been a month since Nike was last seen slipping away into the rain. There was something so poetic about her silhouette running, becoming smaller and smaller to the eye until she disappeared from the horizon. So etched was that image in my head that I made a painting of it. Run, Lady, Run!

"Her husband thinks she's run away to a relative," I said to him. "He received a couple of emails from her, but really, she could be anywhere… anywhere but Lagos if she's smart. I think she is smart."

"A month is a long time to abscond. Do you think she will turn herself in or be on the run for a long time?"

"I don't want her to be found," Maami, in the kitchen, was sympathetic to Nike and, at every opportunity, let us know how she felt. She went on in a strong voice:

"I pity her. Oh, how she must feel alone. The world against her! Poor girl. It's cruel… a moment of anger and her life is ruined. I hope she finds peace. I hope she starts over wherever she is now, somehow."

"This feels like your dad somehow," Somto whispered after a long pause. "You know what I mean, right?" It was as though he had spoken out loud what had been on our minds. If Nike were to never be found and account for Sade's murder, she would have to mirror Father's self-imposed exile, at least. And so far, it's working, and Maami is somewhat content. Perhaps she would disappear to Ghana or Liberia. Meet another man who would change her life and help her along on her new journey. New path.

"It's the reason I received your father with open arms, Deji."

I could only mumble.

"I'm sorry, Deji. I don't mean to be insensitive." Somto was looking into my eyes, and I guess he did not like what he saw.

"It's fine," I said to him. "What annoyed me was that I didn't crack it earlier when we went to Richard's house. I mean, I should have seen it there. He practically told us it was Nike, but we missed it."

"I think you said," he replied, laughing at my expense, "'He is an unreliable witness.' Like the pompous person that you are!"

"Am I really pompous? Modele said something to that effect."

"You don't know?"

I shrugged. "I really thought so at that time. Another time I should have seen through Nike's act early on was when she told me about Sade's pregnancy."

"How could she have known?"

"Exactly. She said Modele told her, but when I accidentally mentioned it to Modele, she was genuinely surprised by the news. I didn't ask her how she knew, but my guess is she overheard it being discussed. If not, then we may never know. That was what I'd been trying to remember all that time."

Somto contorted his face as though I had said something so ludicrous.

"Nike is smart, though," I continued. "She somehow knew I liked the painting in Modele's house and got the arugba lady to dress like the woman in the painting just to throw me off. I give it to her! My only regret is something that completely escaped my mind to ask her."

Somto raised a quizzical brow.

"I have not told you about it, and it's still bothering me to this day. There was a man at our window that night Father showed up. He scared the daylights out of everybody. I want to know if she sent that man to do something nefarious, you know? If she didn't, then who was it?"

Somto laughed so hard it looked like he might go into a fit.

"You think it's funny, eh? Maami was so afraid."

"Ko funny, Somto," Maami shouted irritably. "Iyabo had to sleep in our house because she could not step outside alone!"

"We were so afraid. No be laughing matter, guy!"

"It was me!" he exclaimed after a fit of coughing and continued as soon as he caught his breath. "When I got home that night after your exhibition, my old man said the neighbors were talking about seeing your dad. I thought it was a joke, but he was serious, so I came to see for myself. When I came to the door, I heard a lot of voices. I didn't want to intrude. I think I stood at the window for some time."

"Somto!" Maami cried.

I slammed my fist on the table. "No wonder Rocky didn't bark!"

"It slipped my mind to tell you. How is he, by the way?"

"Fine. You know, without him, I may never have solved this case. I would have been running around in circles. I found help in the unlikeliest of places."

"Me sef surprise."

"A nice stroke of serendipity."

"Does it make you feel better about him?"

I did not hesitate. "Yes, it does. Everything in life is fate, right? It was meant to be. What about your interview?"

"I got the job."

"Wow. Congrats!"

"Thanks."

"How are we celebrating it?"

That evening, over merry conversation at the local bar down the street, I met Somto and an old friend, Dehinde from Ibadan. All three of us had attended the same university. Dehinde was in town for business and ran into Somto by chance.

After we exchanged pleasantries and recalled fond memories, I let slip my desire for another murder to occur.

"So you can try and solve it, eh?"

"Yes."

"You've only had one bottle of beer, man."

"I'm not drunk."

The third party, curious, asked what I meant. Somto explained to him how I solved Sade's murder.

He grew pensive, thinking for a minute or two. "Can you help me with something like this?" he finally said.

"Why? What's wrong?"

"My uncle. Someone in our family is trying to kill my uncle."

I sat back, feeling goosebumps break out on my skin.

"Tell me about it," I said. "Start from the beginning," thinking how much I'd missed Ibadan.

www.ingramcontent.com/pod-product-compliance
Lightning Source LLC
Chambersburg PA
CBHW021125070726
47591CB00014B/1317